DEAD RINGER

BY

PANDORA PINE

Dead Ringer

Copyright © Pandora Pine 2018

All Rights Reserved

First Printed Edition: January 2019

PROLOGUE

Massachusetts Correctional Institution- Cedar Junction
2000 Main Street
Walpole, MA 02070

17 October

Detective Ronan O'Mara
Cold Case Unit
Boston Police District C-6
101 Broadway
South Boston, MA 02128

Dear Detective O'Mara,

My name is Thomas Hutchins. My friends and family call me Tank. You might know me better as The Riverside Ripper. Around here, I'm just known as inmate 889345.

I'm sure you've heard this line a million times before but, I'm innocent. The problem is that I don't have an alibi for the night Lorraine McAlpin was murdered. I was home alone watching the Sox get their asses kicked by the Yankees. My cell phone verifies that I was home, or at least near the cell tower closest to home. The only problem is that Lorraine McAlpin's house is near that cell tower too.

"My" DNA was found at the scene of the crime. I use quotation marks over the word "my" because there's a slight wrinkle in my story. My DNA isn't just my own. I share it with my identical twin brother, Tim Hutchins.

I'm not throwing my brother under the bus here. I'm really not, but if I didn't kill Lorraine McAlpin, then that only leaves one other option. I don't want to believe Tim is capable of committing this crime. Worse, I don't want to believe he's capable of letting me take the fall for something he did.

According to the testimony at my trial, Tim was at home with his wife, Michelle, on the night of the murder. Would my sister-in-law lie for my brother? I can't say for certain. They've got three small children under the age of six. Tim owns his own business and is the sole provider for his family. Life for his family would change greatly if *he* were sitting here wearing an orange jumpsuit instead of me.

I have a new lawyer. His name is Bradford Hicks. You may have heard of him. He successfully got Marco Bishop's conviction in his triple murder case overturned. I've also hired a local private investigator named Jude Byrne.

I'm writing to you because I've heard of your success with your partner, Tennyson Grimm, in solving cold cases. It's too late for your detective work to save Lorraine McAlpin, but it isn't too late to save the next victim of her killer.

It also might not be too late to save me from twenty-five to life as a guest of the Massachusetts Department of Corrections.

I'm enclosing Bradford's phone number and email address. I would like to meet with you to discuss my case if you are available for a consultation. It would mean the world to me, Detective O'Mara, to be able to sit down with you and lay out the facts of this case. As I said, I'm innocent. I *know* you and Mr. Grimm can prove it.

Take care,
Thomas Hutchins
Inmate 889345

1

Ronan

November...

"What the hell is all of this...Stuff?" Ronan shouted. He was trying to work on his vocabulary in an effort to become a kinder, gentler member of the Cold Case Unit. It was only half working.

There was an enormous pile of shit sitting on Detective Ronan O'Mara's desk. "Stuff" was the best out-loud word he could think of to describe the stack of files, mail, newspapers, and other miscellaneous *stuff* that was piled on top of his workspace.

It was the second week in November and technically Ronan had been out of the office since August when he'd been shot by a suspect in a copycat murder case. He'd been a few days away from returning from his medical leave when his future father-in-law had passed away. After that, he and his fiancé, psychic, Tennyson Grimm, had been off to the great state of Kansas to bury the man along with the hatchet in an old family quarrel.

Ronan and Tennyson had ended up staying in Kansas for longer than either of them had expected and when they'd gotten back to Massachusetts, they were two weeks away from the wedding they hadn't even started to plan. Not wanting to get married on the steps of Salem City Hall or at the Witch Museum, Ronan had taken two weeks of vacation time to help Tennyson plan the wedding of their dreams.

Thanks to help from their friends, they'd managed to pull off the perfect Day of the Dead wedding on November 1. The biggest surprise of the day had been the late-arriving Kaye Grimm. Ronan hadn't been sure if his mother-in-law would choose to come to New England for the wedding.

Tennyson's Baptist mother had spent the majority of her life believing homosexuality was a sin. He'd come out to his parents as gay and psychic in the fall of his senior year and Kaye and her husband, the dearly departed David, had kicked Tennyson out of their home on the day of his high school graduation. Tennyson hadn't spoken to either of his parents until David's spirit had paid Tennyson a late-night visit asking him to reconcile with his mother.

The newly married couple had taken a week off after their wedding for a quasi-honeymoon. They were going on a family cruise to Bermuda after Christmas, which would serve as their actual honeymoon. Ronan had figured the week after they got married would be filled entirely with sex and naked time, but instead it had been partially spent helping his boss and son move into their new house.

In truth, it was an offer Ronan couldn't refuse. Captain Kevin Fitzgibbon had been his boss for a little over a year now. He and his adopted son, Greeley, had moved into their house with Tennyson while Ronan had been in the hospital recovering from being shot. The man who shot Ronan had a kill list and Ten, Kevin, and Greeley were all on it. The captain had wanted them all under one roof to better protect them all.

Of course, having two extra people living with you when you were trying to get it on like Donkey Kong wasn't the most convenient thing ever. What Ronan hadn't known was that Kevin and Greeley had been waiting for a house to go on the market in their neighborhood. That very thing had happened when they were all in Kansas and Kevin had put an offer on the house, sight-unseen which had been accepted. The only problem was they couldn't set up a date to pass papers until *after* the wedding.

They'd spent the first three nights after they'd been married in the Honeymoon Suite of the Hawthorne Hotel, courtesy of Jace Lincoln, Captain Fitzgibbon's sort-of boyfriend. According to what Ronan knew, those two crazy kids hadn't really been able to get a solid relationship off the ground.

"For the love of God, Ronan! This is a place of business, not Sesame Street. If you want to play Oscar the Grouch, do it at home!" Captain Fitzgibbon said from behind him.

 "If I'm Oscar the Grouch, that must make you Big Bird!" Ronan turned around and looked up at his boss. Ronan was 6'3", but Kevin towered over him at 6'6".

"Funny! What the hell is all this shit?" Kevin peeked around Ronan's desk looking at the odd grouping of things lumped together.

"I was just asking my esteemed colleagues the same question, but no one was answering me." Ronan's tone was a near-growl.

"Hmm," The captain chuckled. "Guess you're on your own then. I did bring you a coffee, but since there's no place to set it down, I'll just hand it to you. Carry on!" Fitzgibbon handed him the cup from the expensive place across the street.

Ronan was about to zing him with a parting shot when he noticed the name written on the cup. "Newlywed." Fitzgibbon earned a reprieve from his razor-like wit over that one.

He turned back to his desk after taking a sip of the near-volcanic brew. Where the hell did he even start with this pile? Well, what would Tennyson do if he were here? Plopping back down in his chair, Ronan thought that question over.

"Organize it into same-sex piles!" Ronan nearly shouted hopping back to his feet. That's exactly what Ten would do. He grabbed all of the brown accordion-style case files from under the pile and stacked them on his chair. Next, he wrangled all of the newspapers into order from oldest on top, to newest on the bottom. He also grabbed all of the mail addressed to him and made a pile of that.

The rest of the shit on his desk was just that, shit. There were sales flyers from Men's Warehouse and old sandwich wrappers. There was even an ancient cup of coffee with his name written on it. Ronan shivered. That cup was from the day he'd been shot. Christ, couldn't anyone have helped him out by throwing this away? Gathering up all the trash, he walked to the can and dumped it all in.

When Ronan got back to his desk, he organized the piles from tallest to smallest. The mail was the shortest stack sitting in front of him so he grabbed the letters and started flipping through them. What he was concentrating on were the return addresses. He sorted out all of the ones with addresses out of New England.

Notoriety from their reality show and news coverage by the Boston media had made him and Tennyson famous in crime circles across the country. Parents of missing children sent him letters all the time begging for his and Tennyson's help. They were sure that Ten could find their kids like he'd found Michael Frye.

It killed Ronan to read all of the letters. What killed him more was showing them to Tennyson. Sometimes Ten got a lead on the letter-sender's child just by touching them. If that was the case, Ronan took down all of the information and got in touch with local law enforcement and let them take it from there. If Ten didn't get any additional information, Ronan wrote a personal letter to the family and let them know he'd be back in touch if anything changed.

Ronan was nearly finished flipping through the envelopes when one with a return address to the Massachusetts Department of Corrections caught his eye. This was definitely not a missing child letter. His curiosity piqued, Ronan opened the letter and started to read.

"The Riverside Ripper? Jesus Christ!" Ronan muttered, setting the letter down on his desk. He vaguely remembered the case from three years ago. A woman's body had been found on the banks of the Mystic River in Charlestown in July. She been beaten and stabbed. Her cause of death had been exsanguination.

One local news station, famous for their use of alliterative headlines, had dubbed the killer *The Riverside Ripper*, as if this had been an episode of *Criminal Minds* and *not* real life. Of course, the name caught on and soon every media outlet in Boston was using it, even though there had been only one murder with that MO.

There was one thing Tank Hutchins was right about, every con in prison proclaimed their innocence. That fact made him no different from the roughly eight hundred men housed at Cedar Junction. What *did* make him different was the letter sitting on his desk. Hutchins was the first inmate to write to him asking for his and Ten's help in looking into his conviction.

What had really grabbed Ronan's attention wasn't the high-powered Boston defense attorney or the fact that this guy had a private dick working for him, but the fact that he had a twin brother. Twins were the oldest wrinkle in the detective genre. *It can't be me, officer, it was my twin brother...* This, of course, spawned the whole idea of an evil twin versus a good twin.

Ronan was intrigued, no doubt about it. The problem was that he was a Cold Case Detective. There was no way in hell Fitzgibbon was going to let him run off on a field trip to Walpole to interview a man who'd been convicted of a crime. There was no cold case here. There was just a letter from a man desperate to get out prison any way possible and wanting to use Tennyson's gift to do it.

Shaking his head, Ronan shifted his attention away from Tank Hutchins' letter and went back to the rest of the unopened letters stacked on his desk.

2

Tennyson

Psychic Tennyson Grimm was looking at a masterpiece. The beef roast was done to a perfect 145°F. The tiny fingerling potatoes, which were Ronan's favorites, were also perfectly roasted, crisp on the outside and soft on the inside. The baby asparagus tips were steamed and artfully arranged on the plates. The only problem with the perfect dinner was that Tennyson's perfect husband was MIA.

Ronan had sworn up and down that he'd be home by 6pm for dinner, but it was now 6:30pm and there was no sign of him. There had been no phone call, no text, no smoke signal, no message in a bottle, no passenger pigeon with a note tied to its leg.

Ten wasn't worried about his husband. He had the television tuned to the local ABC affiliate and there was no breaking news about a member of the Boston Police Department being involved in anything newsworthy.

He was about to shoot off a text to Ronan when Dixie, their four-month-old Papillon mix puppy raced toward the front door barking her fool head off. That could only mean one thing: Ronan was home.

"Dixie, my little pixie! Daddy missed you, princess!" Ronan cooed.

Tennyson couldn't begrudge Ronan a little time with the puppy. He'd been home most of the day with their little lady. After all the psychic readings Ten had to cancel after Ronan was shot, his calendar was very much open. He'd spent most of the day calling and emailing his client list letting them know he was home from his honeymoon and available to book readings. The rest of the day was spent doing mountains of laundry and making dinner.

"Ten?" Ronan called out.

"In the kitchen!" He lit the candles on the dining room table and waited for Ronan to be wowed by the presentation.

"You are not going to believe what happened in the office today. Some assholes-" Ronan stopped dead when he walked into the kitchen with Dixie in his arms and saw the candles and his husband. "Oh, man." Ronan sucked in a deep breath before he set Dixie down on the kitchen floor. "I totally forgot about dinner. I just got so caught up in getting caught up." Ronan shook his head. "You look..." He sucked in a rough breath.

Ten was dressed in a pair of tight-fitting blue jeans that he'd had to work to shimmy himself into. He wasn't sure how much of his perfect dinner he would be able to eat before he would be undoing the top button, but that was sort of the point anyway. Instead of a shirt, Ten was wearing a blue apron. "I look, what?" Ten stalked toward Ronan, his dark eyes never leaving Ronan's blue ones. "Good enough to eat?"

Ronan nodded, looking too stunned to speak.

"Let's eat before it gets cold." Ten reached for Ronan's hand and tugged his much larger husband toward the table.

"I can't believe you did all of this," Ronan managed to say as Ten pushed him into his usual seat at the table.

"It was your first day back at work. I wanted you to come home to a nice dinner. With our crazy schedules, there aren't going to be a lot of nights when I'm going to be able to cook for you like this." Before Ronan had been shot, they'd worked out a system where Ten would spend two weeks in the office with him working on cold cases and then the next two weeks working at West Side Magick, the Salem, Massachusetts psychic shop he co-owned with his best friends, brothers Carson and Cole Craig. Next week was when Ten was scheduled to go back to work with Ronan.

"It looks so good, Ten." Ronan held up his water glass. "To you, babe. The man of my dreams. My husband!"

"Right back at you!" Ten clinked his glass against Ronan's. "Dig in. Don't be afraid to tell me if it sucks."

Ronan shot him an are-you-nuts look and grabbed his knife and fork. He cut into the prime rib and slid a bite into his mouth. He moaned obscenely.

"Is that good or bad?" Ten narrowed his eyes at his newlywed husband. A moan like that in the bedroom Ten could decipher. Out of the bedroom, fully dressed, was another matter entirely.

"Oh my God! This is heaven!" Ronan didn't even look up from the potato he was stabbing with his fork. "You remembered that I love these little finger taters too!" He didn't waste any time shoving it into his mouth. He moaned again. This time more obscenely than the last.

Ten laughed. He had heard of food porn before but hadn't believed the hype. He knew he needed to get eating if he was going to have enough fuel to get through what was to come tonight. It was all he could do to keep from moaning out loud when he took his first bite of the beef. He'd have to send Bobby Flay an email to thank him for the spot-on recipe. "How was work?"

Ronan frowned. He set his hand on Ten's knee. "We're having a romantic dinner. You don't want to hear about that now."

Ten raised his husband's hand to his lips. He brushed a kiss over his knuckles before sucking Ronan's index finger into his mouth and swirling his tongue around the tip. "Well, I'm sure as hell *not* gonna want to hear about it later, when I'm naked and my mouth is full of dessert…"

Ronan swallowed so hard his throat clicked. He shook his head as if he were trying to remember what they'd been talking about before Tennyson had let the dessert menu slip.

"I think you mentioned something about an asshole when you came into the kitchen." Ten winked suggestively.

Ronan's eyes bugged out. Obviously, Ten's suggestion wasn't helping Ronan's memory. "Oh! Oh yeah, the assholes at work." Ronan shook his head again. "When I came in this morning, my desk was piled so high with shit, I couldn't see O'Dwyer's desk if I was sitting in my chair."

Ten snorted. "What kind of shit are we talking about? Real shit or metaphorical shit? I mean you were out of the office for a long time."

"Funny, babe. There was a shit-ton of mail, newspapers that were deliberately left there as an act of protest, or laziness, and about ten case folders with a letter left on top of them." Ronan leveled his gaze at Tennyson.

Ten stared right back. Without using his gift, he'd guess the files were the guys' way of welcoming Ronan back to work. Opening his gift wide and giving his husband a quick scan, he could see there was more to it than that. He was intrigued. "What did the letter say?" Ten gave him a curious look to try to hide the fact he'd been reading Ronan.

"Don't give me that look, Ten. I know you were using your brain powers to read me." Ronan raised a quizzical eyebrow. "You're lucky we're stuck together forever and eternity." He took a sip of water.

Ten noticed the way Ronan's platinum wedding band caught the candlelight when he raised his glass to his lips. The band matched his own exactly, minus the diamonds. Ronan had said Ten sparkled enough for the both of them. It was true. Ronan shone like a diamond in other ways. He didn't need to put it on public display. "Yes, I read you. You're intrigued by what the letter from the rest of the Cold Case Team said. Obviously, I'm curious because you are. Spill it."

Ronan laughed. He leaned over to kiss his husband. "You're impossible. You know that? Forget it. That was rhetorical, but you knew that." Ronan smiled brightly. "I brought the letter home to show you, but the long and the short of it is that the ten files sitting on my desk were cases that the other detectives worked as far as they could and now they want you to finish."

Ten was silent as he thought that over. He knew what Ronan meant by saying the cases had been worked as far as the other detectives could take them. All of the old witnesses had been re-interviewed, the old evidence had been re-examined and if possible, re-tested. They'd been taken as far as police instinct and their five senses could take them. What these cases needed now was Tennyson to use his sixth sense, speak to the victims, and get some answers. "How do you feel about us being the finishers, so to speak?"

"I'm fine with it since the other detectives are. You know how touchy cops are when it comes to other cops stepping on their toes in an active investigation, but in this case, we're being asked to help. I say let's do it." Ronan sounded convinced.

"Hold on there a second, Columbo. I'm guessing this is in *addition* to your caseload, not as a replacement for what's in your queue, right?" This would lead to overtime and a lot of late nights spent on cases, rather than naked and enjoying newlywed life.

Ronan nodded. "It would be a lot of extra work for us, but I think it's worth it to help these families. I mean, my colleagues got their hopes up by reopening their case and now, unless we step in, the detectives are going to have to go back and tell them that their loved ones' killers can't be found." Ronan grimaced. "I know not every cold case can theoretically be solved, but Ten, with you as our secret weapon, I feel like more of them can be."

Ten hated to admit it, but Ronan was right. "Okay, I'm in, but we pace ourselves. We don't do them all at once."

A slow grin spread over Ronan's face. His cerulean eyes sparkled in the candlelight. He set his silverware down against his plate with a clank and pushed back out of his seat. "Speaking of pacing ourselves, I'm full. How about you?" He held his hand out to his husband.

"Oh, hell yeah!" Ten's pants were already starting to cut off the blood flow to his legs. Now was a good time to stop eating and start working off some of this meal. He placed his hand in Ronan's.

Before Ten knew what was happening, he was being hauled over Ronan's shoulder. "Oh, you beast!" Ten slapped playfully at Ronan's shoulders.

Ronan growled. "You ain't seen nothing yet!" He headed toward the stairs. "Come, Dixie."

"Uhh, Ronan?" Why was Ronan inviting their dog to come upstairs with them?

"Don't want her getting into our leftovers. Nothing ruins a night of hard fucking more than a trip to the doggie ER. We'll move her bed into Fitzgibbon's old room. She'll be fine in there for a few hours." Ronan slapped Tennyson's ass as he started climbing the stairs.

Dixie barked sharply and raced up the stairs after them.

Ten's little princess thought that Daddy Ronan was a threat to him. What the tiny dog had no way of knowing was Tennyson was turned on as fuck. His erection was digging into Ronan's shoulder as he was being carried up the stairs by his newlywed caveman. Let the games begin.

3

Ronan

Ronan had to admit that telling Tennyson all about the stack of files on his desk at work was an effective way to keep his mind and the conversation off the letter from Tank Hutchins. To be honest, it was the only thing Ronan had been able to focus on for most of the day.

In fairness though, he had read every single accordion folder the other detectives had left for him, along with all of his mail, both physical and electronic. The last thing he'd done before he'd gone back and reread the letter from Hutchins was to check on his own work-in-progress cases. Predictably enough, with him on the shelf for the last two and a half months, there had been no movement on any of them.

Ronan didn't want Ten to know anything about The Riverside Ripper's letter. He wasn't sure what he was going to do about it yet and he wasn't in the mood to talk about it.

That wasn't exactly true. Ronan knew what he was going to do about it and didn't want Ten talking him out of it.

"Here we go, little love." Ronan set Dixie down in the spare bedroom that Fitzgibbon had occupied for the past few months. He could still smell his boss's cologne if he took a deep enough breath. He put her pink princess dog bed down in the center of the room and started to back away.

Dixie charged at him. Her black ears were perked up and she was whining for all she was worth. The look on her face was one of pure heartbreak. "Please don't leave me, again, Daddy," it said.

For some reason Ronan couldn't quite figure out, the tiny puppy had chosen him as her person. She liked Ten but she *loved* Ronan. Fitzgibbon had been sure the dog was going to die from grief while Ronan had been in the hospital. It had been the nightly Skype calls between Ronan and Greeley that had saved a grief-stricken Dixie.

Ronan had only been out of the hospital and back home with his one true love for about three weeks before he and Ten had gone to Kansas to bury David Grimm. What should have been a five-day trip, tops, had turned into a two-week odyssey, courtesy of Ten's difficult mother and an even surlier tornado. Dixie was still gun-shy about Ronan leaving her alone for any length of time and they'd been home now for almost a month.

"Daddy Ronan and Daddy Ten are gonna spend some quality naked time together, but I'll be back to get you once we're cleaned up and dressed. I promise." Ronan crossed his heart and backed out of the room. He shut the door on Dixie's cries.

It hurt his heart to hear his baby cry like that, but it would hurt his dick more if it had to stay in this current state of hardness for a minute more without Ten's plump lips wrapped around it.

"Christ, Ronan! Are you coming?" Ten bellowed. "A man could die like this!"

Ronan poked his head around into their bedroom doorway and saw Ten in the center of their king-sized bed, naked as a jay bird, on all fours with his perfect heart-shaped ass perched high in the air. "Someone's a little impatient." Ronan slapped Ten's right cheek.

Ten howled. In pain or pleasure, Ronan couldn't tell at the moment. He thought it was pleasure, but he'd need a second swat to turn his hypothesis into a true scientific theory. He slapped Ten's left cheek a bit harder.

"Oh, fuck!" Ten moaned, burying his face into the comforter.

Pleasure... Ronan grinned at the twin red handprints on Ten's ass. "Sometimes I think you're a mouthy boy on purpose." Climbing up behind his husband on the bed, Ronan swiped his tongue over Ten's eager hole.

"Jesus, Ronan!" Ten was panting now. He pushed his ass back against Ronan, presumably hoping for a repeat performance.

"You're awfully greedy for such a bad boy," Ronan teased. He climbed off the bed. Shit, he was still fully dressed. He could feel his cock soaking his boxers. If he kept going at Tennyson like this, he was going to come in his underpants like a teenager.

"Teasing, bossy, asshole, bastard!" Ten bitched.

"Ah, you forgot one!" Ronan waggled his eyebrows as he unbuttoned his dress shirt.

"Ladies don't say *that* word!" Frustration and need slashed through Tennyson's voice.

"Funny, I was thinking you forgot, 'husband.' What word were you thinking?" Ronan raised a questioning eyebrow as he painstakingly slid his boxers down past his aching cock. It had only been a little more than twelve hours since it had last seen action, but that was far too long where his husband was concerned.

"I, uh, ummm." Ten was staring at Ronan's drooling cock. "What were we talking about?"

Ronan grinned at his distracted husband. It was quite a thing to render your man speechless with your dick. "You want a piece of this?" He slid his hand slowly from root to tip.

Ten nodded.

Ronan crooked a finger at him. He would have crooked his cock, but he wasn't that talented.

Ten sped off the bed in a blitz of color. He sat on his knees in front of Ronan, looking up at his husband, his dark eyes nearly black with need.

"You're gorgeous like this, babe." Ronan ran a hand through Ten's springy, dark curls. He'd never get enough of doing this. "Open up for me."

Ten obeyed, moaning when Ronan slid his cock into Ten's willing mouth.

Ronan hitched his hips forward, fucking himself deeper into Ten's mouth, feeling his cock jerk when his husband gagged. He chuckled. Nothing stroked his ego more than his dick being too much to swallow. He pulled back and out. "You ready to get fucked?"

Ten nodded, wiping off the line of drool and pre-come that had landed on his chin.

"On the bed or here on the floor?"

"Bed, remember the rug burn you got back at the Hawthorn Hotel?" Ten bit his bottom lip at the memory.

Ronan snorted. How could he forget his own wedding night? The rug burn had been epic, but it had been so worth it. He'd come so hard he'd blacked out and Ten spent the next morning feeding him breakfast in bed and sucking his cock. He'd only ended up with tiny scabs on both knees.

Ten licked out at the head of Ronan's cock, a look of longing in his dark eyes. He got back to his feet and walked to his night stand. Grabbing the lube from the top drawer, he snapped open the cap and went to work opening himself up.

"Jesus, Ten!" Ronan felt like he was rooted to the spot. His eyes were glued to Tennyson's fingers and the way his body was responding to them.

"You gonna get your dick ready for me or are you gonna stand there with it in your hand?"

"Who's bossy now, babe?" Ronan loved it when Ten was sassy in the bedroom. Not that he was going to tell his husband that. Oh, no, he had other plans for his mouthy man instead. He peeked into the nightstand drawer that Ten had left open and saw just what he was looking for, the red ball gag he'd gotten after their summer vacation at Sand Dollar Shoal. "You know what mouthy boys get?" Ronan asked, his voice low and menacing.

"Spanked?" Tennyson shivered as he spoke the word.

"We tried that. It didn't work." Ronan nudged his hard-as-steel cock against Ten's loosened hole but made no move to breech his passage. "Open up," Ronan commanded.

"Ronan, what?" Ten squeaked but obeyed.

"That's better." Ronan bent forward, the head of his cock slowly pushing past the first ring of muscle as he set the red ball between Tennyson's teeth. It was hard to concentrate on securing the gag behind his husband's head, but he managed somehow. "You good?"

Ten gave him a thumbs up, their pre-arranged sign when he was gagged and couldn't speak.

Ronan pulled Ten up from all fours onto his knees, wrapping his left arm around his torso and holding onto Ten's right shoulder. He used his right hand to grip Ten's right hip. This left Ten's hands free to signal Ronan or to take the gag off himself if the play got too real for him. "Ready, babe?"

Ten moaned and nodded his head.

That was good enough for Ronan. He pulled back and nearly out and slid back in slowly. Giving a bit of an evil laugh when Ten groaned. "Oh no, babe, this isn't going to be slow and sweet. Bad boys like you don't get that. Hold on, brat. We're going for a ride," Ronan growled low in his ear and set a punishing pace. The only sounds in the room were his own harsh breathing and the slap of his flesh against Tennyson's.

Ten whimpered. His hand went to his cock. Ronan watched over his shoulder as he jacked himself off.

"That's it, babe. Come for me. Paint your chest."

Ten roared around the gag. Come ripped from his cock.

The first blast hit Ten in the face, triggering his own orgasm. Ronan held on tighter, digging his fingers into Tennyson's hip. His cock continued to pulse deep inside Tennyson's body long after Tennyson's storm was over.

When Ronan could suck in a deep breath again, he released the gag.

Tennyson fell forward on the bed and started to laugh. "Holy shit," he muttered into the mattress.

"You're telling me." Ronan backed off the bed and tried to catch his breath. "I keep telling you to be bad more often. I'm glad you finally listened to me."

"I love you, Ronan," Ten called after him as he headed toward the bathroom.

"Love you more, Nostradamus, but you already knew that." Ronan winked at his husband. Round two would be sweet and gentle with Ronan taking his time to thank his man for the romantic dinner he'd taken the time to make for them.

4

Tennyson

Dixie walked into West Side Magick the next morning like she owned the place. Her ears were up as high as they could go, as was her head. She was queen of the store.

"Morning Ten. Your highness!" Carson called out before he bowed to the tiny dog.

"Stop feeding her ego. Ever since Ronan started letting her sleep with us, she's been acting like royalty."

Carson bent down and unclipped her leash. "You are royalty. Aren't you, sweetheart?" He scooped her up and cuddled her close.

Ten watched while his dog loved on Carson. Dixie had stayed with Carson and his husband, Truman, when Ronan had been in the ICU after he'd been shot and also when they'd been in Kansas after David Grimm had passed away. Ten didn't blame his dog for being especially close to his best friend.

"You have a full day, my friend." Carson grinned. He set Dixie down and swiped at the dog slobber on his face with the cuff of his grey shirt. "Totally booked thanks to the rerun of your *Dateline* episode on the Michael Frye case."

"Seriously? I spent hours yesterday calling my client list to let them know I was back in town and it was the *Dateline* rerun that filled up my calendar for the day?" This happened every time some cable network aired that episode. Not that Tennyson was complaining.

"Not just for the day," Cole Craig, Carson's brother, chimed in. "For the rest of the week too. It filled up mine and Carson's calendars with in person and phone readings as well." Cole slapped a hand on Ten's shoulder. "Can't thank you enough, man. Laurel's college fund is getting fatter by the day."

"We wanted to talk to you about that, Ten, before our first appointments show up." Carson wore a serious look on his face.

Ten looked back and forth between the brothers. He'd known there was something important they'd wanted to talk to him about for some time now. With Ronan being shot, then his father passing away unexpectedly, and then with his and Ronan's wedding, there hadn't been time.

To be honest, Tennyson hadn't tried to read either of his partners. His best friends had repeatedly told him that he was the missing third Craig brother. Ten believed them. If it was bad news, he'd rather they just come out and tell him. "Okay, hit me with it." He braced himself for the worst news possible: being kicked out of the Magick shop partnership.

Dixie growled. She ran to Ten's side and stood in front of him. She barked sharply, staring Cole and Carson down.

"Whoa, Cujo." Cole grinned at Dixie. He turned back to Ten. "We're not kicking you out of the partnership."

Ten narrowed his eyes at Cole. He quickly scanned the other psychic and saw that he was telling the truth. Ten turned to Carson.

"On the contrary. We're thinking of expanding," Carson said.

"Expanding how?" The brothers had Ten's attention now.

"Well," Carson said, his blue eyes twinkling, "For starters, I'd like to bring in another psychic or two. We were thinking maybe someone with a different talent than any of us have."

"What, like Broughan Beals and his talent for energy healing?" Ten loved the energy healer. Broughan had been a big help when he'd lost the use of his gift a few months back.

"We thought about him, but we were also thinking about a talent who does astrological readings, birth charts, crystal work, past life regression, or something along those lines."

Ten nodded. Those were all really good ideas. "What about house cleaners?" It was an idea he'd been kicking around in his own head for a long time now. Living in Salem, they would have plenty of clients who inquired about getting unfriendly spirits out of their house. Ten had a bit of experience with that kind of work, but not on the level of a professional ghost hunter.

Cole and Carson exchanged a silent look.

Dixie ran away from Carson's side and happy-barked at thin air. She sat down, and her tail started thumping against the floor.

"Damn, Ten. It's like you read their minds," Bertha Craig cackled.

"Hi, Mom!" Carson and Craig chorused together.

"Is that so, Bertha?" Ten grinned at his favorite mentor from the other side. "Seems like you've also managed to charm my dog." He raised an eyebrow at the spirit.

"Maybe this bit of fluff would love you more if you didn't keep running off and leaving her." Bertha bent down and ran her hand over Dixie's back. The dog yipped and rolled over onto her back.

"Can Dixie actually feel that?" Cole asked.

"Sure looks like it." Carson looked as stunned as his brother sounded.

"Guys, the house cleaners?" Ten said, sounding more impatient than he meant to.

Carson turned away from his mother and Dixie and shook his head as if he were trying to remember the conversation. "We wanted to talk this over with you before we made any decisions about expanding the business. We figured we'd talk to the vacuum cleaner repair shop guy next door and see if he's interested in selling the space to us. From what we've been able to tell, he isn't getting much business. People just go out and buy a new vacuum rather than fixing their old one nowadays."

Ten had to agree there. "What would you put in that space if we could get it?"

"Private reading space for each of us." Cole pointed back and forth between himself and Ten. "Since the reading room here was Mom's I thought Carson should keep it."

"No argument here!" Bertha called out from the floor where she was still playing with Dixie.

"That goes double for me," Ten agreed.

"We'd also put a business office in there and any leftover space could be used for consultations for anyone else we brought onboard." Carson shoved his hands into the front pocket of his jeans and seemed to be studying Tennyson.

Ten knew Carson was reading him or was trying to anyway. He was smart enough to have shut himself down when Carson and Cole had been laying the plan out. "I'm assuming buying the space next door would require some kind of a business loan that the three of us would need to sign together, right?"

Carson nodded.

"I like this idea a lot, but I need to talk to Ronan about this now that we're married." Ten knew Ronan would support him in anything he wanted to do, but when it involved signing his name to a mortgage document and risking his credit, Ronan needed a vote in the matter.

"Same goes for us. We haven't mentioned this to Truman or Cassie yet. We wanted to hear what you thought first." Carson grinned at Ten.

Tennyson was all for expanding and bringing in additional talent. It would be especially helpful when things got crazy with Ronan and one of his cold cases that pulled him away from his work at the shop. Things were quiet now, but Ten didn't need his sixth sense to know they wouldn't stay that way for long.

5

Ronan

Ronan was back at his desk reading Tank Hutchins' letter for what had to be the hundredth time in the last twenty-four hours. He could recite it by heart.

He wanted to jump in the Mustang and hightail it to Walpole, but before he could do that, he needed more information. Pulling up a fresh Google Chrome browser on his computer, he surfed to *The Boston Globe's* website and did a search for The Riverside Ripper. Opening a second browser, he did the same thing on *The Boston Herald's* website.

With his cup of expensive coffee sitting next to his left hand, he began to read.

It took nearly two hours for him to get through all of the articles from *The Globe.* What Ronan found most disturbing of all was that dead serial killer, Rod Jacobson had written an expose on Thomas "Tank" Hutchins that ran on the front page of *The Sunday Globe* back in August of 2015. He'd shivered reading that asshole's byline on the article. As much as Ronan hated that motherfucker, his article had been the most informative and well-researched of everything he'd read.

Born in 1986 in Haverhill, Massachusetts, Thomas and his twin brother, Timothy, had grown up in nearby Methuen. They'd gone to Methuen High School where they'd been standout athletes, lettering in football, basketball, and track. Tank was a standout in the decathlon, while Tim had been a state champion pole vaulter and short distance runner. He still held a Methuen Rangers record in the 100 meters.

The brothers had gone their own way after graduation. Tim had gone to a local technical college and had then apprenticed with Daly Brothers Construction out of Charlestown, Massachusetts. Tank had gone to UMass Lowell on a track scholarship and had majored in finance. He'd graduated near the top of his class and with honors.

Life had gone on from there. Tim had married Michelle and had his three sons, while Tank had been married and divorced, with little drama. According to Jacobson's interviews with the Hutchins family, Tank had doted on his nephews.

Where had it all gone so wrong?

Ronan finished off the rest of his high-test coffee while he read The Riverside Ripper articles in *The Boston Herald*. He didn't learn anything in those articles that he hadn't already read in the other paper. He hated to admit it, but the Jacobson article was the most informative one of them all. He wasn't sure how he'd present that little nugget to Tennyson and Fitzgibbon when the time came. Carefully, he assumed.

His next step was to watch news footage from the beginning stages of the investigation through to the conviction and sentencing of Thomas Hutchins.

Ronan sighed. He picked up Tank's letter. *My friends and family call me Tank...* When had Ronan started thinking of himself as a friend?

None of this made any sense. He was a member of the BPD's Cold Case Unit. The Riverside Ripper case was closed. Tom "Tank" Hutchins had been convicted and sentenced. He had appeals left to wend their way through the court system. He had a new lawyer and some hotshot private investigator. What did he need Ronan for?

For Tennyson. Obviously.

Tennyson was the ace in the hole. Ten would be able to read Tank and know if he'd committed the murder. It was possible that he could connect with Lorraine McAlpin and find out if Tank killed her or not. Although the problem with this case was Tim Hutchins. He and Tank were identical twins.

If Tank's supposition that his twin was the killer was correct, how on earth would Lorraine know which brother had killed her?

Knowing that he'd lost his mind, Ronan grabbed the keys to the Mustang. Fitzgibbon's office door was closed. His boss would never know where he'd gone if he left now. As casually as he possibly could, he made toward the bank of elevators.

Half an hour later, Ronan was pushing the Mustang past 85 M.P.H. down I-95 South toward Walpole, Massachusetts. Ronan had himself an appointment to meet with Tank Hutchins and his dream team at MCI-Cedar Junction.

He'd called the lawyer's office from the parking garage and had been shocked when his legal assistant had put him right through to the big guy himself, no lines, no waiting. Bradford Hicks said he'd see what he could do about getting Jude Byrne to be there for the meeting too. Jude was a busy man, after all with cheating husbands to photograph and totally able-bodied people claiming to be disabled to catch in the act of moving pianos, and all that jazz. Ronan had absolutely no doubt the P.I. would be there today.

What was gnawing at Ronan was that he hadn't told Tennyson about this little field trip. His husband had texted him earlier in the morning to let him know that his day was so overbooked with readings that he might not be home in time for dinner. The same went for Carson and Cole. Ronan would bet the house that their episode of *Dateline* had aired on some cable station last night. That always made appointments at West Side Magick book at lightspeed.

It was the perfect day to make the thirty-mile trip down to the prison to see Hutchins and his dream team. Ten would never know he'd left the confines of the precinct house in South Boston. With a little luck, neither would Fitzgibbon. He would have an easier time explaining this to Ten than he would to Kevin at this stage of the game, although he had a bit of wiggle room now that his boss was also one of his best friends. He hoped. Either way, it was always easier to beg for forgiveness than to ask for permission.

Ronan saw the chain link fence and razor wire long before he saw the white-washed brick structure of the prison. Four guard towers were stationed around the property and he could see the officers manning them were well-armed. He shivered in the bright fall sunshine. It was the first time in his life that Ronan O'Mara had been to a maximum-security prison.

After he parked the car, Ronan spent a few minutes getting himself together. He had spent the near hour-long drive figuring out just what it was he was hoping to get out of this meeting. As he climbed out of the Mustang, he still didn't have a clear answer. The best he could do at this point was agree to sit and listen to what Tank and his people had to say. He'd use his gut instinct to figure out if he was being told the truth or being sold a line of bull.

After he signed the visitor's log and turned his gun over to the corrections officer in charge, Ronan was led out of the main office and down a sterile looking hall. Ronan didn't know what he was expecting, but this pleasant hallway wasn't it.

His only experience with prison was what he saw on television or in the movies. Let's face it, *The Shawshank Redemption* and *Orange is the New Black* didn't really paint a realistic picture of what life was like in a modern-day men's correctional facility.

"This is it, Detective O'Mara." The guard stopped outside a normal-looking door. There were no obvious locks on it. There were no bars and no alarm.

"Where's the security?" Ronan asked softly.

"This is a family visitor's room. Inmates with the best behavior records and those with their attorney present are allowed to have visits in these rooms, rather than in the cubicles with inches of plexiglass and the connecting telephones. Mr. Hutchins is one of our best inmates. When your visit is over just come back to the main desk. I'll sign you out and return your firearm." The officer opened the door for Ronan by twisting the knob. No key was necessary.

Ronan had never seen anything like this on *Law and Order*, that was for sure. The visitor's room had a large rectangular table in the center of it. Off to the side was a lumpy looking sofa and next to that was a bin with some toys.

Ronan wasn't focused on the toys or the furniture though, he was looking at the trio of men sitting at the table. To his left was a man in what he'd guess was a five-hundred-dollar suit. That must be Bradford Hicks. The lawyer was clean shaven with close-set dark eyes and a receding hairline. The man in the center wore an orange jumpsuit. A dead giveaway for Tank Hutchins. The man sitting to his right, by default, must be the P.I.

"Bradford Hicks. You must be Detective O'Mara." He held out his hand.

Ronan shook it, instantly noticing what a weak grip the man had. He hoped for Tank's sake he was a better lawyer than his hand shake indicated. "I am. It's good to meet you."

"I'm Tom Hutchins." Tank stood up and held out his hand.

He shook the offered hand. Ronan noticed he wasn't handcuffed or shackled at all. He remembered the corrections officer saying that Hutchins was one of the best-behaved inmates at Walpole, but he still wished he had his gun clipped to his hip.

"Jude Byrne," The last man said in a deep voice, making no move to stand or shake Ronan's hand. His eyes were an odd hazel color. When he turned his head a certain way, they blazed golden. His hair was so dark it was ebony. He was, in a word, stunning.

Nodding curtly at the rude bastard, Ronan sat down at the opposite end of the table. He took a minute to study Tank. The man no longer lived up to his nickname. He was still tall, Ronan would guess he stood around 6'2" but gone was the bulk that had made him a state champion shot putter and discus thrower. His skin seemed to hang on his now lankier frame and his skin was sallow, having that dusky institutionalized pallor. This was not a man that saw much sunshine. "I got your letter, Mr. Hutchins."

Tom nodded. "Thank you for coming to see me. I wasn't sure you would."

"Why *did* you come, Ronan? And where is your psychic? Or do you prefer to call him your husband?" Jude Byrne asked. His leonine eyes betrayed no hint of emotion. He leaned forward in his seat as if he were suddenly more interested in the Boston detective.

Ronan grinned at the private investigator. In his nearly thirteen years on the police force he'd learned that most guys who ended up doing P.I. work were the ones who'd washed out of the police academy, usually because they'd failed the psych exam. He'd bet a month's pay that Byrne fell into that category. "As I'm sure you can imagine, Mr. Hutchins," Ronan turned his attention back to the convicted killer, "my husband and I get a lot of letters asking for help in matters that require his particular skill set. To be perfectly honest with you, yours was the first letter that I've gotten from a convicted felon."

"I told you I'm innocent," Tank said simply. There was no heat behind his words.

"If I polled the other eight hundred cons in this building, they'd all tell me the same thing, right?" Ronan kept his tone level.

Hutchins nodded. "I suppose they would."

"I read your letter and then I read every newspaper article about your case that I could get my hands on. It's obvious that you know who Tennyson is and what his gift has done to aid in other investigations I've been a part of."

Tom nodded. "I believe in his gift enough to know that he'd see right through me if I was lying. If I were a guilty man, Detective O'Mara, I wouldn't be wasting your time."

Ronan raised an eyebrow at the con. "Here's what I find interesting, Mr. Hutchins. You and your twin share the same DNA. There will always be room for reasonable doubt if you win an appeal and are granted a new trial. There was no fingerprint evidence found with the victim's body, which really could have saved your bacon."

The P.I. snorted. "And how exactly would that have saved his *bacon*, detective?"

Did the private dick even realize he snorted like a pig? It took all of his willpower for Ronan not to roll his eyes. "While identical twins share DNA, they don't have the same fingerprints."

Jude didn't respond verbally, but Ronan saw his jaw visibly tighten. *Touché, asshole!* Ronan was glad he'd done a little research on twins while he'd been stuck in traffic on I-95.

"You're saying one fingerprint could have set me free?" Tank shook his head. "If it weren't for bad luck, I'd have no luck at all here."

"You do realize that even if Tennyson and I agree to work on this case there might not be anything we can do to help you." This had been the one sticking point Ronan couldn't seem to overcome. He was going to need to discuss this case with Ten and with Fitzgibbon at some point in time and this was the one reason both men were going to latch onto as why they should leave this one alone.

"Story of my life, Detective O'Mara." Tank crossed his arms over his thin chest.

"Typical psychic bullshit." Byrne clicked his tongue against the roof of his mouth. "You have to couch your bets in case *the spirits* aren't speaking that day." He made air quotes over "the spirits."

Ronan burst out laughing. He couldn't help himself. This guy was such an asshole. Byrne also reminded him of himself on the day he and Tennyson met.

"My client is looking at twenty-five years to life for a crime he didn't commit, detective. What could possibly be funny at a time like this?" Bradford Hicks asked.

"You're obviously at the end of your evidence here, Mr. Hicks. That, or one of you really believes in psychics. I'm guessing it's you, since Tank probably isn't getting a lot of opportunities to watch *Long Island Medium* here at Cedar Junction. As I said earlier, your letter is the first one we've gotten from a convicted felon. Usually, we're getting requests for help from bereaved family members of the *victim* in cases like this. I wanted to come here today to hear not only what you all had to say, but to look Mr. Hutchins in the eye and see if his story held up to my years of gut instinct.

"This isn't a cold case. It's been fully prosecuted and you've been convicted. It's going to take a hell of a lot to convince Tennyson to come here and for my captain to agree to give us time to look into it. One member of your team thinks what we do is total bullshit and I get that. I was in his exact position a year ago. To answer your question, Mr. Hicks, there is nothing funny about this situation. Courts don't like to overturn murder convictions, especially ones with iron-clad DNA. It takes a mountain of new evidence or a grievous mistake in the first trial for an appellate judge to even consider making that move. As I said, there might not be anything Tennyson and I can do to help."

"What do you mean? All Tennyson needs to do is talk to Lorraine McAlpin. She will be able to tell you I didn't kill her." Tank looked confused.

"How, Mr. Hutchins? I told you that I read every newspaper article I could find on this case. I also watched news footage. I've seen so many pictures of you and Tim together and I'll be damned if I could tell you who was who. If Lorraine saw her killer, she saw *your* face."

Tank's eyes narrowed on Ronan. His eyebrows knit together. Dawning slowly lit in his eyes as if he hadn't thought of that possibility before.

Ronan watched as all of the fight seemed to pass right out of Tank Hutchins. For some reason that made him want to pick up the baton and fight for him. The question was how to get Tennyson and Fitzgibbon to agree to help him.

6

Tennyson

Tennyson was worn to the bone. He'd done five in-person readings and seven more phone readings. He hadn't gotten home until after 7pm. Thankfully, Truman had been able to stop by and pick up Dixie at the shop, otherwise his little lady would have had to go without her dinner until he'd been able to get away.

It wasn't until Ten had gotten home and settled with Dixie that he realized Ronan wasn't home either. He checked his phone for messages and saw there weren't any. It wasn't like Ronan not text him or leave a voicemail at some point during the day. So far as Ten knew, Ronan was going to spend the day in the office going through his caseload trying to figure out which cold case would be the next one the two of them would investigate together.

He dug into his back pocket for his phone when he heard Dixie bark and Ronan's key turning in the lock. Seconds later, the house alarm started its set of warning beeps letting them know they had fifteen seconds to key the code before the real alarm started to wail.

"Ten? Can you get the alarm? My arms are full!" Ronan called from the hall.

Ten sure as hell hoped his husband's arms were full with dinner. He was starving, and it was nearly 7:30pm. He raced from the kitchen through the living room, past his husband, who he noticed was *not* carrying take-out bags. Ten punched in the alarm code and locked the door.

After what had happened in the last few months with Ronan being shot on their front steps, it wasn't like him to be too preoccupied to lock the door and arm the alarm. Whatever it was his husband was carrying had his full and undivided attention.

When Ten walked into the kitchen, Ronan was unpacking several large accordion folders. There were stacks of papers all over their dining room table. From where he was standing, one pile looked like newspaper articles. The next looked like police and evidence reports, and the last stack looked like a trial transcript. Why on earth would Ronan have one of those? Had he been asked to look into an appeal of some sort? "Ronan, what-?"

"Oh, good, you're home," Ronan said distractedly. "We've got a lot to talk about." He went back to sorting through his ton of papers without even looking up at Tennyson.

Ten got his first good look at his husband and didn't like what he saw at all. Ronan's usually tame dirty-blond hair was sticking up all over the place as if he'd been carding his hands through it all day. His white dress shirt was half tucked into his pants and his tie was loosened crookedly. Ronan was a mess. Combine that with his near manic shuffling of papers and Tennyson was worried. He set his hands on Ronan's shoulders and gently pulled him back from the table. "Ronan?"

"Ten, what? Can't you see I'm busy here?" Ronan's eyes flashed annoyance at his husband.

"You just said you had a lot to talk to me about. Why don't you start with explaining what all of this is and why it has you in a near manic state. You're a disaster. When was the last time you ate something?" Ten grimaced. There was probably a better way he could have said that, but there were also worse ways. His husband looked like he was homeless or like he'd lost his shirt gambling at the track.

Ronan looked confused like he had no idea when his last meal was. "That's not important right now. This is."

Ten sighed. "Okay, what is *this*?"

"It's The Riverside Ripper case." Ronan fisted his hands on his hips.

"It's the *what*?" Ten vaguely remembered that moniker, but for the life of him couldn't remember what the case was about. Whatever it was, it couldn't be good. When the word "Ripper" was attached to a murder, it usually meant the scene had been especially gory.

"The Riverside Ripper." Ronan rolled his eyes as if Tennyson should have remembered the case off the top of his head. "Lorraine McAlpin was stabbed to death and her body was left on the banks of the Mystic River in Charlestown three years ago."

Ten nodded. That name rang a bell now that he had a bit more context. "Wasn't someone arrested and convicted of that crime?" It was all coming back to him now. A pretty brunette swam into focus in his mind's eye.

Ronan nodded. "His name is Tom Hutchins."

Ten frowned. "I'm confused then. How is this a cold case if someone has been arrested and convicted? Did Lorraine's family reach out to you at the precinct?" Ten would be more than happy to reunite Lorraine's family with the murdered woman.

"No, Lorraine's family didn't reach out to us. Tom Hutchins did. He sent me a letter. I drove down to see him at MCI-Cedar Junction today."

Tennyson's blood ran cold. Ronan spent the day in a prison filled with killers and rapists and hadn't told him he was going? "You did what?" He took a deep breath hoping that would calm his racing heart down enough to hear Ronan's answer.

"I went to see Tank Hutchins at the prison." Ronan made it sound like going to a prison to see a killer was something he did every day.

"*Tank*?" Ten shook his head, feeling lost. "I thought you said his name was Tom?"

Ronan rolled his eyes. "His friends and family call him Tank."

"Oh, so you're a *friend* now? You're friends with a convicted murderer?" Tennyson felt like he'd walked into an episode of *The Twilight Zone*. What the hell was going on with his husband? For the last thirteen years Ronan's mission in life had been to put criminal behind bars, now all of a sudden, Ronan was trying to get a killer out?

"It's not a big deal, Ten. Tank wasn't even in handcuffs." Ronan shrugged.

"Not in handcuffs? He's a convicted murderer!" Tennyson's voice was shrill. He could feel his own panic rising. What the hell was going on with his husband? It wasn't so long ago that he was lying in a hospital bed with three bullets in his chest. Was this a result of that? He hadn't died so now he felt he was bulletproof? Unstoppable? Ten couldn't believe what he was hearing.

"He needs our help, Ten." Ronan sat down at the table and looked up at his husband.

"And what, you want to give it to him? You want to use my gift to help this cold-blooded killer?" Tennyson's head was spinning.

"Yes," Ronan said simply. "He's innocent. I don't have your sixth sense, but I have thirteen years of my own gut instinct to follow and it's telling me this man didn't kill anyone."

"If he's innocent, who killed Lorraine McAlpin?" Jesus Christ, Ronan wanted him to use his gift to help a killer? What the hell was next? Ronan asking for this week's Powerball numbers? Tennyson was beside himself.

"His twin brother, Tim, killed Lorraine. It's the only other explanation." Ronan pawed through the paperwork until he found what he was looking for and held it up.

"What?" This sounded like one of those *Law and Order* ripped-from-the-headlines episodes. Tennyson shook his head. He had no idea what Ronan was holding up for him to see. He assumed it was a DNA report or a birth certificate for the twin. It could be a report saying that fucking aliens had landed at Fenway Park for all the fucks he had to give at this moment in time.

"He has a twin brother named Tim. There was DNA found on Lorraine's body. The killer cut himself during the attack. If it wasn't Tank who killed her, it had to be Tim." Ronan stood up. "Look, I brought everything home to show you." He spread his arms wide. "Newspaper articles. Police reports. Evidence reports. I even called a buddy at the court and had a copy of the trial transcript sent over. We can call out for Thai and dig into this all tonight."

Ten shook his head. "No!" The absolute last thing he wanted to do after the long day he'd had was to dig into evidence reports and a murder trial transcript. He wanted dinner, a bath, and possibly a quickie hand job before he fell asleep with his head on his husband's shoulder.

"What do you mean, 'no?'" Ronan growled, looking dumbfounded. "We need to help this man."

"I don't need to help anyone." Tennyson shook his head.

"What the hell is wrong with you?" Ronan's eyes narrowed at his husband.

"What's wrong with *me*?" Tennyson shouted. "I'm not the one who spent the day in a prison without telling you. Did Fitzgibbon sign off on this little field trip?"

A guilty look flashed across Ronan's face.

"Jesus fucking Christ, Ronan! You walked into a prison filled with the worst among us and no one fucking knew where you were? Are you crazy?" Ten was starting to feel like he was the one losing his mind.

None of this made any sense. Why had his usually level-headed husband suddenly lost his marbles?

"Why are you so upset about this? I was perfectly safe."

"Upset? Upset!" Ten's head felt like it was going to explode. "Did you think for one second about all of the people you're responsible for sending to Walpole? Not the least of which is your scumbag, child raping, murdering, ex-fucking-husband! Did it ever cross your mind that this was some kind of a set-up? That Josh arranged this to get you into the prison. Or that someone was lying in wait to shiv your stupid fucking ass, Ronan?" Ten knew he was screeching like a fish wife, but he didn't care.

Ronan stared at him with his mouth hanging open. No sound came out.

"We've been married for nine days and you're trying to widow me already." Ten could feel tears streaking down his face. The shocked look on Ronan's face told him that his husband hadn't thought of any of the scenarios that Ten had just laid out for him. "If you had just told me about the damn letter or brought it home, I could have gotten a read on it. Found out if it was genuine or if you were in any danger. But no, you kept it from me intentionally. Why, Ronan?" Ten demanded.

Anger replaced the guilt in Ronan's blue eyes. "I'm a grown man, Tennyson. I don't need your permission to do anything."

"Why did you keep this from me?" Ten asked, this time his voice was more conversational and less demanding. He hoped that would encourage his pig-headed husband to talk to him.

Ronan's upper lip curled into a snarl. "Because I knew you'd say no. Okay? I wanted to hear what this guy had to say, so I went to see him."

"Since when do we help the bad guys?" Ten heard the judgmental tone in his voice and instantly regretted it, but it was too late to take it back now.

"When they're innocent," Ronan gritted out.

"How do you know he's innocent? Are *you* psychic all of a sudden?" Ten winced. He definitely shouldn't have said that.

"How do you know he isn't innocent? You're so damn stubborn, you won't even read any of this stuff." Ronan threw his arms wide to indicate all of the papers he'd brought home with him.

"*I'm* stubborn?" Ten had reached the end of his patience. "You went into a maximum-security prison without telling anyone where you were, to see a convicted murderer who *claims* to be innocent like every other con who ever lived, and *I'm* stubborn?"

"You're being unreasonable. Look at me." Ronan thumped his chest. "I'm fine."

"Jesus Christ, Ronan. This isn't a fucking movie. You're not Dirty Harry. In case you've forgotten you've got four bullet holes in you. We keep talking about our future daughter. If you keep up this kind of behavior, there isn't going to be a daughter, or if there is, I'm going to end up raising her by myself. The only thing she'll have of you beside your stubborn Irish DNA, is the folded flag draping your coffin that some officer in the BPD handed me at your funeral." Ten got up from the table and walked toward the kitchen door.

"Where are you going?" Ronan demanded.

Ten turned around with a sour look on his face. "You don't tell me where you were all day, but I owe you an explanation of where I'm going *now*?" Ten shut his mouth before the words, "How fucking dare you?" could slip from his lips. He turned from his husband and kept walking.

"If you walk out that door don't expect me to be here when you come home," Ronan spat at Tennyson's retreating back.

Knowing he'd say something he could never take back if he opened his mouth now, Tennyson grabbed his keys from the table in the hall and walked out the front door.

They'd just had their first fight as a married couple and Tennyson Grimm-O'Mara felt like shit.

7

Ronan

The sound of the front door slamming echoed loudly in the empty house. Part of Ronan wanted to take off running after his husband, while the other part was glad the harpy was gone. At least now he could listen to himself think.

Even Dixie looked thunderstruck. She stared up at Ronan and then looked toward the empty living room where Tennyson had gone and back at Ronan again. She didn't whimper, didn't bark, she just seemed lost.

"Well, shit." Ronan sat back down at the table. He really hadn't expected Tennyson to walk out. He supposed daring him to do it by saying he wouldn't be there if Ten left really was the last nail in his coffin.

What did he do now? Did he pack a bag and head over to Fitzgibbon's house? Or, did he stand his ground and sleep here? "What do I do, Dixie, my little pixie?"

Dixie, seeming to finally realize Ten was gone, let out a sharp bark and ran to the door. A second later, she let out a howl.

It sounded grief-stricken to Ronan. Not that he blamed her in the slightest. He wanted to howl for Tennyson too.

Step one was to pack up all of the Hutchins material. That was the last thing Tennyson needed to see when he got home. *If* he came home.

Would he spend the night with Carson and Truman? Ronan had no idea. This was the first fight they'd had since they'd moved in together. Their first fight as a married couple.

In the past when they'd have a disagreement, they both had their own apartments to go back to and cool off. Now, they shared the same space. The rules had changed but neither of them had bothered to figure out what the new rules were. Why would they? They were newlyweds and so blissfully happy that the thought of this happening was never on their radar.

Ronan grabbed the printed newspaper articles and shoved them back into the first partition of an empty accordion folder. He hated to admit it, but Tennyson had made several good points while he'd been screaming like an Irish banshee. It had never once crossed his mind that Tank Hutchins' letter could have been a set-up of any kind from one of the killers he'd sent to MCI Walpole or from his ex-husband, Josh Gatlin.

It had been more important to him to get out of the office without Fitzgibbon seeing him than it was for him to have given a thought to his own personal safety. Ronan rubbed a hand against the three puckered bullet scars on the right side of his chest. Three months ago, he was lying in a coma, not knowing if he was going to live or die. Tennyson had every right to worry about his impulsiveness today, but wasn't an innocent man rotting away in a prison cell just as important as his safety?

Tennyson would obviously argue no.

Sighing, Ronan cleaned up the rest of the papers on the table and scribbled his husband a quick note.

He sprinted up the stairs and grabbed his rolling carry-on bag out of the closet in Fitzgibbon's old room and brought it back into their bedroom. He packed for the night and for work the next day. With a heavy heart, he zipped up the bag and rolled it out of the room without a backward glance. He knew it would hurt too much to look back at the bed he and Ten had shared every night since they'd moved into the house.

When he got back down to the bottom of the stairs, Dixie was still sitting in front of the door, waiting for Tennyson. He sat down on the bottom step. "Hey, little girl."

The puppy didn't budge. She didn't even turn around. It was like she hadn't heard him at all.

If his life wasn't lying in ruins at his feet, he would have laughed. Okay, well, this sucked. He picked up the puppy, who went limp in his hands, reminding him of the internet cat videos he'd seen of felines who went boneless after their owners dressed them up in costumes.

He shifted Dixie into his right arm, cradling her against his chest, and walked into the kitchen to pick up the Hutchins files. He walked back through the living room and to the front door. Picking up his keys and grabbing the handle to his suitcase, he armed the alarm and walked out the door.

It crossed his mind to walk three doors down to Truman and Carson's house to speak to his husband, but he didn't want to involve their friends any more than they already were involved. Instead, he walked across the street to Fitzgibbon's house and rang the doorbell.

"Hey, Uncle Ronan!" Greeley Fitzgibbon shouted. He reached out to hug Ronan until he noticed Ronan's arms were full and there was a suitcase sitting on the stairs. "Uh, Dad! I think Uncle Ronan's moving in with us!"

"Funny, kid!" Kevin Fitzgibbon laughed. He came down the hall toward the front door wiping his hands on a red dish towel. He got one look at Ronan and the jovial look on his face sobered instantly. "Don't you have that application to Salem State to finish up?"

Greeley shot his father a confused look, but he nodded anyway. "I'll be upstairs if you need me."

"Come on in." Fitzgibbon grabbed Ronan's suitcase and shut the door behind him.

"Thanks. I was starting to wonder if you both were going to leave me out on the stoop all night."

"I assume there's a story that goes with the suitcase?" Fitzgibbon asked. "Hello, sweetheart." He plucked Dixie out of the crook of Ronan's arm.

"Yeah and it's a doozy." Ronan shook his head, still not quite able to wrap his head around it fully.

"Follow me into the kitchen. I was making dinner for me and the kid. It's no trouble to add another plate to the table."

Ronan trailed behind his boss. He hadn't been to Kevin's house since they'd finished moving in all the boxes and furniture last week. Kevin and Greeley had wanted to set things up on their own. At least that was the line they'd sold Ronan and Tennyson. He'd had a feeling Kevin wanted them to get back to honeymooning. He and Ten hadn't been in the mood to argue. They'd been in the mood for something else entirely that was clothing-optional.

"So, does the suitcase have to do with where you mysteriously disappeared to this afternoon?" Fitzgibbon raised a knowing eyebrow at Ronan.

"Shit, Cap. You should become a detective. Anyone ever tell you that?" Ronan sighed.

"Funny. Now talk. Don't make me suspend you on principle alone."

Ronan shivered at the tone in his voice. It was part disappointed father and part frustrated boss. He dug through one of the accordion folders until he found the cursed letter from Tank Hutchins. "Read this first and then I'll explain. It was waiting for me on my desk when I came back to work after my honeymoon."

Kevin silently took the paper and read it. His green eyes popped up over the top of it after a few minutes, but he didn't say a word. Ronan assumed his boss was reading the contents for a second time.

Fitzgibbon sighed heavily and set the letter down on the kitchen table. "I'm not a psychic, but I'm going to play one in my kitchen. You went to see Hutchins along with his goon of a P.I. and his fancy lawyer. Not only didn't you tell *me* where you were going, but you didn't tell

Tennyson either. Last and by no means least, there are approximately twenty-five cons in that *maximum-security prison* that you are responsible for putting there, including your ex-husband. Tennyson was upset because he didn't know where you were and because you didn't seem to have any concern for your own safety. Am I close?" Kevin crossed his arms over his broad chest. His smile didn't reach his eyes.

"More or less," Ronan mumbled. "He might have mentioned something about the letter having been a trap to shiv my stupid ass."

Fitzgibbon snorted before he burst out laughing. "I'm taking it that was a direct quote from your newlywed and now estranged husband?"

Frowning at the word "estranged," Ronan nodded. "Nothing happened to me, so why is he so upset?"

Kevin stared at Ronan like the man had three heads. "Did you really just ask me that ridiculous question or am I having a stroke?"

Ronan wasn't going to answer that question.

"Three months ago, you were lying in a bloody heap at the bottom of your front stairs, Ronan. I think Ten deserves a little slack for being upset over this. Hell, I deserve a friggen medal for not going off on you myself and suspending your stupid ass for running this errand on the department's time. Not only as your friend but also as your commanding officer, I knew you were working on something and not out betting on the horses, but Jesus, can you imagine the fucking shit storm there would have been if anything had happened to you down there? I would have been standing in front of my superiors with my dick in my hand unable to explain to the brass why you'd gone to Walpole."

Greeley walked into the kitchen and instantly turned back around. "My dad is talking about his dick being in his hand. Guess this is the wrong time to ask about dinner." Greeley grimaced and turned to walk back out of the kitchen. "Wash your hands before you touch the food!"

Ronan snorted. It was the first time he'd laughed all day. It didn't help the fact that he and Tennyson were fighting, but his chest didn't feel quite so tight anymore.

"That kid." Fitzgibbon shook his head. "I swear he's got some kind of sixth sense." He went to the cabinet to the right of the sink and grabbed an extra plate which he set down in front of Ronan. Silverware followed and then a glass and can of ginger ale.

It was odd to see Kevin making dinner in his own house. Ronan had seen him pitch in while he and Greeley had been staying at their house, but this was different. He liked this side of his boss. "You like being the country mouse, don't you?"

"You're changing the subject." Fitzgibbon grabbed the oven mitts but kept his shrewd eyes on Ronan.

"Guilty as charged, Cap. There will be time after we eat to talk about The Riverside Ripper and what I've gotten myself into. I remember a time not so long ago when you swore you'd never be a country mouse, but here you are."

Kevin pulled a steaming casserole dish out of the oven. "Being a father changed me. There was nothing I loved more than living in the city, but once I realized that it was a constant reminder to Greeley of his past, I knew we had to go. Even if you hadn't managed to get your stupid ass shot, again." Fitzgibbon raised a sardonic eyebrow at Ronan. "I still would have wanted to move in with you two crazy kids until we found a house here that we loved. Greeley loves Salem and I've loved watching him blossom here."

Ronan nodded. The kid had been through a lot in his seventeen short years. He'd been taken away from his birth mother, kicked out of his foster parents' house when he'd come out to them, nearly killed twice by a serial killer and once more by his proxy. Greeley was tough as nails but living here in Salem had brought out his softer side. Fitzgibbon was right, the teenager really was blossoming into a remarkable young man. "I'm glad it's all working out for you both."

Fitzgibbon pulled the tinfoil back on what looked like lasagna. "It's all going to work out for you too, Ronan. After dinner, I'm going to sit and go through all of the shit in those files. Then, you're going to tell me about your interview with the convict, the lawyer, and the P.I. After that, we'll figure out how to save your marriage and maybe make some brownies. How's that sound?"

"You know how to make brownies?" Ronan found a smile.

"Nope, but if you can read, you can cook. At least that's what Greeley tells me." Kevin slapped a hand down on Ronan's shoulder and gave it a reassuring squeeze. He walked out of the kitchen and Ronan heard him call Greeley down to dinner.

He'd made an absolute fuck up of this entire day but felt better knowing that Kevin was going to help him set things to rights. He could only hope Tennyson would be ready to hear his apology when Ronan finally figured out the right words to say to the man he loved with all of his heart.

8

Tennyson

Tennyson was never so happy to hear the sound of crying babies in all of his life. It was 6:36am and he'd been lying awake in the guest bedroom at Truman and Carson's house staring at the ceiling for the last two hours.

Fitzgibbon had texted him last night to let him know Ronan was spending the night in his spare bedroom. He could have just gone home after he'd had dinner with Carson and Truman, but he didn't want to sleep in his and Ronan's king-sized bed all by himself.

He was the one who'd walked out on his stubborn husband, but that didn't mean his heart wasn't broken over their fight. When he heard the sound of Carson's voice cooing to the babies, Ten got out of bed and trudged down the hall to help.

"Well, look what the cat dragged in," Bertha Craig cackled. "You're looking like you didn't get any sleep at all, Tenny."

"Good morning to you too, Bertha." Ten grimaced at the spirit of his best friend's mother. He scooped a pissy looking Brian out of his crib and carried the smelly infant to an empty changing table.

Bertha had been the original founder of West Side Magick back in the 1980s. Neither one of her sons had shown any psychic ability when she'd been alive. On her deathbed nearly three years ago, she'd asked Carson and Cole to keep the store open as her legacy. It wasn't until about a year after her death that Carson had his first vision. Cole started developing his own psychic powers after that. The brothers had brought Ten in to help them hone their skills and their partnership had grown into a friendship from there.

"Ten and Ronan had their first married fight last night, Mom," Carson said gently, wiping a mess from baby Bertha's bottom. The baby held out her chubby hands to her Mimi.

"I'm dead, Carson, not blind. I've seen that look before. I might have even worn it a time or two in the years I spent married to your father. That dirty son-of-a-..."

"Mom!" Carson barked.

"For the love of God, Carson. They're haddock. They don't understand a word I'm saying." Bertha folded her arms over her chest.

Carson scooped up his mother's namesake and cuddled the baby against his chest. "They are not haddock!"

"Who's haddock? I like haddock. We should have that for supper." Truman was all smiles as he breezed into the babies' bedroom. "Stephanie, did these mean men leave you all alone with a poopie diaper?" He pulled the baby out of her crib and dry heaved. "Oh my God, child! What did you eat?"

Carson started to laugh. "Mom is here. She says she recognizes the look on Ten's face because Corny put it on her face enough during their marriage."

"Well, that explains everything." The look on Truman's face said that Carson's words clearly did *not* explain anything.

"What happened, Tenny?" Bertha asked.

The last thing Tennyson wanted to do was explain the fight again, especially in the cold light of day. "Ronan got a letter from a convicted murderer asking him to come visit him in prison. He says he's innocent and that I can prove it. Ronan went to see him yesterday and didn't tell me or Fitzgibbon he was going." Ten sighed.

Bertha frowned. "Surely you're not *this* upset because Handsome went somewhere without telling you."

Ten shook his head. "This killer is housed in the same prison as Josh Gatlin and about twenty other men who Ronan helped put away. I freaked out thinking the letter might have been a trap to get Ronan down there where one of those men could have attacked him."

"Okay, that makes more sense. I'm guessing you lost your mind a bit and Ronan doesn't understand why this is such a big deal."

"Yeah. I see those bullet scars every day, Bertha. I was the one sitting by his side listening to that damn machine beep out his heartbeat day after day. We came so close to losing him. There are still days when I can feel that paralyzing fear again like a memory, you know? Ronan doesn't know what that's like. I pray he never does." Ten hugged the baby closer to his chest.

"It's like when your kid makes a break toward the street. You run like hell to save him and snatch him up just before he gets hit by a car. He's safe, but every time you see that part of the road again, you can't help but remember that day. That car. How close you came to losing the most precious thing in your life." Bertha raised an eyebrow at Carson, whose mouth dropped open soundlessly.

Ten nodded. That was how he felt in a nutshell. "It's stone cold fear in my heart, Bertha, but it came out as anger."

"How are you feeling now that you've had a chance to sleep on your feelings?"

"I miss the stupid jerk." Ten grinned.

Truman snorted and started to laugh. "What the hell question was *that* the answer to?" He picked up Stephanie and peppered the baby's head with noisy kisses.

"Bertha asked how I was feeling after I slept on the fight."

Truman frowned. "You cried on my couch for an hour. You picked at my world-famous chicken piccata and barely ate five bites. Not even baby love brought a smile to your face and all you can say after all that is you *miss* the stupid jerk?" He rolled his eyes. "Liar, liar, pants on fire!" Truman turned to leave the room. "I'll be downstairs making breakfast. You'd better eat it. That's all I'm saying!"

"Someone's grumpy when they don't get any!" Bertha laughed.

"You don't know the half of it!" Carson agreed.

"Ew, you talk to your mother about sex?" Tennyson couldn't believe his ears. He looked down at Brian who was looking up at him, his big blue eyes were focused on Ten's face.

"What do you talk to your mother about?" Carson grinned.

"Jesus. What else? She's a Bible-toting midwestern Baptist who still thinks Ronan and are both bound for hell when we die. She's eased back on saying those things out loud since she knows our little miss is on the horizon, but there are times when I know she's mentally measuring Ronan and I up for asbestos suits."

Carson burst out laughing. "I didn't want to say anything, but I got that vibe from her at your wedding too. I was just glad she and your dad came. Did you tell her that David and her future granddaughter were both there?"

Ten nodded. "Sort of. She knows David is always with her. I didn't tell her that you-know-who was also there too."

"You can say her name Ten. We all know she has one." Carson rolled his eyes.

"No, I can't. Ronan thinks if we say it out loud we'll jinx things."

"What?" Carson half-shouted.

"Ten told Handsome what I told you about the future when you were little, Carson." Bertha smiled fondly at her son and pressed a kiss to baby Bertha's head.

"Oh, about the future being fluid and changeable?" Carson smiled wistfully at his mother.

Bertha nodded.

"This baby isn't one of those changeable things. I've seen…" Carson stopped talking as if he didn't want to spill the beans.

"I know what you've seen, Carson. I've seen it too." Ten laughed. "I've tried not to, but my little girl is very persistent. She wants me to see this particular thing, so I've seen it. Several times now. I wake up crying happy tears. I think Ronan's seen it too, but he's never mentioned it to me."

"He might think it's just a dream or he might not remember when he wakes up." Bertha hugged Tennyson and kissed her grandson. "Go eat my son-in-law's fabulous breakfast and then go make up with your husband, Tenny. It's not good to let these things go on for too long. Apologize for being overprotective and emotional. Make sure he apologizes right back for scaring the shit out of you. Then fuck like bunnies!"

"Jesus Christ, Mom!" Carson groaned.

"Eeeeeeee!" Baby Bertha giggled, reaching her chubby arms out for her Mimi.

"I love you too, precious!" Bertha kissed her namesake. "You're gonna have to watch out for this one and Ten's little one. They're going to be formidable when they join forces."

"Oh good. The psychic world's version of The Wonder Twins." Carson pinched the bridge of his nose as if he felt a headache coming on.

"Take my advice, Tennyson! I'll kiss your daughter for you. Toodles!" Bertha was gone.

"You have to admit Mom had some good advice." Carson wore a look on his face as if he couldn't believe his mother had marital advice that was worth a damn.

Ten snorted. "The thing about the bunnies?"

Carson nodded.

Ten slapped a hand on his best friend's shoulder. "Let's go eat. I'm gonna need my strength."

9

Ronan

Fitzgibbon was sitting at the dining room table drinking a cup of coffee when Ronan came downstairs. "Morning, Cap."

"You look like shit." Fitzgibbon grinned.

"Feel like it too."

"Will it make you feel better or worse to know that your husband looks equally as bad as you?"

"You saw Tennyson? When?"

"About ten minutes ago. He was walking back from Carson and Truman's house."

"Shit! I told him if he left, I wouldn't be there when he came home."

"Look, Ronan. I know we spent all of last night reading and talking about the Hutchins case, but do you really need me to tell you what you did wrong here?"

Ronan sighed and looked down at his bare feet. "I should have told you and Ten about the letter. I should have let Ten get a psychic read on the letter. I should have told him where I was going and I should have gotten your okay before I left the precinct instead of sneaking out like a booty call in the middle of the night."

"Agreed, but Ronan?"

The exhausted detective looked up wordlessly at his boss.

"When you tell these things to Tennyson, look him in the eye and throw in the phrase, 'I'm sorry.' You'll be surprised how far that will take you. Maybe promise never to go to bed angry again."

Ronan chuckled. "Last night sucked. Not that I don't appreciate your hospitality, but I missed falling asleep with Ten's head on my shoulder."

"Stop wasting time telling me that. Go tell him."

"What are we going to do about the Hutchins case?" Ronan knew he was skating on thin ice just by asking the question.

Fitzgibbon drummed his fingertips on the table. "I'll leave that ball in your husband's court. Technically, there is no case. Tank Hutchins is just a convicted murderer who sent one of my detectives a letter. What that detective and his psychic husband decide to do with that letter in their spare time is their business."

"What if we find something?" Ronan had expected that kind of answer from his boss. There really was no case. It was fine and dandy for Tank to have a new lawyer and a P.I., but until there was new evidence for an appeal, the case was dead in the water.

"*If* you find something, you bring it straight to me. Do not bring it to the shark lawyer. Do not bring it to the sleazy P.I. Am I understood?"

Ronan nodded. "I can't imagine this is going to go much further than this discussion, Cap. You didn't see how upset Tennyson was last night."

"The sunrise has a way of shedding new light on a problem, Ronan. Listen to him. Don't talk over him. Hear me?"

"Yes, sir." Ronan found his first smile of the day.

"Round the conversation out with that stack of dead files on your desk. Now, those are people the two of you can for sure help out. I'm assigning those cases to you since the other detectives have worked them as far as their five senses can take them."

"I had a feeling you were going to say that." The cases were tailor made for them. All Ten had to do was use his gift. All of the usual cold case legwork had already been done.

"I'll set up a meeting to talk about this with the two of you on Monday when Tennyson is back in the office with us." Kevin stood up. "Text me later to let me know how this goes." He yanked Ronan into his arms and gave him a rough hug.

"What the hell was that for?" His boss had never hugged him. Not even after he'd gotten shot.

"For luck. I don't want to play host to you for a second night." Kevin laughed.

***

Ronan stood at the foot of his front steps. His house looked the same as it had yesterday and the day before. He sighed and climbed the brick stairs. He used his key to unlock the door. Dixie started barking and the alarm started chirping simultaneously. "Ten?"

"In the kitchen," Tennyson's tired voice answered.

Leaving his suitcase and the Hutchins' files in the hallway, Ronan kept Dixie under his arm and headed into the kitchen. Ten was sitting at the dining room table with a cup of tea in front of him. Ronan could smell the earthiness of Ten's preferred brand of green tea. "Hi."

"Hi." Ten stood up from the table. "I don't need to be a psychic to see that you didn't get much sleep."

Ronan shook his head. "The spare bed at Fitzgibbon's is too hard. You don't look like *you* got a lot of sleep either." He set Dixie back down on the floor.

"Truman snores, remember?"

"Yeah, how could I forget the night Truman spent in the hospital with me after he'd been attacked?" Ronan had nicknamed him *Little Deuce Coupe* because he'd sounded like a revving car engine.

"Beats me how Carson gets any sleep at all." He'd had enough of this beating around the bush bullshit. He walked to Tennyson and pulled his husband into his arms.

"I missed you," Ten whispered into his ear. "Even if you are stubborn."

"Yeah, well we're equally matched then, because you're stubborn too, but I understand now where you were coming from." Ronan pulled back, taking Ten's face in his hands. "I love you. I'm sorry I was an inconsiderate asshole."

"That's not a half bad apology." Ten shot his husband a shy smile. "I'm sorry too, for flying off the handle like I did even though you were safe. I just remember what it was like seeing you in that hospital bed, not knowing if you were going to survive. I'm not in any hurry to be back in a situation like that again."

"I know, babe. To be honest. It never crossed my mind that the letter from Tom Hutchins could be anything but genuine."

"It never crossed my mind that the letter could be anything but a ruse." Ten shrugged. "This case is like a role reversal. Usually I'm the Pollyanna of the group, thinking everything is rainbows and unicorns. You're usually the skeptical son-of-a-bitch." Ten rested his head against Ronan's heart as if he needed to hear it beating for himself.

Ronan wrapped his arms around his husband and held him close. He'd missed this last night. "You're right. I can't argue with a single thing you just said. The only excuse I have is that I read Tom's letter. It was genuine. We talk all the time about your gift versus my years of gut instinct. I went with my gut."

Ten pulled back from Ronan. "Did you explain all of this to Kevin?" He sat down at the table and took a sip from his tea.

"Yeah. I told him all about our fight and then after we had dinner, we sat down and went through the whole case file."

Ten held up his hand. "I don't want to hear any of it."

Ronan's brows knitted together. "Wait, I thought we were making progress here."

"We are. If I'm going to come into this Hutchins thing, I don't want to be influenced by what you or Fitzgibbon think."

"Are you saying you want to read the letter and the file?"

Ten nodded. "I don't have any readings scheduled until this afternoon, so I was planning on grabbing a couple hours sleep in my own bed. Maybe we could call out for pizza tonight and I could read the file after dinner?"

Ronan liked the sound of that. He only wished he could go back to bed too. "Yeah, that works. I'm gonna run up and grab a shower before I have to head in to the office for the day."

"Are you really going to work or off on another wild convict chase?" Ten grinned up at his husband.

"I'm going to work. I swear." Ronan held up his pinkie finger. "Cap has some new files he's assigning to us. He's going to meet with us about them on Monday when you're back in the office."

Tennyson perched on his tiptoes to press a kiss to Ronan's lips. "Can't wait."

Neither could Ronan.

10

Tennyson

Tennyson was pleasantly surprised to see Ronan was home when he got back from the Magick Shop a little after 5pm. Not only was Ronan home, but the house was spotless and so was Dixie.

"Shit, Fitzgibbon didn't fire your ass, did he?" Ten asked as he scooped his fresh smelling baby into his arms. Dixie responded by bathing his face in her love.

"No, of course not. I hightailed it out of the city around 3pm after I spent the day working on the new cases the captain assigned to us. I also spent some time putting together bullet points for each one of them so you'd be able to catch up quickly and we could hit the ground running."

"Sounds good." Ten wrapped his arms around Ronan. "Why are you really home early?"

Ronan laughed. "Because my ass is dragging. I slept for like ninety minutes last night and O'Dwyer taped me snoring at my desk. He told me if I didn't get my ass home, he'd put the video on Facebook. So, I packed up and came home. I've got my laptop so I can work from the sofa while you read the Hutchins stuff later."

"You mean you'll turn the computer on, open documents and fall asleep in front of an episode of *Ozark*?"

"Or *Fuller House*." Ronan shrugged. "How many eighteen-hour shifts have we put in when we've been on a case? Plenty! It's not a big deal for me to miss a few hours here or there because I was a big, fat jerk." He pulled his phone out of his back pocket. "Hawaiian pizza from Greek Life?"

Ten shook his head. Pineapple wasn't floating his boat tonight. "Why don't we get the Mediterranean pie with the feta and plum tomatoes?"

"Sold!" Ronan punched the contact on his phone and placed their order. In addition to the pizza, he also ordered a Greek salad.

Tennyson loved ordering out from Greek Life. It was a small, family-owned place over by the Salem State campus. They did a lot of business over at the college and it was because they had the best pizza in town.

"While we're waiting for the food, why don't you show me the letter from Tom Hutchins."

Ronan shot Ten a questioning glance then ran out of the kitchen. When he came back a minute later, he was carrying the two accordion files he had last night. He set them down on the kitchen counter and pulled out a single sheet of paper, which he handed to Tennyson.

Shutting his eyes, Ten set his right hand down on the piece of paper. He could feel desperation and sadness emanating from it. He wasn't surprised. If he were facing life in prison, he'd feel those emotions in spades.

What was of bigger importance to him was what he *didn't* feel when he touched the letter. There was no malice. No anger. No obvious signs of deceit. If Ronan had given him this letter the night before he'd taken his little field trip to Cedar Junction, he would have felt better about his husband making the visit.

"Well?" Ronan sounded impatient.

"I don't feel any deceit or ill will in this letter." Ten opened his eyes. "He's not trying to snow you or trick you into coming down to meet him."

"So, if I'd shown you the letter, you would have been okay with me going down to see Tank and his dream team?"

Ten raised an eyebrow. "I would have felt better if you were wearing a Kevlar suit and had Fitzgibbon and the nastiest Belgian Malinois on the police force with you, but yes, I would have been okay with you going down there to see him."

Ronan let out a sigh of relief.

"You realize how many pitfalls there are with this case, right?" Ten shook his head. "Twins are never an easy thing to deal with. They have the same DNA, but not the same fingerprints. Not to mention the family dynamics."

"I mentioned the twin issues to Tank. He'd already considered the DNA issue. It was a bit harder explaining what Lorraine saw, or more specifically what she would tell *you* she saw the night she was killed. If Lorraine McAlpin saw her killer, she's going to say it was Tank, even if it was Tim. I've seen a ton of pictures of the brothers together and they're impossible to tell apart."

"That's what the defense attorney is going to count on. I'm surprised he got convicted at all. Usually the explanation about twin DNA is enough reasonable doubt for any jury to acquit." What was that old saying about putting your fate in the hands of twelve people too stupid to get out of jury duty?

"Well, I won't spoil anything for you then. You can decide how you want to look at everything I brought home." Ronan was about to open his mouth again when the doorbell rang. He dug his wallet out of his back pocket. "What do you mean 'family dynamics?'"

"If Tank didn't kill Lorraine then that means Tim did. Tank's own brother sat by and watched his twin get arrested, tried, convicted, and sentenced to twenty-five to life. Talk about tearing a family apart. How do you ever forgive your brother for doing that to you?" This was one of those moments Tennyson was thrilled to pieces he was an only child.

11

Ronan

Ronan had to admit the pizza choice was excellent. What wasn't so excellent was the wait for Ten to read through all of the Hutchins documents.

Fitzgibbon had sped through everything last night. Ronan supposed that after nearly thirty years on the force you knew how to read evidence reports and trial transcripts quickly and, in a way, that you were able to cherry pick the relevant data. Knowing Tennyson, he was reading every damned word.

He was sitting on the living room couch, with Dixie curled up next to him, watching an old episode of *Law and Order*, of all things. Whatever network he'd landed on was showing a marathon of episodes. In the time he'd been watching, Detective Stabler had beaten up three suspects, chased another one down an alley, and had taken his shirt off twice. Ronan was beginning to see why Ten liked this show so much.

"Okay, I'm finished," Ten said from the kitchen doorway. "I'm exhausted. Can we go to bed now?"

Ronan laughed and patted the space next to him on the couch. "You read it all?"

Ten nodded. He curled up next to Ronan and reached out to scratch Dixie behind her ears. The dog scrambled into his lap. "I could have never been a lawyer. What a boring-ass job."

"Did you get anything from the trial transcript with your gift?"

"You mean aside from the fact that the judge is having an affair with the stenographer? No. Nothing that will help us figure out who killed Lorraine McAlpin."

"Do you think it's worth a trip to Walpole for you to meet Tank?"

Tennyson didn't move. He barely breathed. "I've never been to a prison before."

"Neither had I before yesterday." Ronan didn't want to keep harping on the fact that he'd been to the prison yesterday.

"Is it like *Oz*? With men getting raped and stabbed all over the place?" Ten shivered.

"I saw very little of the place. Just the main office, a hallway, and the visitor's room where I met with Tank, his lawyer and the P.I." Ronan hugged Ten closer. "Since when do you watch *Oz*?"

"When I was single and home alone on Friday nights. Detective Stabler was in it before he was on *Law and Order*."

Well, that explained it...

"Speaking of Stabler, it looks like you've become quite the fan." Ten pointed at the television.

"No way. That was Dixie. It was her turn with the remote. This is what *she* picked. Right Dix?"

Dixie's head popped up from Tennyson's lap. Her mouth dropped open and she yawned at Ronan. An obvious affirmative answer.

Ten raised an eyebrow. "Oh sure. *Law and Order* has a huge canine fanbase. What does Fitzgibbon say about this case?"

Ronan shook his head over Ten switching gears so quickly. "He said technically it isn't even a case. Tank has been convicted and sentenced. He says the ball is in your court. If you want to look into it, he says we have his permission so long as it doesn't interfere with our regular work. Anything we find though, he wants us to bring to him, not to the lawyer."

"I get that you want to help but tell me you understand just how difficult this case is."

"I do," Ronan affirmed.

"If Lorraine McAlpin didn't know either of the brothers, she won't know which one of them killed her. The DNA evidence doesn't differentiate between them. All we'll really have to go on is my reading of them which is inadmissible in court. It sure as hell isn't enough to get the original verdict overturned."

"What if someone other than the Hutchins brothers killed her?" Ronan asked. "If that were the case Lorraine would be able to tell you neither of the brothers killed her."

"Then how do we explain the DNA?" Tennyson asked.

"Cross contamination," Ronan answered quickly. "You hear about that kind of lab mix up all the time in the news."

"Christ, don't tell that to Lyric Vaughn. She'd have a conniption fit if she thought her lab made that kind of mistake. After the lab passed the state exam with flying colors, rumor has it she's in line for a big promotion."

"There are other ways DNA gets to crime scenes, Ten. Maybe Tank or Tim knew this woman. Maybe one of them was having an affair with her on the down low. I know there was no evidence of either of them in her house, but maybe they met at hotels?"

Tennyson sighed. "Or maybe the evidence is right. Maybe the Boston Police Department and the Suffolk County DA's office got it right. Maybe Tank Hutchins killed Lorraine McAlpin."

Ronan had to admit Tennyson had a very valid point. "Yeah, maybe you're right."

Ten rested his head back on Ronan's shoulder. "Call his lawyer in the morning, Ronan. I'll agree to meet with Tank and read him. Just promise me we'll both be safe."

More than anything Ronan wanted to make that promise, but he knew it was one he might possibly have to break. Things went wrong in maximum-security prisons all the time. Riots broke out. Prisons went into lockdown. Weapons were smuggled in or fashioned out of bed frames or toothbrushes. The only thing they could do to stay safe was to stay alert. Ronan hugged Tennyson tighter and kept his mouth shut.

12

Tennyson

If Tennyson had to pick his least favorite month in New England it would have to be November. Even though he'd gotten married on November 1st, the rest of the month sucked with its cold, harsh rains. He would almost rather have December's snow instead of November's raw, bitter days.

He and Ronan were driving down I-95 South toward MCI-Cedar Junction in Walpole. He was staring out the window at the trees. Gone were the vibrant red and yellow foliage colors of October. What was left now on the trees that still had their leaves, was a rusty brown color. If he were being whimsical, he'd call it russet. All of New England was drab now and would be until the first snows of December changed the landscape from fall into winter.

"Penny for your thoughts, Nostradamus." Ronan set a hand on Tennyson's thigh.

"Just thinking about how crappy the weather is in November. What about you? You've been awfully quiet on this ride."

"I was thinking about what you said the other night about our little miss." Guilt tinged Ronan's words.

"Ronan, I didn't mean to scare or upset you about her." The last thing Ten wanted was for Ronan to walk around acting like a China doll because he was afraid that Ten would end up raising their daughter as a single father.

Ronan shook his head. A smile blossomed across his face. "I mean I agree with you that I need to think a bit more carefully about my actions and how they will affect the future of our family, not to mention my career. I got damn lucky that Fitzgibbon didn't suspend my ass."

"Yeah, you did." Ten couldn't disagree with him there. Investigating something that wasn't a cold case on the clock was definitely cause for a suspension. "So, if you're not thinking about how you need to change your behavior to be a better future-father, what *were* you thinking about."

"That!" Ronan crowed. "That right there. You used the word *future*. You always use the word future. Future-daughter. Future-father. I'm sick of hearing that word, Ten."

Ten shifted toward his husband. "What are you saying, Ronan." He had a feeling he knew what Ronan was driving toward, but he didn't want to read him. He wanted to hear Ronan say the words.

"Why can't the future be now? I want the future to be *now*." Ronan took his eyes off the road for a second to look at his husband.

Wow... Ten hadn't been expecting Ronan to say it like that. He could see how serious Ronan was. "You want to have a baby now? We've only been married for eleven days."

"I couldn't sleep when I was spending the night in purgatory at Kevin's house, so I did some research. From the time a couple with no fertility issues starts looking into in-vitro fertilization via surrogacy until the day their baby is born takes on average about eighteen months. That's the average. So, it could be two years from now until we're holding our little miss in our arms. I want her in our lives now."

"I had no idea you wanted to start a family this soon." Tennyson had been gung-ho about the idea from the moment he'd realized Ronan was the man he was going to marry. He figured that after Ronan's rocky first marriage, he wanted things to go a bit slower. He guessed he should have asked the question instead of assuming.

"So many different things have gone into me making this decision." Ronan flipped on his blinker and changed lanes.

"Like what?" Ten couldn't wait to hear Ronan's thought process.

"You know how much I love spending time with Truman's babies. Even when all three of them are blowing chunks out of both ends at the same time, I love being with them. The first time they recognized who I was and reached for me, did something to my heart. I've also seen how much closer those little people have brought Truman and Carson."

Ten couldn't argue with any of the points Ronan had made. He'd seen all of those things for himself, not to mention the changes those babies had made in Ronan. "What else?"

"Fitzgibbon and Greeley. I know Kevin didn't raise Greeley but seeing their father-son relationship from an adult level rather than from a child level is fascinating. I can't wait until we can sit down and have conversations with our daughter." Ronan shook his head as if the thought of that was too overwhelming for him to fathom.

It had been an education for Tennyson watching Fitzgibbon and Greeley's relationship as well. Kevin had met the boy at the age when his own relationship with his parents had ended. He understood where Ronan's emotion was coming from. "Is there more?"

Ronan nodded. "The final straw for me was our trip to Kansas. Seeing the way your mother treated you was the deciding factor."

"That makes no sense, Ronan. My childhood was so screwed up. I had to deny who I was on two levels for my entire life. When I had finally built up enough self-confidence to confess my secrets, both of my parents hated me for it. You want to have a baby with a man who has almost no good parenting experience to fall back on."

"Bullshit, Tennyson Grimm-O'Mara. I'm throwing the bullshit flag on that one." Ronan laughed. "Yes, your parents sucked. Obviously, you're not going to model the parenting style you grew up with. You're going to be the most loving father this world has ever seen. Our house is going to be the cool house. All of the kids are going to hang out with you. I can see it so clear in my mind. Laurel, Carson's three kids, Fitzgibbon's future kid, our kids, and all of the other neighborhood hellions, they'll all be at our house because of you, Ten."

Ten rolled his eyes. "I'm hardly Mary Poppins."

"You're better. You won't fly away because the winds changed or whatever the hell the reason was she left. You'll be the parent the other parents in the neighborhood come to for advice and cookie recipes and stuff like that. You watch. That's my one and only psychic prediction."

Ten leaned forward in his seat and shimmied around until he was able to pull his wallet out of the back pocket of his jeans. He pulled out his grocery store card and then his CVS card until he found what it was he was looking for. He held up the grey business card for Ronan to see. "Carson gave me this when their surrogate was six months pregnant with the triplets. That was the October before I met you."

Ronan absently rubbed at his left shoulder where he'd been shot by Manuel Garcia. His eyes narrowed with the memory of that day. "When in October?"

"You won't believe it, but it was the day you were shot. The reason I remember it so clearly was because I was driving home from the Magick shop when the breaking news of a BPD officer being shot in South Boston came over the radio. I prayed for you, Ronan, and I didn't even know your name."

"Does it surprise you that fate working like that *doesn't* surprise me anymore?" Ronan laughed.

Ten shook his head. "No. We were moving toward our future and we didn't even know it."

"We've got about twenty minutes until we get to where we're going. If we agree about the future starting now, why don't you call the number on that card? If they've got a redheaded surrogate who's looking to carry a baby for a gay couple, then we'll know our time is now, right?" The tone in Ronan's voice was hopeful.

Butterflies rioted in Tennyson's stomach. He knew without a doubt this was the right move to make. Having Ronan's absolute vote of confidence in him as a father was the icing on the cake. He unlocked his phone and started to dial the clinic's phone number. "Hi, my name is Tennyson Grimm-O'Mara. My husband and I would like to make an appointment to talk about having a baby."

13

Ronan

Just knowing that they had an appointment at the fertility clinic on December 4th made Ronan feel lighter. Not even the sight of the razor wire coming into view could darken his mood today.

"Is that it?" Ten asked. His voice sounded anxious.

"Yeah, that's Cedar Junction." Ronan pointed to the building as it came into view.

Ten shivered. "Pull over. Now!"

Hearing the alarm in his husband's voice, Ronan didn't hesitate to obey.

Ten was out of the car before Ronan had put it in park. He ran into the grass next to the road and started throwing up.

Ronan could hear him retching from the car. Undoing his seatbelt, he ran to join his husband. "Shit, Ten, are you okay?"

Bracing his hands on his knees, Ten shook his head no. Physically, he was fine. Psychically was another matter. "It's the energy from the prison."

"What do you mean the *energy*? From the convicts inside or from the spirits of the dead ones haunting the place?" Ronan had no idea energy could do this to Tennyson. What had he done by bringing his husband here?

Ten retched again. His entire body shook with the force of it. "Both," he managed to mutter before wiping the back of his hand over his mouth.

"I'll be right back. Stay here." Not bothering to waiting for an answer, Ronan ran back to the Mustang. Popping the trunk, he grabbed a bottle of water from the cooler he'd packed and grabbed the roll of paper towels he kept back there for emergency clean ups. Sometimes it paid to be anal about car maintenance.

"Here you go." Ronan opened the bottle and poured some on a folded paper towel which he slapped on the back of Ten's neck. He handed the rest of the bottle to Tennyson.

Ten nodded and washed his mouth out before taking a tentative sip. "Thanks."

"Are you feeling better?" Ronan asked. In his opinion Ten sure as hell didn't look better. He wanted to put his husband back in the car and drive home. This interview with Tom Hutchins and his team wasn't worth Ten's health.

"A little." Ten managed a weak smile.

"Did you forget to shut your gift down?" It wasn't like Ten to be that careless.

"This happened with it shut down." Ten shook his head. "The prison opened in 1955. That's sixty-three years of the worst of humanity being housed here. Leaving their imprint on this place, their energy, their evil." Ten shook his head. He stuck his hand in left pocket and started rummaging around.

Ronan could hear the sound of rocks sliding against each other. "What did you bring with you?"

"Black tourmaline. It wards off negative energy and psychic attacks. I don't think I brought enough of it with me."

"Yeah, you're still looking a little green." That was an understatement. Ten could pass for the Wicked Witch of the West's brother.

"That's why I only had a piece of toast this morning." He stood up straight and took a deep breath. "I'm ready to go. The sooner we get this done, the sooner we can get the hell out of here."

Ronan wrapped an arm around Ten and led him back to the car. He hadn't even considered how hard this might be on him. He knew hospitals and morgues were difficult places for Tennyson to be because people had died there. It never occurred to him that a prison could be worse.

***

Twenty minutes later, they were being escorted down the hallway of the prison toward the visitor rooms. Today more than his first visit, Ronan hated being without his gun. It was safely locked in the main office. He had the key to the locker holding all of his and Tennyson's personal possessions in his pocket.

Ronan could feel the nervous energy pouring off Tennyson. It was as if he were expecting cons with homemade shivs to be jumping out at him from around every corner.

"This is it, gentlemen." Officer Thorne stopped in front of a wooden door with a rectangular window built in. "Check in at the main office when you leave."

Ten nodded, looking too sick to speak.

"Are you going to be okay to do this? If you're not, we can leave right now." Ronan had half a mind to do it anyway even if Tennyson said he was good to go.

"For the tenth time, Ronan, I'm fine. I said we'd do this and we will. Just don't expect it to be a long interview. In and out, okay?" Ten smiled.

"Just so long as you never say that sentence in the bedroom. I'm okay with that." Ronan winked and opened the door.

All of the usual suspects were in the room. Tank Hutchins was dressed in his usual gaudy shade of orange. Bradford Hicks was wearing another expensive suit and Jude Byrne was looking surlier than the first time they'd met. Ronan had no idea it was possible to look that pissed off and that drop-dead gorgeous at the same time.

"This is my partner, Tennyson Grimm. Ten, this is Bradford Hicks, Tank Hutchins and Jude Byrne." He pointed to each man as he said their names. Ronan hated not introducing Ten as his husband, but for the sake of this investigation, he figured less was more. He took a step back while Ten shook everyone's hands.

"Don't you mean this is your *husband*, Ronan?" Jude asked. His typical sneer was back.

Tennyson took the seat directly in front of Tank. "You must have graduated top of your class in private *dick* school, Mr. Byrne." Ten barely looked at the man, instead focusing on Tank Hutchins instead. "Tell me why you wanted to meet with me and Detective O'Mara, Tank."

Ronan was impressed with Tennyson. He knew how hard being in the prison was for his husband, not only physically, but also knowing that Josh Gatlin was here too, along with the other men Ronan had a hand in locking up over his career. He was handling it like a champ.

Tank made eye contact with the psychic. "I've seen and heard about your work with the BPD on the news and I've read about you in the Boston papers. So has my lawyer. I believe in your gift and I know that once you read me, you'll see that I'm innocent."

Ten was silent. He seemed to be studying the man. He turned to Bradford Hicks. "I didn't realize you were a fan of my work, Mr. Hicks."

"I'm a fan of justice, Mr. Grimm. I don't have any of your talents, but just sitting and speaking with Tom, I can see and hear that he was not responsible for the murder of Lorraine McAlpin."

Ten turned to Ronan, making eye contact with him briefly. "I've read all of the evidence reports, as well as the trial transcripts. If Tom didn't commit this murder then there is a good chance that his twin brother did. Are you prepared for those ramifications?"

Hicks nodded. "It's something we've wrestled with, but we can't worry about that now. All we can do is find the evidence that will clear Tom and get him the hell out of this place."

Ten's dark eyes moved to Jude Byrne who was slouching in his chair, a cocky look in his golden-hazel eyes. Ten frowned, giving a slight shake of his head. "I assume that's where you come in, Mr. Byrne. What have you uncovered so far?"

"How is *that* any of your concern, ghost whisperer?" Jude shot back.

"Okay, so you've got nothing." Ten turned back to Tank who wore a shocked look on his face. "Why do you look so surprised. I thought you said you believed in my gift."

"I do, it's just no one's ever spoken to Jude like that before." Tank grimaced, seeming shocked by his own candor.

"What? Like he's full of shit and it's overflowing?" Ten shrugged. "Okay, let's get down to it." He took a deep breath and closed his eyes.

Ronan wanted to laugh out loud, but he kept his mouth shut. He could see Ten was trying to find his Zen and in a place like this, knew that was going to be next to impossible. He set his right hand on Ten's thigh and started breathing with him in hopes it would help.

"The night Lorraine was killed you stopped off at a liquor store on Bunker Hill Street in Charlestown and got some beer and chips. You paid with your debit card. After that, you went home and called out for a sandwich. You paid cash, which is unfortunate. There's no electronic record of the transaction. You spent the rest of the night watching the Sox on live television, which is unfortunate too. If you'd used the DVR or accessed the menu, the cable company would have a record of that." Tennyson sighed and opened his eyes. "You didn't kill Lorraine McAlpin, Tank."

Tank nodded. His shoulders slumped while his right hand came up to shield his eyes.

"Hold on a second," Ronan said. "Tank, you were watching the baseball game. I know when I get up to go to the bathroom or if someone," Ronan inclined his head toward Tennyson, "starts talking to me, I hit the button on the remote to pause live TV. Do you remember doing that at all? Did you access the TV guide or the DVR?"

"I don't know." Tank's hand fell away from his misty eyes. "That night was so long ago and so much has happened since then."

Ronan pointed at Jude. "Start with that. Go to the cable company and get his records. There might not be any evidence there, but it's a good place to start."

A muscle started ticking in Jude's cheek. "I don't work for you, O'Mara," he said from behind clenched teeth.

"No, you work for me, do it. What's with the dick measuring contest anyway?" Tank had an incredulous tone in his voice. "I can't remember if I used the remote for anything more than turning the television on, but if I did and the cable company has a record of that, it's worth a shot to dig up the records."

The muscle was still ticking, but Jude's look softened. He nodded and started tapping the screen of his phone.

"What else did you do that night, Tank?" Ronan asked. "I know you lived close enough to Lorraine that your calls and text messages would have pinged off the cell tower closest to her house, so that's moot. Did you play a video game online with friends? Did you surf the web on your computer? Look at porn? Buy anything on Amazon or eBay? Were you on Tinder? Or social media? Did you do anything on your work computer?"

Tank shut his eyes. The room went quiet. Ronan didn't think this line of questioning was going to pan out when all of a sudden, Tank slammed a hand down on the table. Ten jumped and squeaked in reaction.

"I had a client who was looking into investing in Japanese textiles and electronics. Martin Penkis was his name. He was from Brookline. Big player in the U.S. Stock Market and wanted a footprint in Asia. I told him Japan was a good place to get his feet wet. Anyway, the Japanese Market opens at 8pm Eastern Time. I logged on to my work computer for about ten minutes to check the opening numbers for a few stocks I thought would interest him. Low risk, high yield options that would get his foot in the door overseas. I jotted down the prices and logged out of my computer." Tank wore a hopeful look in his eyes. "I remember thinking I should have just written an email to send Martin those numbers, but the Sox had the bases loaded with no outs. I made a mental note to send the email in morning."

Sending that email could have kept him from being convicted, but that was the last thing Ronan was going to say out loud. Water under the bridge now. "What did you write the figures down on?" Ronan asked. His mind was spinning, trying to remember the inventory contents of what had been seized from Hutchins condo.

"It was a yellow legal pad I kept on the coffee table. I never ripped pages off of it, just flipped over to the next page."

Ronan frowned. He couldn't remember if there was an item like that in the inventory. He turned to Tennyson. "Do you remember if we have that pad in our inventory?"

Ten shook his head. "I don't remember reading about it, but that doesn't mean it's not on the list."

"Some psychic you are." Jude snorted. The look on his face was pure annoyance.

Ten raised an eyebrow at the private investigator. "Being psychic doesn't mean I have an eidetic memory."

"Guys, enough." Ronan wanted to punch the P.I in the throat, but they had bigger fish to fry at the moment. "We've got some good leads to go on here at the moment. Jude can get the information about Tank's cable account while Tennyson and I look for the legal pad in our evidence log. Bradford, what happened to the rest of the things in Tank's condo?"

"Tim boxed up everything and has it all in a storage locker somewhere. Somerville, I think." Hicks started flipping through notes in his file.

Tank nodded. "He would have kept everything too, except for what was obvious trash."

"Tank, do you think your brother would let me read him too?" Ten asked cautiously.

"Why would you need to do that? You already said that Tom didn't kill Lorraine, that's all we need to get him a new trial." The sour look was back on Jude's face.

Tennyson shot him an are-you-for-real look. "So, all you care about here is getting Tank off? It doesn't matter to you that Lorraine's real killer is still out there somewhere? It could be Tim, or it might be someone else entirely. They could be stalking their next victim right now. It's been three years since Lorraine was killed. It's possible this killer has already struck again."

"What are you saying, Ten?" Ronan wanted to know if Ten was speculating here or if had some sixth sense knowledge.

"The one thing I didn't really like about this trial is how little information was put out there about Lorraine and her lifestyle. I'm never one to blame the victim, but the prosecution was never able to explain how this woman would have come into contact with her killer. They seized on the fact that there was DNA and I'm convinced that was what convicted Tom. Well, that and the fact that Tom lived closer to Lorraine than Tim did."

Tennyson had a good point. DNA was an awesome tool in the pursuit of criminal justice, but sometimes Ronan wondered if it was used as a tool to make arrests and convictions to the exclusion of all other evidence or lack thereof. Jurors heard the phrase "DNA match," and that seemed to seal the deal for them in this case, even when there were two men with the exact DNA profile.

"I agree with Ten, we need to interview Tim as well. If the legal pad isn't in our evidence, we're going to need to meet with him anyway." Ronan found himself looking forward to getting the opportunity to meet Tim Hutchins. It didn't matter that the sleazy P.I. only wanted to clear Tank. Ronan wanted justice for Lorraine McAlpin and he was going to see that she got it.

14

Tennyson

It wasn't until they were out of Walpole and driving through Norwood on I-95 North that Tennyson finally started to feel almost human again. The nausea was gone and so was the pounding headache at the base of his skull. He was starting to get his appetite back too. "Enchiladas!"

"What?" Ronan looked at him like he'd lost his mind completely.

"I just got out of prison. I want enchiladas." Ten started to laugh. It wasn't pretty to think about spending time in that place and he'd only seen a tiny fraction of it. Just walking outside and seeing all the chain link and razor wire, not to mention all of the guards armed with high-powered rifles was enough to make him never want to jaywalk ever again.

"I take it that means you're feeling better?" Ronan reached out for Ten's hand.

"Once we hit the Walpole town line, I was good as new. How crazy is that? Not that we're ever going to move but living in a city with a maximum-security prison is definitely out of the question." Ten shivered. It was something that had never crossed his mind. In all of the years he'd lived in Massachusetts, he'd never visited the town of Walpole. So far as he knew, he'd never even driven through it.

"I'll keep that in mind for when we're looking for a place to retire in sunny Florida."

"You want to retire to Florida?" Ten didn't know that about his husband.

"Of course, don't you? I don't want to be in my sixties and still shoveling snow. You don't have to shovel sunshine, Nostradamus. Didn't you know that?" Ronan laughed at his own joke.

Tennyson laughed along with him. "Surprisingly, yes, I did know that. Can you imagine us retired? No more bullets flying at your body. No more trips to the ER. No more brown accordion files or excursions to the morgue, although, I will miss Vann Hoffman. He made the morgue fun."

"That's the first thing I look for in my coroner, a sense of humor." Ronan slapped a hand on the steering wheel.

"What's the second thing?" Ten couldn't wait to hear this answer.

"Abs of steel. What else?"

"Of course." Ten had never seen the good doctor without his blue scrub top but knew enough about the man to know there were abs to spare under it. "Vann was the medical examiner on the McAlpin case. We're going to need to read his report at some point."

"Agreed," Ronan nodded. "What did you think about Tank? What were your impressions of him, beside what you read?"

Meeting and then reading Tank was another thing contributing to Ten's queasy stomach. "I liked him. He's a good man who didn't kill anyone. I can't imagine being arrested for a crime I didn't commit and then being tried and convicted for it too."

"The worst part though has to be knowing that your brother, your twin, no less, is the one who killed this woman." Ronan shook his head. "You hear so much about the twin thing and how close identical twins are and I just can't get over the fact that Tim is letting Tom rot in prison."

"Let's not string Tim up by the neck just yet. He could be innocent too. He had an alibi after all." Ten found it hard to believe that one brother would do this to another, but he'd grown up as an only child and had nothing to base his theory of sibling loyalty on except reruns of *The Brady Bunch* and *Eight is Enough.*

"His wife was his alibi, Ten." Ronan shot him a look of disbelief. "Spouses are notoriously bad alibi witnesses."

"Are you kidding me, Ronan? No offense here, but if I thought you killed someone I wouldn't want you in our home or sleeping in our bed. That would go double if we were parents. I can't imagine Tim's wife, Michelle, wanting him home with their three young sons if there was even a shred of doubt in her mind that he did this awful thing."

"Come on, Ten. Don't be so naïve. We watch those trashy daytime shows all the time where the wives are convinced their husbands are faithful to them and it turns out that the men are cheating on them left, right, and sideways."

Ten snorted. "How exactly do you cheat on someone sideways?"

"I'll show you tonight." Ronan winked at his husband. "But before we can get to that, the first thing we need to do is talk to Fitzgibbon. Can you call him and put it on speakerphone?"

Ten dug his phone out of his pocket and dialed the number.

"Hey, Ten, how's prison treating you? Any chance they decided to keep Ronan? I sure could use a few days off from his constantly running motor-mouth." Kevin sounded downright jovial.

"Hilarious." Ronan deadpanned. "That's no way to treat your best detective, boss. Ten and I were just talking about living in Florida."

"You were? Hell, why didn't you say so! I'll start writing your letter of recommendation now. Take my best detective, *please*!" Fitzgibbon laughed.

"Ten, take him off our Christmas card list, would you? And buy extra eggs and toilet paper when you go grocery shopping this week." Ronan winked at his husband.

"It's like working with preschoolers." Ten shook his head. "We have intel for you, Cap."

"Intel? Christ Ten, this isn't the CIA. Or is it? Have you been drafted by The Company?" Fitzgibbon asked.

"That's above your paygrade, Cap."

Ten whacked Ronan's shoulder. "You're grounded, so hush. If you and Greeley don't have any plans, why don't you come over for dinner tonight? Ronan and I will fill you in on what happened."

"Are you cooking, Ronan, or calling for take-out?" Kevin laughed.

"Probably calling for take-out. Why?" Ronan asked.

"No reason," Fitzgibbon sounded relieved. "We'll bring dessert. See you at six. Bye!" The phone beeped three times to signal Kevin had ended the call.

"What's his problem?" Ronan sounded genuinely puzzled.

"No clue," Ten said gently. Ronan had been taking cooking lessons from Truman, but so far only knew how to make three things. Everyone was full up on shrimp and grits, spaghetti and meatballs, and black bean chili. "You didn't tell me Jude Byrne was so..." Ten was having a hard time picking out the right word to describe the difficult man. There were so many adjectives to choose from.

"Handsome?" Ronan supplied.

Ten turned to Ronan with his mouth hanging open. "*Noo*, that wasn't the word I was going for." That didn't mean it was untrue though. Jude Byrne, with his leonine eyes and bad attitude was gorgeous, no doubt about it. There was something about him though that Ten couldn't quite put his finger on.

"Okay, open mouth, insert foot." Ronan laughed. "What word *were* you going for?"

"He is handsome with those eyes. I'll give you that. There's something different about him, aside from his bad attitude." Ten cocked his head to the side, still trying to puzzle out what he was trying to convey to Ronan.

"What do you mean *different*?" Ronan sounded curious.

Ten shook his head. It had been bothering him since he'd met the surly P.I., but there had been so much else going on in his head that he hadn't had time to examine it fully until now. "I couldn't read him, Ronan."

Ronan looked confused. "What do you mean you couldn't read him? Did he have his guard up?"

Ten shook his head no. "Some people are harder to read than others. Some shield their thoughts or try to hide things when I'm around. Jude was different though. This guy was a blank page."

Ronan took his eyes off the road to give Ten a shocked look. "What does that mean? Is he a talent too and he's blocking you?"

Ten grimaced, shaking his head. "I don't think that's it. I think there's something more to it than that. I need to talk to Carson about him."

"You're freaking me out here, Ten. Is he dangerous?"

"I have no idea. I think we should do a little internet research on him and look him up in your criminal database at work on Monday. He's a literal blank page, Ronan. I can't tell if he's friend or foe or something else entirely."

It was the something else entirely that scared him.

15

Ronan

The first thing Ronan did when they got home, after taking Dixie out for a walk, was to look up Jude Byrne on the internet. The first and maybe the most interesting thing Ronan learned was that Jude wasn't his real first name. "Uh, Ten?" Ronan carried his laptop into the kitchen where his husband was tidying up for their guests.

"Let me guess, Jude isn't his real name?" Ten grabbed for a dish towel to dry his wet hands.

Ronan sagged. "I hate when you do that."

Ten held his hands out in a who-me gesture. "What? Make an educated guess?"

"No, take the wind out of my sails. Did you know that's what I was going to tell you or did you really guess?" Sometimes it just wasn't any fun living with an all-knowing, all-seeing, oracle.

"I really guessed. Remember I told you that I couldn't read him at all."

Ronan was about to remind Ten that he was psychic and probably read *him* instead. Thankfully, the doorbell rang, saving him from sticking his foot in his own mouth. Again. Dixie barked and raced toward the front door. "Hi, Cap," Ronan greeted when he opened the door. "Hello, sweet Lola!" Ronan took Dixie's sister from his boss and brought her into the house. Dixie danced at his feet.

"Hello to you too, Uncle Ronan. Don't mind me. I just brought dessert." Greeley grinned and headed toward the kitchen with a bakery box from Holy Cannoli.

"Hi, Greeley," Ronan managed between dog kisses.

"You don't look any worse for wear from your trip to Walpole." Kevin sat down in the high-backed chair across from Ronan and the dogs.

"I'm fine. It's Ten who had trouble." Ronan's look darkened. He remembered the way Tennyson had ordered him to pull over and way his entire body had shaken when he was getting ill on the side of the road.

"What do you mean trouble? Did someone try to hurt him?" Fitzgibbon was instantly in cop-mode.

Ronan shook his head. "No, nothing like that. He got really sick when the prison came into view. Ten said it had to do with the energy of the place. Sixty plus years of evil men leaving their residue on the place. He actually made me pull over so he could get sick."

Fitzgibbon grimaced. "I had no idea that kind of thing could happen."

"Neither did Tennyson until he was yelling at me to stop the car." Ronan hoped to God they didn't have to go back to visit Tank again. Or, if they did, that he could go alone.

"How did the reading go? Did Ten find out if Thomas Hutchins killed Lorraine McAlpin or not?" Kevin leaned forward to balance his elbows on his knees.

Setting Lola down on the floor, Ronan looked up at Fitzgibbon. "According to what Ten saw, Tank was home all night watching the Sox game just like he said. We did get two small leads. Tank thought he might have used the remote to pause the Red Sox game, so Jude Byrne is going to try to get access to Tank's cable records. They might keep records of that kind of thing. Although with the way Tank's luck has run here, I'm going to doubt the cable company can give us that kind of data, or if they can, it's been wiped out after three years."

"Jude Byrne? Is he the private investigator?"

"Yeah, he's a bit of a wildcard in all of this. I had just thought he was an arrogant prick when I met him the other day, but then Ten said something to me on the way back today that has me wanting to dig deeper into his background."

"What did he say?" Fitzgibbon sounded intrigued.

"Ten can't read Jude at all. It's not that Jude is blocking him or anything like that. Ten says he's a literal blank page. He's going to talk to Carson and Bertha about this phenomenon and see if they know anything about it." Ronan hadn't liked the look in Ten's eyes when he was talking about this guy. He was equal parts freaked out and fascinated.

"Check into him on Monday, just don't send up any red flags. Byrne isn't the subject of this investigation, but to cover our own asses we have to make sure he isn't wanted in any other criminal investigation and doesn't have any warrants out for his arrest either."

Ronan nodded.

"You said you had a couple of small leads. What's the other one?"

"This is actually the more interesting of the two. Tank remembered logging on to his work computer to look at the Japanese Stock Market at 8pm the night of the murder. He said he made notes about some shares on a yellow legal pad on his coffee table. I told Tank that I'd look at the evidence inventory and see if we had the pad in custody. If we don't, the lawyer told us that Tank's twin brother has everything from his condo boxed up in a storage facility over in Somerville."

Fitzgibbon was silent. He rubbed his hands together while he seemed to be thinking over what Ronan had told him. "Is there any chance Tank's firm would still have a record of his time online that night?"

"It's worth asking the question, don't you think? I'm wondering if that request would be better coming from us or from Tank's appeal lawyer? You said to bring everything we found out to you first, so I haven't made a move on this evidence. I didn't even check the inventory sheet to see if we have a yellow legal pad in evidence."

"Let me think about who the request should come from. In the meantime, go check the inventory and see if we have the legal pad." Fitzgibbon sat back in his seat.

Ronan crossed the room to the table where he'd stashed the Hutchins' files. Dixie and Lola were at his heels. "Well, hello, ladies." He stepped around them as he walked back to the couch with the files. Both dogs hopped up beside him when he sat back down. One on either side of him.

When he opened the first accordion folder, Lola stuck her head into the first partition. "Not helpful, honey." Ronan pulled the folder away from her, only to come face to face with Dixie on his other side. She offered him a doggie grin before licking the side of his face.

Fitzgibbon burst out laughing. "This has to go on Facebook!" He had his phone up recording the whole thing. "My best detective being bested by puppies!" He was laughing so hard the phone was shaking.

Snarling his lip, Ronan dove into the file and found the inventory list. He scanned through it but did not see a yellow legal pad. "It wasn't collected. So that means it's probably in a box in that storage locker. How helpful will the notation be anyway? Unless Tank dated it?"

Fitzgibbon nodded. "In conjunction with proof from his company's IT department showing he was online at that time and with whom, it could be corroborative, but alone it won't be enough to get him a new trial."

"Makes me wonder though why no one thought of this the first time around. Or why Tank didn't remember himself." Ronan scratched behind Dixie's ears. Lola climbed into his lap and nosed her head under his other arm.

Kevin shrugged. "You know how those trials go. In the confusion and anger of it all, Tom might not have remembered going online and looking at the Japanese stocks. When you're innocent, you think it's all going to work out in your favor. He could have had a shit trial attorney or he could have had a good one who thought his client was innocent too. Then there was the DNA. I still can't believe that with twins sharing the same genetic material the jury didn't find room for reasonable doubt."

That had bothered Ronan too. Tank Hutchins had no criminal background. Not one witness called to testify had a bad word to say about the man. The only shred of evidence against him was his DNA on the murder victim. This jury was not sequestered and there had been no rumors of trouble in the jury room. Usually stuff like that had a way of leaking out after the verdict, but nothing like that had ever come to light. The five men and seven women considered the facts in evidence, voted, and all agreed that Thomas Hutchins killed Lorraine McAlpin.

"I think the request for the IT records should come from the attorney. If I make the call, it's going to look like the Boston Police Department is reopening the case, which we're not doing." Kevin sighed. "You're putting me in a tough spot here, Ronan."

"I know, Cap." Ronan agreed. "Aside from the episode we were in about Michael Frye, you ever watch *Dateline*?"

Kevin shot him a confused look. "No, and I barely watched the episode we were in."

"Bullshit!" Ronan laughed. "You've got it saved on your DVR! I saw it there the other night when I couldn't sleep."

"What's your point, Ronan?" Fitzgibbon's hackles were up.

"Aside from the fact that I'm a kick ass detective?" When Fitzgibbon's frown only deepened, Ronan pressed on, "They talk about old cases on that show sometimes, where the wrong person was convicted. Whenever they interview the original detectives on the case, they always, to a man, stick by their original conclusion that the person they arrested was the murderer, even when there's stone-cold, irrefutable proof that person is innocent of the crime."

Fitzgibbon rolled his eyes. "You're saying that you don't want to be *that* detective when *Dateline* comes back to town to interview people for the McAlpin murder?"

"Something along those lines." Ronan shook his head. "We're in this job to arrest criminals. There's no crime in admitting we made a mistake. Granted, this wasn't our case." Ronan pointed back and forth between himself and Kevin. "It was a BPD case with rock-solid DNA evidence. It just might be that we got it wrong. What was it that Thomas Jefferson said about letting guilty men go free?"

"It was Benjamin Franklin, and he said, 'It is better that one hundred guilty men should go free than one innocent man should suffer.' Or something along those lines. Not that I agree with the hundred guilty men part, but I see what point you're driving toward. You do realize that I'll be in for a whole lot of butt hurt when the commissioner gets wind of this off-the-books investigation, right?"

"I had no idea he swung that way!" Ronan grinned.

"Not funny, Ronan." Fitzgibbon's lips were curling into a smile.

"I know. I know. We'll figure out how to spin it when the time comes. *If* the time comes. The Massachusetts Court of Appeals is notoriously stingy when it comes to overturning verdicts from the lower courts. From what I read in the trial transcript there was nothing glaringly wrong in any of the judge's rulings or in the way Tank was represented. The only way he's going to be granted a new trial is if new evidence comes to light."

Fitzgibbon nodded. "I know, but I'll be working on my letter of resignation anyway. On a positive note, I already know who my successor will be." His grin was as wide as the Charles River.

"You do?" Ronan had a sinking feeling about this.

Fitzgibbon pointed at Ronan. "There's no better man for the job. I'll even leave a new bottle of lube in my top drawer for all the butt hurt you'll be in for."

16

Tennyson

"Now I know how Charlie Brown feels, Uncle Ten." Greeley pouted as he walked into the kitchen carrying the box from Holy Cannoli.

"Did someone pull a football away just as you were about to kick it?" Ten took the bakery box from him, setting it on the counter, and gave the sulky teenager a hug.

"No!" Greeley whined dramatically. "My dog likes Uncle Ronan better than me."

Ten laughed and hugged the boy tighter. "Don't feel too bad. My dog likes Ronan better too. I'm chalking it up to Dixie having no taste at all. If Lola likes him better than you, it must be bad genes."

Greeley burst out laughing. "That's for sure." He pulled back from Ten. "You don't feel so good, huh?"

"Why do you say that?" Ten narrowed his eyes.

"I don't know. I could feel it when I hugged you. Not physically like you were shorter or had a lump or something else weird. You're just off, somehow." Greeley ran a hand through his dark hair and seemed to really be studying Tennyson.

"Well, you're right. Do you know anything about where Ronan and I went today?" He was torn about telling Greeley any of this, but it was leading him toward something else he'd been meaning to talk to the teenager about for a while now.

Greeley shrugged his narrow shoulders. "Sort of, but not really. I know Dad's kinda pissed about some dumbass thing Uncle Ronan did."

Ten barked out a rough laugh. "Yeah, that explains this situation in a nutshell. Let me call out for dinner and then I'll give it to you in a bit more detail."

"What are you ordering?" Greeley's eyes glowed. He rubbed his hands together as if he couldn't wait to eat.

"Couple of pizzas and salads from Greek Life. Is there anything else you want me to add?" Ten knew it was dangerous question to ask. Greeley ate like a plague of locusts.

"Hot wings! Get the biggest order they have with extra hot sauce on the side."

"If I do that you have to promise to fart out on the deck." Ten felt his dry heaves return. The last time they'd had hot wings with Greeley, he'd had to use up an entire bottle of Febreze to get rid of the stench. At one point, he was afraid they'd have to get a new couch.

"Seriously, Uncle Ten?" Greeley giggled.

"Your ass is a weapon of mass destruction. Do we have a deal or not?" Ten was not standing down on this point.

"Fine." Greeley sat at the table and sulked harder while Ten called in the order.

After he got off the phone, Ten grabbed drinks out of the fridge and joined Greeley at the table. He set a Coke in front of the teenager and kept the bottle of water for himself. "Uncle Ronan got a letter from a convict at Walpole asking for our help because he was innocent of the crime he was convicted of committing."

"Ohhh, so that's why he spent the night with us. You were pissed that he went down there. It all makes sense now. Continue." Greeley folded his hands in front of him.

Ten couldn't help thinking this kid was something. "It all makes sense now?"

"Yeah, that's the prison where Uncle Ronan's dirtbag ex is housed, right? Along with other baddies that he's locked up over time. I can see why you'd be super pissed that he went. It could have been a trick so that some asswipe with a homemade weapon could have killed him. That's how cons get street cred on the inside." Greeley nodded like he knew all about it. "I watch *Lockup Raw* on MSNBC. You learn a lot about prison life on that show."

Tennyson had never seen that particular program before and was thanking Christ for it now. "You're right about who's housed there. Anyway, Ronan met with the man who wrote the letter. His name is Thomas Hutchins. Ronan got the vibe from him that he was innocent and asked me to go back down there with him and read Tom to see if he actually killed the woman he was convicted of murdering."

"That's where you both went today?"

Ten nodded. "A few seconds after the prison came into view, I got sick. I made Ronan pull over and threw up on the shoulder of the road. I was psychically overwhelmed."

Greeley's eyes narrowed. "Like when I had too much homework in my GED classes and I just lost my shit?"

Ten chuckled. "Something like that. I would liken it more to those video game arcades down at Salem Commons. There are so many sounds and flashes of light, combined with the crush of people. All of those things are bombarding your senses all at once. It was psychic overload with evil energies."

Shivering in the warm kitchen, Greeley reached out for Ten's hand. "That sounds awful. How did you fight it?"

Ten reached into his pocket and pulled out some black stones. They weren't polished like most of the crystals he carried. They were in the raw. "Both pockets were filled with this."

Greeley let Ten's hand go and picked up one of the stones. He closed his fist around it and shut his eyes.

Amazement and pride flowed through Ten as he watched the young man work with the crystal.

"This is off the hook!" Greeley's eyes were sparkling when they popped back open. "What is this stuff?"

"It's black tourmaline. It's good for blocking negative energy and psychic attacks. How did you feel when you held it and centered yourself with the stone?" Ten was interested to see how the crystal made Greeley feel.

The teenager was silent, as if he were choosing his words carefully. "This is going to sound strange, but in my mind's eye, I could see it moving through my body, cleansing me."

"It's been called a disinfectant for the soul, so I can see where you'd get that impression from the stone."

Tennyson pushed the small pile of stones toward Greeley. "Why don't you keep these? I have a feeling you're going to need them. Keep one under your pillow. Carry one in your pocket. Put one in the car when you get one."

"Thanks, Uncle Ten." Greeley scooped the dark stones up and held them in his hand. "So, the stones alone didn't work for you today?"

Leave it to Greeley to come back to what was wrong with him. "Not really. I had to push back against the dark energy with my own light. It's an exhausting process. I managed to get through the interview with Tom Hutchins. He didn't kill the woman he was sent to prison for murdering."

"That totally sucks." Greeley shook his head. "Being in prison for a crime you didn't commit. Of course, everyone on *Lockup* says they're innocent too, but come on, they're totally not." He rolled his eyes dramatically. "You're not going to have to go back there again, are you?" The concern was genuine in Greeley's eyes.

"Not right now," Ten breathed a sigh of relief. "There's a lead Ronan's going to look into and another one that Hutchins' private investigator is checking out, so I should be in the clear for now."

"Wow, this con has a private eye? What a cool job! Slinking around and getting the dirt on people."

Ten tilted his head. "Jobs like that can drag a man down rather than lifting him up. After a while, you start to think the only kinds of people in the world are the ones who cheat on their spouses or fake disability claims. A man with your kind of light would drown in a career like that."

Greeley nibbled his bottom lip for a minute. "I guess you're right, Uncle Ten. Stakeouts look so cool and those guys always carry around those cameras with the big ass zoom lenses and drive pricey sports cars."

"You hear that, Ronan? My son thinks stakeouts are cool!" Fitzgibbon laughed as he walked into the kitchen. Ronan was right behind him.

Ronan snickered. "Good, I'll let him sit in the Mustang all night with a take-out bag from Taco Bell and their thirty-two-ounce soda. Just make sure you piss on the neighbor's tree, not ours."

"What? Those guys take a leak outside? And you know what happens when I take a run to the Border. It's followed by a run to the bathroom! Gross! I definitely don't want to be a P.I. now." Greeley wore a skeeved out look on his face.

Fitzgibbon slapped a hand on Tennyson's back. "I owe you big time for that. How can I ever repay you? With a Ferrari maybe? Christ, my blood pressure would have been through the roof if he'd become a private investigator."

"What was the other thing you wanted to talk to me about, Uncle Ten?"

"Why do you think there's something else?" There was, but Ten wanted to know what gave Greeley that impression.

"Every time I see you, there's this look on your face like you want to ask me something, but you don't have the right words to do it. Am I right?"

Tennyson laughed. The kid was so spot on, it was ridiculous. "There is something I want to ask you about. It's about something that happened at mine and Ronan's wedding."

It was Greeley's turn to laugh. "That whole day was wild, Uncle Ten. There are parts of it I'm still trying to process myself. That's why I haven't said anything to you when you had that word constipation look on your face."

"Word constipation?" Fitzgibbon grabbed a bottle of water out of the fridge and joined them at the table.

"Yeah, you know when you're trying to think of a word and it just won't come. Just like when you're in the bathroom trying to take a-"

Fitzgibbon held up both hands. "Got you loud and clear."

Tennyson wasn't sure where he wanted to go with the conversation. It was not a case of word constipation, but a case of maybe more happening with Greeley than just him having been able to see who was walking Ronan down the aisle. He'd been so busy dancing his first dance and cutting the cake and enjoying the wedding that he hadn't had his eye on the teenager during the whole reception. "I saw one thing in particular that made me curious, but you saying the whole day was wild has me even more curious."

Greeley took a long slug from his Coke. His hands twisted around themselves after he set the can back on the table. "I'd read a lot about The Day of the Dead and All Souls Day. I knew that veil between the spirit world and the physical world was at its thinnest on that day. I also remember what we talked about in Kansas, Uncle Ten, with you thinking that I had above average intuition and how that would serve me well as a social worker."

"You put two and two together and opened yourself up to the possibilities of the spirit world, didn't you?" Ten couldn't keep a smile from blooming across his face.

"Yeah, I did. I wasn't sure what would happen or if anything at all would happen." Greeley glanced up at his father who had a spellbound look on his face.

"Tell me what you experienced," Ten urged. He was sitting on the edge of his seat.

"When I got to the Hawthorne Hotel, I had a feeling I was being watched. You know, like you hear about in those old horror movies. It wasn't scary or anything. I was just aware that spirits were around. I had never felt anything like that before and haven't since."

Ten nodded. He knew exactly what Greeley was describing. He'd gone through something similar when he'd first gotten his gift only the feeling of being watched stayed with him and developed into something much greater.

"Then, when Uncle Ronan was walking down the aisle, he wasn't alone." He turned to Ronan, "I know we talked about your mother's spirit walking with you, but I almost lost my mind when I saw her on your arm in that blue dress."

Ronan laughed. His blue eyes were misty with the memory. "You could see her?"

Greeley nodded. "Not only her, Uncle Ronan, but the other redhead too. Who was she? I haven't seen any pictures of her before. She looked a lot like Erin."

Ten exchanged a watery look with Ronan, who appeared to be on the verge of losing it. "That was our daughter."

Fitzgibbon's mouth dropped open. "I-I." His mouth shut with an audible clack. "How?"

"I don't know the exact hows and whys of it either, but Bertha was somehow able to use her power to make Erin visible to Ronan for a short time while he was getting dressed. He was able to catch a glimpse of our little miss then. She was somehow able to do it again when they were walking down the aisle because I could see them both too. Bertha and Erin have been telling me that they've been visiting her soul and I guess they thought we should have glimpse of our future on our wedding day." A rogue tear slid down Tennyson's cheek.

Fitzgibbon opened his mouth to speak again, but no sound came out. He made eye contact with his son, but still no words came out of his mouth.

"Dad wants to know if Bertha or Erin have seen my sister? The one that Madam Aurora told him about?" Greeley squeezed his father's shoulder. Fitzgibbon nodded, but didn't say a word.

"I'll ask them about that the next time I see either of them. It might help matters along if you and Jace got your acts together!" Tennyson shot Fitzgibbon a knowing look.

"Well, the two of you aren't making things easy on me with your serial killers and ghosts of serial killers and all of these god damned bullet holes." Fitzgibbon absently fingered the scar on his chest over his shirt.

"Good point. I have an idea that might make up for all of that."
Ten nudged Ronan's knee under the table.

"Oh, right! I almost forgot about our idea." Ronan shook his head
as if he was still stuck in the memory of his wedding day. "Ten
and I have been trying to figure out where to go on our actual
honeymoon."

"The two of you took a week off. Wasn't *that* your honeymoon?"
Fitzgibbon shot Greeley a confused look.

"Seriously, Kevin?" Ten raised an eyebrow. "We spent three days
helping the two of move into your new house and the rest of the
time rubbing each other down with Icy Hot."

Fitzgibbon shuddered. "TMI, guys. I don't need to know your
cutesy nicknames for sex."

"Jesus, Kevin, Icy Hot isn't a cute nickname for sex." Ronan rolled
his eyes. "It's that pain gel Shaq hawks on television. We were so
sore from hauling boxes we could barely move."

"This was a mistake," Ten said with a sparkle in his eyes.
"Whoever had the brilliant idea to take our friends to some
tropical destination over the winter break should have their
head examined. Ronan and I can just go alone to a place with a
nude beach and all the free coconut oil we can slather on each
other."

"Wait! You were going to take all of us on your honeymoon too?" Greeley's green eyes popped wide open. "Seriously?" He elbowed his father. "Apologize, Dad."

Fitzgibbon laughed. "You want us all to go away together?"

Ronan nodded. "When was the last time you actually took a vacation?"

"When we moved into the house. You helped us move, remember?"

"Allow me to rephrase that. When was the last time you left New England to go on vacation? And don't say when you went to Kansas with us, because that was *not* a pleasure trip. Between dealing with Kaye and solving the Bradley case, it felt like all we did was work." Ronan gave his boss a triumphant smile.

"Ah, then the answer would be never." Fitzgibbon folded his arms over his broad chest. "Smartass."

"Ditto for me!" Greeley agreed.

"Talk to Jace, Kevin. See what he thinks about coming on this trip too. I know he's had a lot to do after the death of his father with settling his estate but try to break him away from all of that. Make some time to get this relationship off the ground."

"I could even have my own cabin so you and Jace could get jiggy with it." Greeley seemed thrilled with his plan.

"And how do I know you and some crazy-haired teenager wouldn't also be getting *jiggy* with it?" Kevin leaned forward in his seat.

"Where's the trust, Dad? Where's the love?" Greeley tapped on his father's chest.

"Trust? Who was it that was looking at porn on the internet last night?" Kevin raised a skeptical eyebrow at his son.

Greeley snorted. "That was Kaye."

"What?" Tennyson started to laugh. "My mother was looking at porn?"

"I know, right!" Greeley looked stunned too. "She told me she was looking something up online and all of a sudden this video popped up. I told her to share her screen with me so I could see what was going on and that was when Dad came into my room. He saw three guys going at it and went ballistic."

Ronan was laughing so hard he was having trouble breathing. "What...was...she...looking...up?" He managed on a wheeze.

"Daddy Bears," Greeley said simply. "I found out today she meant to type in 'teddy bears.' I guess she wants to send something to Truman's babies. They had a nice talk at the wedding. Anyway, she wasn't wearing her reading glasses and typed it in wrong. Teddy came out as Daddy. She clicked on the first link that came up and voila! Instant supersized three-way."

"You mean the guys were really tall?" Ronan asked.

Greeley bit his bottom lip and shook his head no slowly. He didn't answer Ronan's question. He just held his hands a foot apart.

"Sweet Jesus!" Tennyson muttered. He guessed that him and Ronan holding hands at Kaye's dining room table paled in comparison to the big-dicked gangbang Kaye had unwillingly witnessed.

"That's what Kaye kept saying too!" Greeley burst out laughing.

17

Ronan

Ronan was lying in bed looking at different cruise line websites while Dixie was curled up on his right side. What was missing was Tennyson curled up on his left.

After Greeley and Fitzgibbon went home, Tennyson had disappeared upstairs. Ronan heard the water running while he'd cleaned up from dessert, but when he'd followed with Dixie and his laptop, Tennyson hadn't been waiting for him in bed. The door to their office was closed, so Ronan had assumed Ten was in there soothing his kundalini or something similar.

"That's okay, pixie-girl, right? You'll help Daddy Ronan pick out the perfect spot for a tropical vacation we can't take you on." Ronan nuzzled the puppy's fur and clicked on a cruise that would take them to the Panama Canal.

As Ronan read through the trip itinerary, he couldn't help thinking about Greeley's experience at their wedding. He knew Bertha Craig made it possible so that he could see and speak to Erin on that special day, but what would it be like if he could talk to her everyday like Tennyson could?

"Hey, babe." Ten walked into the bedroom looking refreshed and relaxed.

"Well, hello to you too, Icy Hot!" Ronan set down the computer to ogle his husband. Ten was shirtless and wearing tight yoga pants.

Ten crawled up on the bed next to Ronan. Dixie scampered over to see him. "Hello, precious." He buried his face in her black and white fur. "What are you doing?"

"I was looking up cruises for our winter trip. What were you doing in the office?" Ronan reached over to the nightstand to grab his phone to snap some pictures of Tennyson and Dixie.

"I was meditating. I really like how we turned half of that room into a meditation space for me. My Buddha statue is right at home near that sunny window and my yoga rug fits perfectly beneath the sill. Did I ever tell you you're the best husband ever?" Ten kissed the dip in his collarbone.

Ronan laughed. "As a matter of fact, you haven't." When they'd first moved into the house, Ronan had moved his old desk and futon into that room. While Greeley and Fitzgibbon had been staying with them, the teenager had slept on the lumpy futon. After they'd moved out, Ronan decided to ditch the crappy thing. That was when Ten mentioned what a great meditation space it would be for him.

Ronan was more than happy to turn half of the room over to Ten. He couldn't help noticing how calm and completely relaxed his husband was when he finished meditating. He'd tried a bit of meditation when they'd gone on their little vacation to the Cape back in July, but he had been distracted by the sound of the ocean waves and the smell of the culinary creations the hotel's chef, Gregor Allen, was whipping up in the kitchen. Mostly though, he was distracted by Tennyson sitting right next to him in the same black yoga pants he was wearing now, looking good enough to eat.

"You know you're welcome to join me in there anytime. My mat is big enough for two." Ten said, seeming to read his mind. "Learning how to meditate now and work on your chakras will be very beneficial when we start going through the process of trying to get pregnant. Not to mention in dealing with our day-to-day stressful lives."

"You're right, Ten. You look so loose and relaxed when you come out of that room."

"It's time that I take for myself. I know you're getting back to running and working your body again and that's how you take care of yourself, but it's just as important to take care of the spiritual side of yourself too."

"And my ass will look banging in a pair of those pants, just like yours does." Ronan brushed a kiss against the hot skin of Tennyson's neck.

"My ass looks banging?" Ten looked back over his shoulder. "Ronan O'Mara, are you trying to seduce me?"

"Is it working?"

"Almost." Ten laughed. "Tell me about the cruises before I give in to your male charms and the bulge in your pants."

"There are a couple of choices that I really like. There's this trip to the Panama Canal. You go to a couple of islands on the way there like Aruba and then you go through half of the canal and spend the rest of the day in Panama. The last day is in Costa Rica. Can you imagine getting to see the rainforest?"

"That sounds like an amazing trip, but maybe not with four kids under the age of two."

Ronan frowned. "Good point. Howler monkeys and babies don't exactly mix."

"Those babies *are* howler monkeys sometimes. What else do you have?"

"Just regular Caribbean itineraries where you go to places like Martinique, St. Lucia, and Barbados, but that's a lot of island hopping for the babies. What would you think of Bermuda?"

"There's a cruise that just sails around that one island?" Ten didn't look convinced that was a good plan either.

Ronan shook his head no. "All of the Caribbean cruises sail out of Fort Lauderdale, but this one sails right out of Boston, so we wouldn't need to fly. Then the ship sails to Bermuda, which takes a day and a half. It docks at Hamilton and stays there for the whole trip, so it's like a floating hotel. All of our meals are paid for and we never have to worry about catching the boat, except on the day we sail back to Boston." He turned the computer toward Ten to show him the pictures of the crystal-clear azure water and the pink sand beaches.

"Wow, that looks amazing. And we wouldn't be at sea as much in case anyone gets seasick."

"Yeah, and if we like the cruise, you and I could go other ones in the future. I really like the idea of you and me in the Caribbean, babe. Sugar sand beaches and balmy breezes blowing through the palm trees."

"We've been so busy with this Hutchins thing that I didn't get a chance to tell about Carson and Cole wanting to expand the business. If we got this off the ground it would free me up for a bit more time off."

"Expand how? By making the space bigger or by adding more talent?"

"Yes." Tennyson laughed. "The biggest thing is that they want to buy the shop next door from the vacuum repairman. Carson thinks that the business is on its last legs anyway and he might be looking for a way out."

Ronan nodded. It was rare he saw customers coming or going from that store. "I would agree with Carson there. If he agrees to sell that would involve a loan, I'm guessing?"

"It would, but with Carson wanting to bring in more talent, that would also mean more money. Plus, the loan would be taken out between the three of us."

"You know I'm behind you one hundred percent in whatever you do. Cole and Carson are smart businessmen. If they think this is the right move for the business, then I'm sure it is."

"But?" Ten asked nervously. "You've said all these really great supportive things, Ronan. I'm just waiting for the but."

Nibbling on his upper lip, Ronan thought hard about all of the things Tennyson had just told him and what the possible risks were to their family and personal finances. "But my balls are so blue right now they ache, so do you think you could possibly do something about that?" Ronan flashed him a brilliant smile.

"That's it? I can go all in on this loan if I suck your dick?" Tennyson look skeptical and scandalized, but mostly skeptical.

"No! You can go in on this loan. Period. Please suck my dick. I'm sorry if you thought the one thing was contingent on the other." Ronan winked at his husband and shut the lid of his laptop. "Be naked when I get back!"

Tennyson laid back on the bed and went for the waistband of his yoga pants.

"Dixie, come!" The puppy hopped off the bed and followed him out of the room. He led her into the spare bedroom where they kept her doggie bed for times like this. "Time for you to meditate, little girl. I'll see you later. Time for Daddy Ronan to get him some." He shut the door behind him on Dixie's cries.

He made a mental note to tell Ten later how much he believed in him and the business he was building with Carson and Cole, but right now, he was going to focus on getting down with his new husband.

18

Tennyson

Ten was naked as the day he was born before Ronan had left the room with Dixie. He felt bad that the puppy needed to be shut up in the spare bedroom, but on the other hand, he didn't need an audience or a wet nose where a wet nose didn't belong either.

"Are you nekkid, boy?" Ronan called.

What was this, *Deliverance*? "Come find out for yourself!" Ten shouted back. "I thought you were going to fuck me sideways! Remember?"

Ronan's laughter bubbled up from the hall. "Oh, yeah. I did, didn't I?"

"You have no idea how to do it. Do you?" Ten sure as hell had no idea what the phrase, 'cheated on me left, right, sideways,' meant in the literal sense.

Ronan's head popped around the corner into the bedroom. "Do too. I'll prove it to you." He strutted into the room with his fat cock bobbing against his abdomen. "Lay on your side."

"Oh, so that's the sideways?" Ten giggled but obeyed. Before he rolled over, he'd seen the devious look in Ronan's darkening eyes. From behind him, he could hear his husband digging through his nightstand drawer for the lube and then the cap popping open.

Ronan knelt behind Tennyson on the bed. "Bend your leg and put your right foot flat on the mattress." He bent to press a kiss against Ten's right shoulder.

Slick fingers probed at Ten's entrance. He relaxed and let Ronan's magical fingers do their work. It wasn't long before he felt the heat of Ronan's chest against his back and the blunt head of his cock pressing against his eager hole.

"Let me in, babe." Ronan eased his hips forward until he was pushing past the ring of muscle. "That's it, just like that." When he bottomed out, Ronan wrapped his right arm around Ten's chest. "What do you think?"

"I like sideways. Maybe we'll have to try right and left sometime."

Ronan hummed his approval against the hot skin of Tennyson's back. He took his time with the movement of his hips. "Ten..."

Tennyson rolled back, his eyes meeting Ronan's over his shoulder. "Just like that. Slow." He pressed back further to kiss his impossible husband. The man he loved with his entire heart and who gave him everything his heart desired in return.

Ronan obeyed his command to go slow. So much of the time they'd spent in this room lately had been hurried. Fucking hard and fast to get to the happy ending, forgetting that the journey was the most important part. Even at this pace though, Ten knew he wasn't going to last long. This position had Ronan's cock nudging his sweet spot constantly.

"Should have done this sooner, but my husband doesn't let me watch porn for new ideas. All of my moves are old." Ronan kissed Ten again, tugging on his bottom lip with his teeth.

"Oh, so *that's* the reason you watched porn, to increase your repertoire. I never would have guessed."

Instead of responding to Tennyson's snarky tone, Ronan reached for Ten's leaking cock.

"Oh God, Ronan," Ten moaned, resting his head back on his husband's chest. "More, please."

"Oh, no, babe. You were the one who said to go slow. Your wish is my command." Ronan slowed the pace of his hand and hips down even further.

"Sadist," Ten muttered, knowing full well Ronan was the furthest thing from that.

"That's only going to make me go slower to prove your point." Ronan bit Ten's shoulder, not hard enough to break the skin, but hard enough to let Ten know he was there.

Ronan was true to his word. Ten could feel the slow drag of Ronan's cock as he bottomed out all the way back until he nearly pulled out. It was maddening. It was also the best fucking thing he'd ever felt in his entire life.

"Love you," Ten whispered. He knew he was getting close and might not remember to say those words at the critical moment. He shut his eyes and concentrated on Ronan. It felt like his husband was everywhere at once. Ten's back was pressed entirely against Ronan's front. His hand was still slowly stroking Ten's erection.

"Love you too." Ronan pressed a kiss to the hollow of Ten's shoulder. "Need you to come for me. Can't last much longer."

"So then make me come. Isn't that your job, husband?"

Biting his husband again, Ronan responded by hitching his hips harder, but not faster.

Ten moaned in response. Ronan was fucking him hard, but slow. How was that even possible? At this moment in time, Ten didn't care. He was so close, he could practically taste it.

"Hurry up. Not waiting," Ronan muttered.

Knowing damn well his husband wasn't going to come without him, Ten clamped down his muscles, tightening his passage and making Ronan have to work harder to move. It also felt fucking amazing.

"Jesus, Ten, gonna come," Ronan cried out.

Ten felt Ronan's cock jerk deep within him. Felt his husband's teeth dig into his shoulder. That was when his own release hit him. Ropes of sticky come splattered against his chest and stomach while Ronan kept moving his hips and muttering Tennyson's name. He wrung every last drop from Ten before his hand dropped away. "Christ, Ronan, are you still alive?"

Ronan groaned, but didn't move.

That was good enough for Tennyson. He'd have to remember this move for the cruise ship. He bet it would be dynamite on the water.

19

Ronan

Ronan was bright-eyed and bushy-tailed when he walked into the office on Monday morning. This was the start of the two weeks when Ten would be back at work with him and he was walking on sunshine.

The first thing on his agenda was to sit down at his desk and pretend to read the paper while all of his colleagues congratulated Tennyson on their wedding. It never bothered Ronan that the detectives in the squad room like Ten better than him. Ten was more of a people person, after all.

There were shouts of congratulations and lots of hugs. A lot of the guys showed Ten pictures they had taken on their phones during the wedding and the reception. That was quickly followed by Ten giving the cop his information so they could send the pictures along. It was more fun for Ronan watching Ten work the crowd then it would have been being in the middle of it.

"Jeez, I sure the hell hope he doesn't run for governor. He could give Charlie Baker a run for his money." Fitzgibbon sat down in the chair Tennyson always sat in. "I kind of dig him when we have blizzards and he wears a sweater in the emergency bunker. He's so strict when he tells people not to crowd the plow. Makes me want to do it just so he'll have to punish me. Oh, Daddy!" Kevin growled.

"Ah, Cap? We're sitting in the middle of the squad room, you might want to tamp *that* down." Ronan pointed in the general direction of Fitzgibbon's zipper.

"What?" Fitzgibbon turned to Ronan with a bit of a lost look on his face.

"We were talking about Charlie Baker." Christ, had Fitzgibbon been daydreaming out loud the whole time?

"We were? I like it when he wears those sweaters during blizzard press conferences." Kevin smiled at Ronan.

"You don't say." Ronan rolled his eyes and reached for his copy of *The Boston Globe*.

"You're going to talk to Ten about the dead files the others left for you?" Kevin pointed to the stack of files on Ronan's desk.

Ronan nodded. "That's the first thing I'm going to do when Evita Grimm gets his happy ass back over here."

"Loved by all of his people, that's for sure. I'd watch out if I were you. I don't think people would cry for you, Ronan. Him, yes. You, not so much." Kevin stood up from Tennyson's usual seat.

"Thanks for the vote of confidence."

Fitzgibbon slapped Ronan's shoulder. "Anytime. You hear anything back from that private dick yet?"

"Can you be a bit more specific? I know a *lot* of dicks, Cap."

Fitzgibbon barked out a surprised laugh. Ronan saw every cop in the room turn and look at him. It wasn't often the big man laughed like that.

"What's so funny?" Ten asked. Fitzgibbon shook his head and laughed harder.

"I'm not quite sure. Do you think I broke him?" Ronan shot a guilty look at his husband.

"I don't know, but we need proof of this moment, otherwise, it never happened." Ten held up his phone to their still laughing boss.

"Ah, Jesus Christ, that was funny," Fitzgibbon shook his head. "Byrne, Ronan. Have you heard anything from Jude Byrne?"

"No. Not yet. I'll let you know when we do. Ten and I would like to get out and walk the crime scene during our lunch hour today. I'm interested to see if he'll pick anything up."

Fitzgibbon nodded and headed back to his office.

Ronan turned back to Ten. "You're the hit of the ball, huh?"

"They were all so excited to show me pictures they'd taken at our wedding and to say what a great time they'd had. They're gonna send over their favorite pictures so we'll have them too."

All of the fellow officers that had come up and spoken to Tennyson has been in the office last week when he'd come back to work. Not one of them had shown him any pics or told him what a great time they'd had at the wedding. Ronan had no doubt everyone in this room would have his back or take a bullet for him, but maybe he should work on his "indoor" attitude.

"So, what are these dead files you keep mentioning but never actually give me any details about?" Ten sat in his usual seat and focused all of his attention on Ronan.

Ronan pointed to the double stack of files in front of him. There were ten files in all. "These are the coldest of the cold cases."

"Frigid cases," Ten muttered.

"Yeah, that's what the other detectives in the unit have implied. They worked these cases the same way I do and were never able to develop new leads or find new DNA or fiber evidence thanks to advances in testing technology. That's where you come in."

Ten nodded. "It's pretty amazing how far they've all come when you think about how hostile everyone was to me in the beginning."

Ten was dead on. Eleven months was a long period of time to change minds and perceptions and Tennyson had certainly done that. "Fitzgibbon is hoping that your sixth sense can give us new leads that will make it possible to close some, if not all of these cases. In addition to our regular caseload."

"No pressure then." Ten gave his head a little shake. "How about if I read through them and see if anything pops out at me and you can do the same with the regular cases. We'll compare notes later."

"Sounds good, Nostradamus." Ronan wanted to lean forward and kiss his husband, but they were in the middle of the office. He powered up his computer instead.

As the morning progressed, Ronan kept an eye on Tennyson. He was taking notes on each case file which he would tuck into the folder when he was finished working on it. He'd stack it on the floor next to his feet when he was finished with it and grab for the next file.

Ronan, for his part, had settled on what he thought would be the next case they would tackle together. It was the case of Morse Hines, a twenty-nine-year-old newlywed father of one who'd died under suspicious circumstances six years ago. The young man had been working on his car in his garage when the vehicle slipped off the jack and crushed him. There hadn't been enough evidence to prove if the "slip" had been accidental or if it had been helped along by someone else.

He was about to check in with Tennyson to see when he wanted to break for lunch when his phone jingled with an incoming text message. He couldn't help snorting when he saw who the message was from.

"What's so funny? It can't be one of our cases." Ten set down the evidence report he was reading.

Instead of answering him, Ronan nudged his phone across the desk.

"Who the hell is Fiery Dick and what crime scene does he want us to go walk?"

"Jude Byrne. Get it? Not just his name, but I swear when he's pissed off his eyes look like they're on fire. Dick because he's a P.I. and because he's a dick."

"I noticed that about his eyes too," Ten said, skipping right over any talk of dicks.

"It's interesting he wants to walk the crime scene but he doesn't mention anything about what he found out from Tank Hutchins cable company."

Ten's eyes narrowed. "Maybe he's one of those types who doesn't trust cell phones. Any information he has he'll give us in person rather than over the phone or in written form that can be traced back to him."

That was an interesting point, one that Ronan hadn't considered. "That sounds awfully paranoid to me."

"Just because you're paranoid, doesn't mean they're *not* out to get you. That, plus the fact we're not Jude's client. Tank is. He could be breaking his own bond of confidentiality by talking to us."

Two more good points from his husband. Ronan sank back into his chair. "How'd you get to be so smart?"

Ten shot his husband a conspiratorial grin. He looked around to make sure no one else was listening in on their conversation. "Osmosis from all the bone-jarring sex we have."

Ronan burst out laughing. "Grab your coat. I'll text Jude back that we'll meet him in ninety minutes. I'm gonna need to face this guy on a full stomach."

"Yeah, we all know how bitchy you are when you're hungry." Grabbing for his jacket, Ten stood up.

Slipping into his own coat, Ronan realize he had no witty comeback for that. When Ten was right, he was right.

20

Tennyson

Usually, the only view Tennyson got of the Mystic River was from high above, coming into Boston on the Tobin Bridge or on Route 93. From up high, the river was bustling with the port business of the city of Boston.

The view of the Mystic River was different from its banks. Looking out over it from the site where Lorraine McAlpin took her last breath, it was beautiful and bucolic. If you didn't know where you were, you'd never guess the city of Boston proper was a mere two miles behind you.

Brick row houses were backed up against the high banks of this part of the river. A five-foot-tall stone wall protected the properties against rising waters during snow melt or heavy rains. About twenty-five yards down was a footbridge which led to the park Tennyson was standing in. The park was popular with dog walkers and runners.

It was one of those early morning athletes, training for the Boston Marathon, who discovered the lifeless body of Tammy McAlpin and called 911. Tennyson could see Lorraine's townhouse from where he was standing. It was to his right about seventy-five yards down river.

"Are you using your mind powers?" Jude Byrne asked suddenly from behind him.

Ten stiffened, trying hard not to yelp out loud. He shot the private investigator an annoyed look. Instead of engaging with him, Ten turned the tables. "You get anything from Tank's cable company?"

Jude frowned. The muscle in his jaw was ticking again. "Nothing yet. Bastards haven't returned my call. Might get a better response if the call came from a member of the BPD."

Ten knew it cost the man a lot to say those words out loud. He nodded briefly. "I'm not trying to use my gift, I'm just trying to get a feel for the scene. Lorraine's house is down there." Ten pointed. "So, how'd she get here?"

"According to the autopsy, she weighed one hundred sixty-two pounds. Not a tiny girl, but for someone of Tank or Tim Hutchins size, easily movable," Ronan chimed in, coming to stand on Tennyson's right.

"This is an active place. People with dogs would walk them at all hours of the day and night. I have to imagine dragging a woman or carrying her over your shoulders like a sack of potatoes isn't something you'd want to get caught doing here." Ten turned around to survey the park. There were benches spread throughout and smaller, young growth trees. There wasn't a lot of privacy here for a murder.

"You're thinking she was lured here instead?" Ronan asked.

"Why not? From what I read in the newspaper article it was a hot July night. Perfect for a walk. No one in the neighborhood would have looked twice at a couple out for a stroll."

"There were no fingerprints or foreign DNA in her condo, Grimm," Jude said with a sneer.

Ten turned a sunny smile on the private dick. "I realize you might not have many friends, Jude, so I'll roll play the scenario with Ronan." Ten rolled his eyes and turned to his husband. He made like he was pressing a pretend doorbell. "Ding, dong."

Ronan acted like he was opening a pretend door. "Oh, hey, Tennyson. It is so good to see you." His voice was deliberately mechanical.

"Would you like to go for a walk in the park with me?" Ten imitated his husband's stiff language.

"Sure! Let me grab my keys." Ronan turned and gave Jude a see-nothing-to-it look.

"Doing it like that, the killer never came into the house. And before you say it, he never had to touch the doorbell either. He could have used a knuckle or used the fabric of his shirt to cover the pad of his finger so he wouldn't leave a print or touch DNA."

"God, you two are assholes." There were the beginnings of a smile on the P.I.'s face.

"We aim to please." Holding up a picture of the body, Ten walked over to where it had been found. There was a dense outcropping of trees next to the bank of the river. It was a pretty spot to stand and watch the water pass by.

From out of nowhere, someone grabbed Ronan, slipping a hand over his mouth and shoving something sharp into his lower back. He tried to buck out of the death grip but couldn't.

"Okay, Jude. I think you made your point," Ten sighed. "You can let him go now."

"Just one more minute? I'm kind of digging the quiet." Jude released Ronan giving him a small shove at the end.

"Jesus, you could give Ironman a run for his money. You eat steel bars for breakfast or something?" Ronan gave his shoulders a shake.

"We know from the autopsy that the victim was stabbed in the right kidney. The blow incapacitated her. Neighbors didn't recount hearing any screams. For a stabbing this brutal you would think there would have been some sound."

"Unless the wind was knocked out of her." Ten turned to Jude with a wicked smile on his face.

"Oh, no! No! This guy is built like a concrete linebacker. I'm still recovering from being shot three times in the chest." Ronan held up both hands and took a quick step backward.

"Jesus, Ronan, don't be such a baby. You're fine. Your endurance wasn't a problem last night when you were...Never mind." Ten felt color flaming his face. It was a good time to shut up, as Carson would say.

"When he was what?" Jude asked with the first real smile he'd flashed in the time Tennyson had known the surly man.

"That's none of your business, Ironman. Just do it but watch my jewels. I've got a baby to make," Ronan grumped, turning around and bracing for impact.

Jude backed up a few paces and winked at Tennyson before he came at Ronan. He hit the detective full-force, driving him to the ground. Ronan hit chest first, but the way Jude drove him down, he landed on his knees, straddling Ronan's backside with his hands on Ronan's back. When Ronan was down, Jude continued to demonstrate how Lorraine was stabbed.

"Can't...breathe...dickhead..." Ronan gasped.

"Ah, the sound of silence," Jude mused before hopping up off of Ronan and helping the panting detective to his feet.

"As painful as that looked," Ten grimaced, shooting Ronan a sympathetic glance, "maybe now we know why no one heard Lorraine cry out for help the night she was killed."

"Yeah," Ronan half-growled as he brushed himself off. "Are you feeling anything here, Ten?"

Tennyson's nerves were jangled for some reason. He tried to close his eyes and get a read on this place, but he wasn't getting anything at all. It was like there was a strange kind of interference. This feeling reminded him of when he'd be stopped at the set of lights near his bank in Salem and the XM Radio signal would inexplicably go out. Out of the corner of his eye, he could see Jude Byrne lurking around and couldn't help but wonder if he was the culprit.

Instead of trying to focus in on Lorraine McAlpin, he tried to get a read on the private investigator. Nothing. Aside from being able to gather data with his five senses, Ten was getting nothing at all. In all of the years since he'd first gotten his gift, he'd never met a human being who'd been able to block that gift as effectively as Jude Byrne was doing. It was eerie.

"Tennyson?" Ronan nearly shouted. He was waving a hand in front of his husband's eyes.

"Sorry, I was lost in space there for a minute." He offered his husband a weak smile.

"Yeah, you were." Ronan looked concerned. "What were you thinking about?"

Ten could see Jude standing a few feet behind them and wasn't going to talk to Ronan about this in front of the man. "I was thinking how messy stabbing Lorraine like Jude showed us would have left the killer. Yes, it was dark, but he still would have been pretty bloody."

Ronan narrowed his eyes, but kept his mouth shut.

"If it was dark enough and the killer was wearing black, people who encountered him might not have noticed he was bloody. Or he could have had a backpack with him that he could have shoved the stained shirt in," Jude suggested.

"He could have changed at his car." Ronan pointed to the parking lot behind them. "It's possible he parked here, crossed the bridge, and walked to Lorraine's house this way. He would have avoided parking on her street."

"Where does Tank live in relation to where we're standing?" Ten asked.

Jude turned toward the footbridge and pointed. "Five blocks in that direction. It's about a ten-minute walk from here. Tim lives on the other side of town. It's about a fifteen-minute drive at that time of night," Jude said, seeming to read Tennyson's mind.

That put Ten even more on edge.

"Are you okay?" Ronan whispered.

Ten gave his head a little shake. He wasn't feeling okay at all. Jude was really putting him off his game. Not being able to pick up one bit of information from the P.I. was completely unnerving him. Whether there was something physical to it or that was all in his head remained to be seen.

21

Ronan

"Okay, Nostradamus. You want to explain to me what happened back there?" Ronan had barely shut the door to the Mustang before those words were out of his mouth.

"Hi, babe. How was *your* day?" Ten raised an eyebrow and pulled his seatbelt over his shoulder.

Ronan sighed. Okay, maybe he was being a bit of a pill. "Fine. I'm a rude bastard, but I'm worried about you. Can you blame me? You were standing out there, staring into space like Cindy Brady when the game show camera turned on."

Tennyson burst out laughing. "Okay, that's probably an apt description of how I looked. It's Jude Byrne."

"Don't tell me you were standing there fantasizing about that golden-eyed Adonis." Ronan rolled his blue eyes.

"Seriously, Ronan? You described him twice as Ironman and now as an Adonis and you think *I'm* the one having fantasies about him?"

Figuring the best defense was a good offense, Ronan turned the key in the ignition. "I'm sorry, babe. Were you able to get a read on him at all today?"

Ten shook his head. "No," he whined. "I got nothing. What's worse, he made me feel edgy. Not the way I do when you're being annoying, but him being close to me put me on edge."

"Like you were attracted to him? That kind of on edge?" Ronan wasn't worried that Ten would leave him for the golden-eyed private dick, but he still needed to know what his newlywed husband was feeling.

Ten shook his head. "I really don't know how to explain it. I'm on edge psychically, like there's something about him that's upsetting my sixth sense."

"Upsetting like disturbing it?" Ronan pulled out of the parking lot and turned the car toward the highway. "Like there's a disturbance in the force, Luke?"

Ten laughed. "Maybe. I'm thinking its time I talked to Carson and Cole about this. Bertha and Erin too if we can round everyone up."

Ronan reached a hand out to Ten. "We'll figure it out and even if we don't, it's not like we're going to be stuck with this guy for the rest of our lives, right? We'll finish the Hutchins case and then we'll never have to see him again. Piece of cake."

Ten had a weird feeling in the pit of his stomach it wasn't going to be that easy to get rid of Adonis Ironman, Jude Byrne.

***

An hour later, Ten and Ronan walked into absolute chaos at Truman and Carson's house. From the sound of things, a fight was about to break out any second in their kitchen.

"The only way to cook a turkey is to brine it!" Fitzgibbon shouted. "It makes the meat more juicy."

"Deep frying!" Truman hollered back.

"Whatever happened to stuffing it?" Carson challenged.

"I just want gobbler sammiches the next day," Cole said.

"I want to spatchcock it, like Bobby Flay!" Greeley chimed in.

"What the hell is *that*?" Cassie practically screeched.

Ronan slapped a hand over his forehead. "You want to go away on a tropical vacation with this group of knuckleheads?"

"RO!" Laurel called out, as she toddled toward him on unsteady legs.

"Busted. Too late to go back home now." Ronan scooped up Cole and Cassie's daughter. "Hello, cutie pie. What's all the fuss about?"

"Loud!" The two-year-old put her hands over her ears while Ronan carried her into Carson's busy kitchen.

"Guys, what's all the ruckus? My niece would like to file a formal complaint!" Ronan giggled and poked Laurel's tummy.

The baby laughed and wrapped her arms around Ronan's neck.

"We're discussing Thanksgiving. Pull up a chair. I'll grab you a bottle of water." Truman moved to the fridge.

"Discussing?" Ten grimaced. "I'd hate to hear your definition of fighting. I could hear you from the sidewalk."

"Well, why don't you offer an opinion about the bird then." Cole raised an eyebrow.

"I think they all sound good."

"That's such a cop out, Uncle Ten. Trying to be a people person." Greeley waved a hand at him.

"I don't think Ten was trying to cop out of anything," Ronan said. "I think he sees an opportunity to start a family tradition." Ronan took the bottle Truman was offering him.

"He does?" Greeley looked confused.

"Yeah, I do?" Ten looked equally confused.

Ronan nodded, while he twisted the cap off his bottle of water. "Cap, you brine a bird. Tru, you deep fry one. Greeley will slap and tickle a bird, and Carson will do one the traditional way."

"Uh, that's spatchcock, Uncle Ronan."

"Uh huh. That sounds like a made-up word to me. Just an excuse to say *cock* in mixed company."

"Cock!" Laurel announced in her sweet little voice.

"Nice going, butt wipe," Cole muttered, yanking his daughter out of Ronan's arms.

"Uncle of the year!" Ronan crowed. "Vote early. Vote often. Anyway, you all make the birds. Mc and Ten and Cassie and Cole can make the sides. There will be plenty of turkey left over for sammiches and soup and casserole, or whatever else you crazy people want to do with it. What do you think?" Ronan looked around the kitchen.

"I like the idea of starting family traditions," Carson said. "This is the babies' first Thanksgiving. I was thinking of coming up with an idea that we could go with every year that they would think of as special."

"Me too," Truman agreed. "Having our crazy family around sure counts. I want lots of pictures of them with yams splattered all over their little faces." Truman pressed a kiss to Carson's face.

"Count us in." Greeley pointed back and forth between himself and Fitzgibbon.

"Invite Jace," Ten said.

Kevin blushed, but managed a brief nod.

"Cole, what do you and Cassie think?" Ronan asked.

"I don't know." He pressed a kiss to his daughter's head. "Do you want to have Thanksgiving dinner with your loudmouthed Uncle Ronan, sweetie?"

"Ro!" Laurel shouted, reaching for the man in question.

"Ha!" Ronan plucked the toddler out of his arms. He peppered her face with kisses.

"Fine, we're in too." Cole laughed. "What kind of sides are we making?"

"Traditional stuff like mashed potatoes and gravy. Yams for Uncle Truman. Maybe a root veggie mash." Cassie was all smiles.

"I like cornbread," Ten chimed in.

"Green bean casserole!" Truman called out. "The real thing though. Not that crap out of a can."

"Bobby Flay has a kick ass recipe for that, Uncle Truman." Greeley started tapping on his phone.

"Swear jar, buddy! You can be the one to research the recipe though." Truman grinned.

"I'll do research on other recipes too. Thanksgiving sides from around the country. Same with dessert. I want to try pecan pie."

"That's my favorite too, honey," Cassie smiled. "We're trying pie orders for the first time this year at the bakery. Pecan is one of the pies I'm offering."

"Do you need any help? I know a teenager with too much time on his hands." Greeley pointed at himself.

"Do you have any experience working in a bakery?" Cassie asked.

Greeley's happy attitude deflated. "No, sorry."

"You're hired!" Cassie and Truman shouted together.

"I am?" Greeley looked shocked.

"My mom always says if you can read, you can cook. Tomorrow morning 5am. I'll put you to work." Cassie slapped a hand on the teenager's shoulder.

"Dad, can you drop me off?" The smile on Greeley's face was so big, it practically split his face in half.

Kevin nodded. "That's about the time I need to leave for work anyway."

"Awesome! Thanks guys."

Ronan loved the look on Greeley's face. He'd been talking about getting a part-time job and working at the bakery would be perfect. The holiday season was their busiest time.

"So, we settled Thanksgiving and got Greeley a job. Anything else you all need my help with?" Ronan looked around the room.

Standing next to him, Tennyson raised his hand.

22

Tennyson

Ten hated the idea of breaking the jovial party up with his problem. "I've got something I wanted to talk about. I'm not sure if you can help me though."

"We're here for you, Tenny!" Bertha Craig said from behind him.

"Thanks, Bertha." Tennyson was so happy to see her.

"Mimi!" Laurel screeched, reaching her chubby arms out to her grandmother.

"Hello, little princess." Bertha pressed a kiss to her oldest granddaughter's head and then did the same to Ronan.

"She's loving on me, isn't she?" Ronan asked.

"Yup." Ten managed to laugh.

"It wouldn't be a day ending in "Y" if I wasn't loving on you, Handsome." Bertha cackled.

"Oh, jeez, Mom. No wonder his ego is the size of Texas." Carson sighed.

"She's talking about my butt, right!" Ronan laughed. "Now that I'm running again, I'm getting some of my tone back." He looked over his shoulder.

Cole groaned and slapped a hand over his face. Laurel mimicked him perfectly.

"Tell us what's going on, Ten," Truman said.

"It's this Jude Byrne. He's the private investigator Thomas Hutchins has working on his murder appeal."

Truman nodded and started tapping on the touchpad of his phone.

"There's something about him I can't put my finger on but being near him puts my gift on edge. The strangest thing about him is that I can't read him."

Carson frowned. "Maybe he's just one of those people whose good at blocking talent like us."

"I thought so too when I met him at the prison the first time. Granted I was sick from all of the negative psychic energy of that place. I figured it was a combination of the bad energy and of me not feeling my best. Then when Ronan and I met with him again today, I was convinced it was more than that."

"His real name is Judas Byrne," Truman announced. Holding his phone up for everyone to see. "Says here that he's originally from a place called Kingdom City, New Mexico."

Ronan shivered. His eyes popped wide open. Laurel jiggled in his arms for a second before he settled her back against his hip again.

"Jesus, are you okay?" Ten wrapped an arm around his husband.

Ronan nodded. "It's the name. You don't hear it every day."

"It's a brave name, don't you think?" Kevin asked. "Or named by a mother who has no obvious tie to Christianity."

"Or has a darker tie," Cole said. "Judas was a traitor. Maybe his mother saw her infant son as one too and that in combination with the name of the town? Kingdom City?"

Ten shook his head. "As interesting as the possible origin of his name is, that has no bearing on my inability to read him. Religion never has had any kind of effect on my gift."

"Explain this to me, Tennyson," Bertha said. "What exactly are you feeling when you try to read him?"

"The only way I can explain it is that he's one big, blank page. When the babies were newborns, they were so peaceful to hold because they had pure auras and no spirits glommed on to them. They had no real thoughts to read, but I could still hear other spirits and feel other psychic vibrations around me. They were the closest thing I could get to quiet time until Madam Aurora taught me how to shut down my gift on command. Jude is different though. He's like a dead zone."

Carson and Cole exchanged a silent look.

"What?" Ten asked. He could feel his anxiety starting to ratchet up.

"It's probably nothing," Carson said.

"I'm sure it's nothing," Cole echoed.

"JFC, guys spill it. You're scaring the bleep out of me." Ronan cuddled Laurel tighter.

"KFC!" Laurel announced. She turned a big smile at Ronan.

Ronan laughed and pressed a raspberry to her neck, making the baby squeal with laughter.

"Shifters." Carson looked over at Bertha.

"What?" Ronan's mouth dropped open "You've got to be shitting me. Those are just dirty books that I read when I'm bored, about werewolves and werebears and dragons getting it on."

"All fiction is rooted in truth somewhere," Carson said quietly. "And I'm not necessarily talking about wolf shifters."

"What do you mean you're not necessarily talking about wolf shifters. What else is there?" Ronan wore a look of alarm tinged with interest.

Carson exchanged a silent look with Cole. "Not shifters in the traditional sense where people are bursting out in fur or scales."

Ronan opened his mouth, but Tennyson held up a hand to stop him.

"Okay, so let's say shifters are real," Ten took a deep breath. This was a pretty big leap for him here. "What does that have to do with me not being able to read Jude Byrne?"

"If the myths are real, people like that can't be read by people with our gifts," Carson said quietly. "Truman just said Jude was from New Mexico, that could explain what's going on here. Native American tribes from that part of the country have mythology about spirit animals."

"You mean like totems? An animal spirit guide?" Tennyson asked. That made a lot more sense to him than people magically transforming into a panther or a T-Rex.

Cole shrugged. "Like Carson said, a lot of myth is rooted in truth."

"Bertha, you're awfully quiet." Tennyson looked up at his mentor.

"I don't have much to say here. Native American spirit dinosaurs aren't exactly in my wheelhouse. I liked it better when we were talking about starting family traditions and my little munchkin was calling my name. If you want my advice on this Byrne character, try getting to know him instead of trying to antagonize him. It could just be he's one of those people who doesn't like psychics and has an extra high wall up against you, Tennyson."

"What's my secret love saying, Ten?" Ronan asked.

Ten snorted. "She thinks we should get to know Jude in case he's mistrustful of psychics and has a high wall up."

"Oh damn, Bertha! Just when I thought we were building something, you had to go and ruin it by saying something like that. Jude Byrne is the most egotistical, high and mighty butt munch I've ever met in my life."

"The two of you obviously have a lot in common then. Toodles!" Bertha was gone.

Tennyson burst out laughing. He couldn't argue with Bertha's logic but wasn't about to share it with his husband either.

"Butt munch!" Laurel crowed, raising her little fist high in the air.

23

Ronan

Ronan was lying in bed with his laptop and Dixie. She was resting her head on Ronan's arm. Tennyson was finishing up in the shower. Ten had invited Ronan to join him, but in an uncharacteristic move, Ronan had declined.

He'd spent the last twenty minutes going back and forth between candied yam recipes, thinking about why he wasn't in the mood to ravish his husband in the shower, and the possibility that shifters were a real thing. Who the fuck knew?

He looked down at Dixie who was staring at him with her big dark eyes. "You're not going to turn into a person, Dix, are you? Be some tiny naked woman with boobs and whatever else you got going on downstairs?" Ronan grimaced.

"What is wrong with you?" Ten asked from the bathroom door. He was wearing blue and red flannel pants and a weird look on his face.

"This shifter thing has me freaked out. I was just wondering if I was gonna wake up and Dixie would be gone and, in her place, would be a naked woman."

"*That's* why you wouldn't take a shower with me?" Tennyson sat down on the edge of the bed. Dixie scampered over Ronan and the laptop to get to him. "That's my girl. Daddy Ronan's lost his mind. Hasn't he?"

"I've just got a lot *on* my mind." Ronan turned the computer around to show Ten all of the recipes he'd been reading.

"Why are you looking at ten recipes for the same thing?" Ten rested his head on Ronan's shoulder.

"In addition to shifters, I was thinking about Thanksgiving too."

"You don't think the turkey's gonna turn into a naked man, do you?" Ten lifted his head up to look his husband in the eye.

"No, don't be ridiculous. In all of the books I've read, shape-shifters only seem to be predators."

"I beg your pardon, but to a wild berry, a turkey *is* a predator." Ten pressed a kiss to Ronan's neck and settled back down to his shoulder.

"Okay, Jack Hanna. I meant the shifters I read about are carnivores: wolves, panthers, bears, lions. I guess I don't understand what Carson and Cole were talking about and that's what's got me rattled. So, instead of showering with my gorgeous man, I was looking up spirit animals and wondering if Dixie was one."

Ten laughed. "Native American mythology is fascinating. The idea of spirit animals has more to do with the lessons we can learn from that animal and people identifying with the animal than anything else. There are some myths that say the Native Americans were born from animals and therefore have animal blood in them."

"You're saying that's where the shifter stories come from?"

Ten nodded against Ronan's shoulder.

"If that were really true, if Jude Byrne theoretically had mountain lion or Gila monster or road runner blood in him, why wouldn't you be able to read him?"

"I don't know, Ronan. Why do I lose Elvis Radio on XM when I'm stopped at the light near Bank of America on Essex Street?"

"There's gotta be something in the bank that interferes with the signal." Ronan paused and thought about that for a minute. "Jude Byrne is your kryptonite. Is that what you're saying?"

"Maybe *he* isn't, but something inside of him is." Ten shifted and pulled Ronan's computer closer. He clicked off the Native American mythology pages Ronan was looking at and clicked back over to the recipes. "Why are candied yams so important?"

"All of that talk at Carson's about starting family traditions got me thinking about our little miss. She will be born into established family traditions by the time she gets here and I want them to be good ones."

"And that starts with yams?" Ten turned to look at his husband.

Ronan nodded. He blinked up at the ceiling hoping Tennyson wouldn't see the emotion in his eyes. "When I was growing up it was just me and my mom and her parents for Thanksgiving. It was the same generic meal every year, turkey, stuffing, squash, mashed potatoes, gravy and cranberry sauce. It was the yams that made it special. The recipe had been handed down from Grammy's family back in Ireland. It was never written down and when my mom died, the recipe died with her. That's why I've been looking at every recipe on the internet. I'm trying to find the one that is the closest match."

"Babe, all I have to do is ask Erin about the recipe the next time she stops in to see me. I'm sure she'd be thrilled to pass it down to us, especially when she hears why you want it."

Ronan wiped his eyes. "It was such an amazing thing getting to talk to her the morning of our wedding, Ten. We only had a few minutes together, but aside from saying, 'I do,' it was the best part of the day. I miss her so damn much."

Ten slipped an arm around Ronan's chest. "I know you do, sweetheart. I know how much she wishes she were here with us too. Which of course brings me to a rather uncomfortable question."

Ronan snorted and started to laugh. He knew exactly what question Tennyson was going to ask him. "It's about Kaye. Isn't it?"

Ten nodded. "I know she's settling in back in Kansas to her new life without my father. She's working twenty hours a week at the shelter and trying to figure out which animal she wants to adopt. She's driving to church and having dinner at the Main Street Café again. I just wonder if she'd want to come out here for Thanksgiving."

Ronan sighed. Having Kaye out here for the few days after their wedding had been an exercise in patience. Thankfully, Truman and Carson had been kind enough to take her on and play host. Greeley had played tour guide, when he wasn't busy helping Fitzgibbon move into their new house. He knew what the right answer was in his heart, even if his brain was not on board with that plan. "If you want to invite her out here, I'm willing to pay the price."

"What?" Ten shot him an angry look.

Realizing what he'd said had a double or even a triple meaning, Ronan sat up and pushed the computer onto the comforter. "No, I mean I'll pay for her ticket. She's more than welcome to stay in the guest room. Although I'm sure she'd be happier with Greeley and Fitzgibbon."

"What if she doesn't want to come, Ronan?"

It was entirely possible Kaye wouldn't want to come to Boston twice in a month for a number of reasons, one of which was that she was still struggling with the fact that her son was gay and now married to a man. "If she doesn't come then we make new traditions and amazing memories with the family that is here celebrating with us."

Ten nodded and rested his head on his husband's shoulder.

24

Tennyson

Ronan was scowling over his phone when Tennyson walked into the kitchen the next morning. "Well good morning to you too, grumpy cat."

"It's not you. It's Ironman." Ronan's demeanor didn't brighten when he glanced up at his husband.

"What's he want now? A date at the roller-skating rink?" Tennyson laughed.

"No," Ronan's eyes narrowed. "He wants us to find some way into Lorraine McAlpin's house."

Ten's mouth fell open. "You're kidding me." How on earth were they going to find a way into Lorraine's house? "So, does he want us to just come right out and tell her family we're working for the defense team of her convicted killer? Or does he want us to break in like cat burglars?"

"Oh, it gets better from there. He also wants us to speak to her family. 'Dig up some dirt,' was how he put it."

"He's out of his Gila monster mind." Ten threw his hands up in the air. "I'm making tea. Do you want a cup?"

"Hell, no! If I need to convince a murdered woman's mother to let us poke around in her life, I'm gonna need something with higher octane than green tea." Ronan strode across the kitchen and pulled his husband into his arms. "Good morning."

Ten kissed him hard. "Good morning to you too, caveman." Ten studied his husband for a minute. "If you were a shifter, what kind would you want to be?"

Ronan rolled his eyes. "You don't get to pick. You're born a wolf or a panther. If I could pick, I'd want to be a dragon."

"Of course, you would. Magnificent and silver scaled, sitting on your pile of treasure, able to breathe fire and incinerate your enemies." Ten knew that would be Ronan's best-case scenario.

"Hmm, maybe that's what Jude is, a dragon. Byrne. He's got those golden eyes that turn kind of fiery when he's pissed off. I bet that's it. I bet his spirit animal is a dragon. Or he's an actual dragon and that's why you can't read him."

Ten was starting to wish he hadn't asked Ronan what kind of shifter he would be if he could choose. "Dragons aren't real, Ronan." If they were, he was going to need something stronger than green tea to talk about it.

"Hey, Carson was the one who said all myth is based in fact. What if he's not a dragon like Smaug or like modern mythology portrays, but it's something else? More like the Chinese myths portray, smaller and more snake-like?"

"I suppose it's possible. What's more important is Lorraine McAlpin. We can deal with Fiery Dick later."

Ronan burst out laughing. "Okay, fine, but we're not done talking about him being a dragon. Promise me."

Ten couldn't help feeling like his husband was a giant toddler half the time. What was next? Pinkie swearing? "I promise we'll talk about this shifter business again after I get a chance to spend more time with Jude, okay?"

Ronan held up his left pinkie finger.

"Seriously, Ronan?" Ten sighed dramatically but wrapped his little finger around Ronan's.

"You *know* you love me."

Ten knew it too. "How are we going to get Lorraine McAlpin's mother to talk to us?" Ten skipped right over inflating Ronan's ego. It was big enough as it was.

"That's the easiest part of all of this. You're going to offer to do a reading."

Ronan was right. The reading was the easiest part. What was harder was getting their foot in the door. "How do you propose we approach her? Ring the doorbell and offer her a reading like we're some kind of door-to-door psychics, like the Jehovah's Witnesses or Avon ladies?"

"Okay, I guess I didn't think about that. Mrs. McAlpin is going to want to know why a Cold Case Detective and a psychic are showing up on her doorstep when her daughter's murderer has already been tried and convicted."

"Tank was convicted two years ago. His first parole hearing isn't for another twenty-three years. Think about that, Ronan. These people have settled back into some semblance of normal life. If we go and knock on their door out of the blue, we're going to blast that new normal to hell." Ten knew the McAlpins probably thought about their daughter every day, but Tank Hutchins was probably the furthest thing from their minds.

"You may have a point. Those people are also gonna blow a gasket when they find out we're working for Tank."

Ten frowned. "Explain something to me."

"Anything."

"You just said that the McAlpins are going to blow a gasket and I agree with you. They totally are. Don't they want to see justice served here as much as we do or do they just want a warm body in prison serving time for Lorraine's murder?"

Ronan was silent. He tapped his index finger on the kitchen counter. "You know what it's like to go through a criminal investigation. We do all of the leg work, identify a suspect and find evidence to prove that this person committed the crime, right?"

Ten nodded, not wanting to interrupt Ronan's train of thought.

"The murder victim's family is along for that same ride in all of this. The detectives who investigated Lorraine's murder identified Tank Hutchins as the suspect. They found enough evidence to have an arrest warrant sworn out, a grand jury voted to indict Tank and the case went to trial. The McAlpins spent the entire year leading up to the trial thinking that Hutchins was the killer. Then the trial starts, and they hear all the evidence against him. Lastly, the jury convicts him. Do you see where I'm going with this, Ten?"

"I do. You're saying that the McAlpins have had the last three years to think of Tank as Lorraine's murderer. It's just that you see stories on *Dateline* where the cops and the family of the murder victim continue to think the innocent man was the killer long after other evidence is uncovered proving otherwise."

"What I just explained to you is the reason why people get it stuck in their heads. It's not just the emotional family, but the detectives who invest time and themselves in these cases that can fall victim to that trap too. Just because we know Tank is innocent doesn't mean the McAlpins are going to be happy to hear it. If he's innocent, then who killed Lorraine? Now there's no one to pay for her senseless murder."

"An eye for an eye," Tennyson muttered.

Ronan shrugged. "It might not be right, but when you've been wronged, it's one hell of a platitude to hang your grievances on."

Ten couldn't argue with that. "When does Jude want to meet?"

"Whenever we're free."

"Good, tell him to meet us up here. It's high time the rest of the gang meets him, Carson, Cole, and Fitzgibbon especially. If he wants us to do something for him, he's gonna have to work for it."

Ronan raised an eyebrow. "That your version of an eye for an eye?"

"Yeah, maybe so. I think we're going to need to use him to get our foot in the door with Lorraine's family."

Ronan grinned from ear to ear. "What do you mean?"

"What if we set Jude loose on them? He uses his usual brand of *charm* on them and then we sweep in like heroes to clean up his mess."

"That's pretty devious, Ten. Just because he's an asshole to me, doesn't mean he's going to treat everyone like that. I can't imagine him being a total dick to the grieving family of a murder victim."

"I thought you hated this guy?" Ten was confused. If anyone could grease the wheels here, it had to be Jude. Didn't it?

"You have to admit I'm a dick at times too. It's part of my unique charm and half of the reason you fell in love with me."

Ten grumbled a half-assed, "Maybe." It was all he was willing to concede.

"Like attracts like, as my mother would say. It's probably why Jude and I bounce off each other the way we do. We're too much like each other. Only he's a bit more gruff and closed down than I am. Why don't we invite him up here, let him meet everyone, and then ask him what he thinks about getting in to see Lorraine's family?"

Ten shook his head. "When the hell did you turn peacemaker?"

"Must be osmosis from sleeping next to you every night. What can I say? You make me a better man just by standing next to me." Ronan pressed a gentle kiss to Tennyson's temple. "Dixie, my little pixie? Who's ready for walkies?" Ronan sang out.

An excited bark sounded from under the kitchen table as Dixie scrambled to her feet and raced toward Ronan.

Ten watched in stunned silence as Ronan hooked their excited puppy up to her harness and led her toward the front door.

25

Ronan

It turned out it wasn't as much of a hassle for Jude Byrne to meet at their house as Tennyson hoped it would be for the private investigator. He lived in Cambridge, Massachusetts which was only a twenty-six-mile drive to Salem. Jude had seemed upbeat about making the trip especially when Ronan mentioned providing dinner.

He'd run out to the grocery store and grabbed the biggest, juiciest rib-eyes he could find. Dragons loved red meat according to every shifter novel he'd read, so he was going to tempt the dragon with what he loved. He'd also grabbed baking potatoes and fixings for a salad in case he'd completely gone off the deep end with this dragon bullshit.

Fitzgibbon and the Craig brothers were coming for dinner, so they'd be able to get their two cents in as well when it came to the mysterious private dick. Ronan snorted. Before long he was laughing out loud.

"What's so funny?" Ten looked around the empty kitchen and then behind himself. Dixie was sitting at his heels staring up at him.

Ronan shook his head.

"This isn't good if you're alone in a room and laughing hysterically? Are you hearing voices? Seeing things that aren't there? Have you lost your shit?"

Ronan shook his head again, this time making the universal gesture for jacking off.

"Well, fuck you and everyone who looks like you too, sweet cheeks!" Ten grinned at his husband suddenly turned hyena.

Ronan took a deep breath, desperate to share the joke with Ten. "Byrne," he managed to gasp.

"I should have known that dick was involved in this somewhere." Ten rolled his eyes.

Ronan, still laughing too hard to talk, tapped his nose and pointed to Tennyson.

"Dick? This has to do with the dick?" Ten narrowed his eyes.

Ronan nodded.

"Private dick?" Ten guessed.

"Yessss!" Ronan managed.

"What the hell is so funny about a private dick?"

"Aren't all dicks private?" Ronan finally said.

"Unless you're a porn star." Ten cocked his head to the side, as if he were thinking hard about public dicks. "Or a flasher."

Ronan started laughing again. He was about to suggest guys who piss in public, but the doorbell rang.

"Christ, he's not one of those early dicks, is he?" That's all they needed was for Jude to be this early. Carson wasn't even here yet with the food.

"No, it's Carson and Truman. I'll get it. You stay here and keep obsessing over dicks."

"That's what I do all the time anyway!" Ronan called back. It was true. Most of the time, anyway.

"Da Da Da Da!" Came little shouts from the living room.

"Oh, good, Jude *is* here!" Ronan crowed as he walked into the living room.

"Ronan, it's the babies. They've learned how to say my name," Truman rolled his eyes.

"Ah, in case you've forgotten, *husband*, Daddy is my name too." Carson was laying down a blanket and setting out toys for the now ten-month old triplets.

"They're obviously talking to me, *wife*!" Truman shot back, grinning from ear to ear.

"Oh good, so this is going to be a multi-dick party then." Ronan scooped baby Bertha up and snuggled her close. "You know, if you just learned how to say, 'Ro,' you'd save everyone a lot of hassle."

"Eeee!" Bertha screeched instead.

"Mimi's here, isn't she, princess? Just what we need. The perfect person to judge the biggest dick contest." Ronan rolled his eyes heavenward.

"Still heavyweight champion," Carson said with a grimace. "Mom, I sure the hell hope Ronan's a metaphorical *heavyweight* champion."

Tennyson burst out laughing.

"What did she say, Ten?" Ronan asked. He could feel a blush creeping up his neck.

"I'll tell you later." Ten's face was flaming like a lobster that had just come out of a pot.

"Where do you want the cold cut platter?" Truman asked, once the babies were settled on the floor.

"In the kitchen." Ronan led the way after he set the baby down with her siblings. He'd picked up rolls, condiments, and chips earlier in the day. They'd figured it would be easier to have a do-it-yourself sandwich bar, rather than calling out from Greek Life.

"What's news?" Truman asked, after he set the platter down.

"It's so weird being on this side of a case." Ronan shook his head. He still couldn't believe they were helping a convicted killer, rather than the grieving family of the victim.

"Tennyson said he's innocent though, right?" Truman wore a look that said that was all that was important to him.

"Yeah, but Lorraine McAlpin is still dead." At the end of the day, Ronan knew that was the only fact that would matter to the McAlpin family.

"I get that, but you're still on the side of justice."

That was true enough. He and Tennyson were now turning their efforts toward trying to exonerate an innocent man. "The piece of the puzzle that we're missing is usually the first one we place."

"Talking to the victim?"

"Right. Ten and I can't seem to come up with a way to convince Lorraine McAlpin's family to let us read her spirit, so we haven't reached out to them yet."

"If I can help you with that, will you change my name to Genius Dick in your phone?" Jude Byrne asked from the kitchen door.

Ronan burst out laughing.

26

Tennyson

Tennyson couldn't decide if letting Jude in to the kitchen without telling Ronan he was here was a good idea or one that would get him spanked later. Either way, he was going to come out a winner.

When he heard Ronan laughing his ass off, he knew he'd made the right decision. Jude had gotten to the house at the same time as Fitzgibbon and Greeley. They hadn't rang the doorbell, they'd just walked in. Ronan would have had no idea Kevin and Greeley, let alone the dick of the hour, were here.

"What the hell is their issue anyway?" Carson asked, pointing toward the kitchen. "Doesn't Ronan know they're destined to be BFFs?"

"Jesus Christ, Carson! Whatever you do, don't tell Ronan that." Fitzgibbon laughed.

"I disagree." Greeley wore a wicked grin. "Tell him, but make sure you're recording it. We could win a lot of money on *Funny Videos*! Of course, ABC would have to beep out most of the words in order to show it on the air..."

"Let's go see what's so funny." Tennyson picked up Brian from the floor and headed toward the kitchen. He knew the babies' reaction to their guest would go a long way to telling the tale of Jude Byrne.

"Marry me, Bertha?" Greeley tickled the baby and scooped her up from the floor.

"That boy is a natural. Just like you, Tennyson." Bertha Craig said from behind him.

"Christ, Bertha. Don't tell Fitzgibbon that. Let's hope there are a lot of years before we see Greeley with one of his own."

"I thought the boy was a bone tooter? It's not like he's gonna go out and make one of those the old-fashioned way." Bertha patted Tennyson's shoulder. "Sometimes I worry about you, Tenny."

Carson was standing in the kitchen doorway with a shocked look on his face. "All I heard was bone tooter and not going to make one of those the old-fashioned way. Do I want to even know what my mother was talking about?"

"Greeley." Ten laughed.

"Of course. Who else would she have been talking about but a seventeen-year-old, gay boy. Jesus Christ." Carson carded a hand through his blond hair.

"What do you think of Jude?" Tennyson half-whispered.

"He's hella gorgeous. He knows it too. Man, those eyes..." Carson trailed off as if he were in a trance.

"Are you going to pick up your daughter or leave her on the floor for Dixie to watch?" Ten couldn't help but laugh over the way Dixie was standing at Stephanie's head, standing guard. The baby kept reaching for the puppy's ears, which Dixie would perk up at the last second to keep out of her pudgy grasp.

"What?" Carson shook his head.

"Your baby." Ten pointed.

"Hmm." Carson scooped her up. "Those eyes, Ten."

"Are you in an actual trance?" Ten shifted Bertha to one hip and waved his free hand in front of Carson's eyes. "What's our secret code word?"

"Seriously? Prickly pear." Carson looked like he thought Ten had lost his marbles.

Ten relaxed a bit. "Would you still be able to remember their code word if Jude were exercising some form of mind control over you?" Ten whispered.

"I'm not exercising mind control!" The dick in question shouted. "Can we eat please? I'm so hungry that this little baby is looking quite tasty!"

"That dirty bastard!" Carson raced into the kitchen.

Jude was sitting at the dining room table and laughing his ass off. "Guys, I know what's going on here."

"We're about to grab pitchforks and torches," Carson said, with his dander up.

"Why don't we grab some food instead?" Truman offered. He pried the plastic lid off the cold cut tray.

"Good idea." Ronan opened the chip bags and started grabbing condiments out of the fridge.

"Oh, and by the way, I have supersonic hearing or whatever." Jude flashed Tennyson a wicked grin. "You wanted your friends to check me out, right, O'Mara?" Jude asked.

"Something like that," Ronan admitted.

"Why?" Jude seemed genuinely surprised. "I've been a P.I. here in Massachusetts for three years now. My license is in good standing. Bradford Hicks wouldn't have hired me to work on such a high-profile case if my credentials weren't stellar. So, what the hell is *your* problem?"

The room went silent. Everyone looked around at each other without making eye contact with Jude.

"Come on people. I'm clean. I don't eat kids and I don't have a hump on my back. Yeah, I can be a bit surly at times, but that's no crime." Jude looked around the still quiet room.

"A *bit* surly?" Ronan asked under his breath. He looked up at Tennyson.

Ten took a deep breath. "Do you believe in my gifts?"

Jude threw his hands up in the air. "What the hell does that have to do with anything?"

"Answer the question, butt munch. It will make things go easier on you," Fitzgibbon half-growled.

"Yes. No. I don't know." Jude sighed. "I've read about you in the papers. I've seen stories about you on television and I saw what you did with Tank in the prison. You've never read me and told me I was a Zulu warrior in a past life, so I don't know if I personally believe in what you do."

Ten nodded. It was an honest answer. "That's the problem, Jude. I can't read you."

Jude pushed out a harsh breath. "Well, you don't have to be such an asshole about it."

Fitzgibbon put a heavy hand on Jude's shoulder. "He's not saying he *won't* read you. He's saying he *can't*. Who's the asshole now?"

Jude cocked his head to the side. "I don't understand."

"When I meet strangers, usually my spirit guides and my own intuition give me some clue about the person. Are they good or bad? Do they have something to hide? I got none of that when we met in the prison. To be honest, I was sick that day from all of the negative energy there. Fifty years' worth of residue from killers and rapists was making me physically ill."

"I didn't know that could happen." Jude sounded sympathetic.

"I didn't know it could either. Not to that level, anyway." Ten shrugged. "I figured I would be able to get a better read on you the next time we saw each other, but that day in Charlestown, I couldn't read you then either."

"Explain that to me." Jude leaned forward in his seat. All of his attention was tuned into Tennyson.

"Right now, I know Ronan wants me to hurry this up because he wants a sandwich. He's thinking about how he wants to get it on later. He's also thinking that your cologne is off the hook." Ten raised an eyebrow at his husband. "No, asshole, I'm not wearing it for *you*."

Ronan started to laugh.

"Those are just the PG-13 rated things he's thinking. His left foot is asleep and he's got an itchy left ear." Ten smiled at his husband.

As if on cue, Ronan scratched.

"When I try to read you, Jude, I get nothing at all. You're completely blank."

Jude's frown deepened. "So, what, that puts you on edge with me? Or it makes you think I'm a bad person or not trustworthy because you don't have the upper hand? You're just a regular guy when we stand toe to toe and you don't like that, right?"

When Jude put it that way, it made Tennyson sound like the dick and not the other way around. He took an involuntary step back.

"Why don't we all make a sandwich?" Truman offered.

"I want an answer to my question." Jude demanded.

"Fine! I do feel a bit off kilter when you're around. I don't know if you're friend or foe or what skin you've got in the game with Hutchins. Tank *or* Tim!" Ten could feel his temper starting to get the best of him and knew it was time to shut up.

Jude looked around the kitchen at all of Tennyson's friends before his gaze landed back on the psychic. "I always think the best way to find out the answers to questions like that is to ask. Start an open and honest dialogue with spoken words, instead of poking around inside my head, uninvited. How does that sound?"

"Not as dickish as I thought it would," Ronan blurted out. "Now we can eat." He got up from the table and started the line himself, leaving Jude alone at the kitchen table.

"Wow, that makes me sound like I'm king of the assholes, doesn't it?" Ten took the empty seat next to Jude.

"Only a little. I know who I am and what I stand for, Tennyson. I get where you and your overprotective squad are coming from." Jude sounded genuine. "I'm a total stranger and you've got no reliable data on me."

"How did you get tangled up with Tank Hutchins and Bradford Hicks." It was the question Ten had been dying to ask the P.I.

Jude laughed. "A man's gotta eat and keep a roof over his head. I was at a point where I couldn't afford to be picky."

Tennyson had certainly been there a time or two in his early career. "Are you working toward getting Tank exonerated?"

"That's the plan. Although I don't mind telling you it's a weight off my mind to find out he really is innocent." Jude shrugged, leaning closer to Tennyson. "I've been in the P.I. game for a long time now. Everyone says they're innocent. Ronan must hear that all the time too. It restores a tiny bit of my faith in humanity to find out that one guy actually *is* innocent."

"Get away from my husband, dick!" Ronan bellowed, sounding half serious.

"For the love of God, Ronan. We're just talking."

"He's halfway to kissing you, Nostradamus." Ronan winked at his husband.

"As if." Ten got up from his seat.

"What's this great idea you have for getting us in to see Lorraine's family so Tennyson can speak to her spirit? It's the reason we let you into the house in the first place." Ronan set his sandwich down on the table.

"Is he always this pleasant?" Jude asked.

"No, usually he's worse." Carson took the seat opposite Jude and seemed to be studying the newcomer. "Answer the question."

"Call the family and tell them you've been approached by Tank's new sleaze ball defense team. Say we've asked you to work for us and that we're mounting a strong appeal. Tell the mother that if you could read Lorraine it might help to counter that appeal if it comes back to the BPD for further investigation." Jude stood up from his seat and headed over toward the sandwich bar. Tennyson thought he could hear the P.I. whistling.

Ten exchanged an impressed look with Ronan. "That might be enough to get our foot in the door. What do you think?"

Ronan wore a sour look on his face that said he should have thought of that idea himself.

Ten bit his lower lip to keep from laughing. He didn't need his gift to read his husband like a well-worn copy of his favorite book.

Love or hate Jude Byrne his idea was a good one. First thing in the morning, Tennyson was going to give it a try.

27

Ronan

Ronan stood on the stoop of his townhouse, waving goodbye to Jude Byrne as he drove off in his black 1966 Ford Thunderbird.

"Wow! That's one hell of a car," Truman said from behind him.

"Yeah it is! I thought about buying one of those before I came across the Mustang in one of those used car magazines." Say what he would about Jude, the man had good taste in cars.

"Is that how you ended up with the 'Stang? I'd always wondered."

Ronan nodded and turned around to look up at his best friend. He took a seat on the brick steps and stared out at their neighborhood. A second later, Truman joined him.

"What did you think?" Ronan knew he didn't need to explain himself any more than that.

Truman sighed. "He's not as bad as you made him out to be. I was half expecting him to have horns and eat Brian for lunch." He laughed dryly. "There's a story there. That's for sure. People fall into jobs for all kinds of reasons. Private investigators are in a class all by themselves. Usually they're washed out cops or failed members of society who work better alone or like catching other people with their pants down, so to speak. I think he got lucky with Tank being innocent. I'm guessing not all of his clients fall into that category."

Ronan nodded. "Ten talks a lot about psychic residue sticking to people. When you think about all of the cheating spouses he's investigated some of their ick must have rubbed off on him over time. Not to mention his own baggage."

"What do you mean?" Truman took his eyes off the Mustang to turn to Ronan.

"Well, he's a handsome guy. Everyone pointed that out. Repeatedly. No ring. No mention of a family, not even parents or siblings. I peg him at about twenty-seven years old. Looks like he's traveled some. He's definitely not a native New Englander and let's face it, being a P.I. is a universal trade. He can do it anywhere."

"I got that vibe too. He's not from around here. He doesn't have a New England accent and doesn't say things like wicked pissah."

Ronan laughed. "Truman, we live here and we don't say wicked pissah either. Do you think Carson was able to read him?"

Truman shook his head no. "I don't think so. He got bitchier as the afternoon wore on. That's never a good sign. Is that why you're sitting out here? Because you don't want to go back in for the post-mortem?"

"How'd you guess?" Ronan laughed.

"Why the hell do you think I followed you out here?" He snorted. "We're birds of a unique feather. Men married to psychics. Our own merry band of brothers."

Truman made a good point. There were things they understood about each other that other married men would never comprehend. "I think I stashed some brownies in the vegetable crisper. Let's go find out if they're still in there or if Tennyson snapped them up in the middle of the night." Ronan stood up and stretched his back.

When Ronan and Truman walked back through the living room, Dixie, Sadie, and Lola were standing guard over naptime. Three portable cribs were set up against the far wall and the dogs were taking turns standing sentinel. None of them left their posts to greet their owners.

"I used to be Dixie's favorite," Ronan grumped.

"Ditto for Sadie," Truman agreed.

"Come on, let's see what's cooking in the kitchen." Ronan let Truman go ahead of him so he could snap a couple of pictures of the dogs with the babies.

"Well, there you are!" Ten laughed. "I was starting to wonder if you ran off with Jude, like a modern-day Thelma and Louise."

Carson laughed. "My money was on you being gagged and tied up in his trunk."

"No!" Cole howled with laughter. "My guess was that Ronan was burying the asswipe in your backyard, Carson."

"Why in *my* backyard?" Carson shot his brother a confused look.

"Because Truman was with him and he knows where you keep the shovel!"

"You all thought I was either running away with Jude, kidnapped, or committing a crime and you all stayed in the house? Thanks, guys!"

Ronan rolled his eyes and headed toward the fridge where he was praying the brownies were still hidden.

"Someone had to watch the babies." Ten laughed.

Finding what he was looking for, Ronan pulled the tub of brownies out of the vegetable crisper.

"What have you got there?" Carson asked.

"My precious, so piss off!" He pried off the plastic lid and held a brownie up to his nose.

"If you don't share then I don't share," Carson gloated.

"We already know you couldn't read Jude either, Carson." Truman grabbed a brownie out of the bucket and shoved the whole thing into his mouth.

Carson's mouth dropped open. His bottom lip quivered.

"We really should share, Ronan. He is the father of my children after all." Truman laughed.

"He thought Jude kidnapped me and was content to sit in here gossiping like a clucking hen!"

"Ah, psychic, remember?" Carson tapped his skull. "We would have found you, Ronan! Eventually..." Carson trailed off.

"Eventually?" Ronan half-roared.

Tennyson plucked the brownie bucket out of Ronan's hands. "The babies are sleeping, remember? Be a good host and share." Ten whacked Ronan's rear end and set the treats on the table. "Now, can we talk about what Carson and Cole got from Jude?" His voice was on edge.

"You didn't discuss that already?" Ronan took the seat next to Tennyson.

Ten shook his head. "We were waiting for you and Truman so we only had to go through this once."

"I experienced a lot of what Tennyson did." Carson sounded frustrated. "I wasn't getting so much a blank page from him but static, like when you're between radio stations. When I realized I couldn't read him with my sixth sense, I used my regular intuition. It seems to me like the Hutchins case is just a job to him. He's got no other stake in the case than a paycheck. He's got no roots here in Massachusetts. Nothing that ties him here. No love interests. No family. No Mr. Right Now."

"*Mr.* Right Now?" Fitzgibbon asked.

Carson nodded. "That was one vibe that came through loud and clear. Come on, Fitz, weren't you picking it up too?"

Kevin blushed like schoolgirl. "My son is sitting right next to me, Carson," he said through gritted teeth.

"Even I noticed he was totally digging you, Dad." Greeley elbowed his father.

Fitzgibbon mumbled something under his breath and reached for a brownie.

"I got the same thing," Cole said. "The static when I tried to read Jude, I mean. I didn't turn my gaydar on. I didn't get anything malicious in him, but not being able to read him psychically really puts us all at a disadvantage. This must be what it feels like when Thor's hammer doesn't work."

"Or when Captain America's shield is in the shop," Carson agreed.

"Oh please." Ronan rolled his eyes. "You all are rock stars every day. I trust your instincts as much as I trust my own. We're only going to be working with Byrne until the end of this case anyway. I just need to know Ten is going to be safe. I can take care of myself."

"Oh, really? Says the man with four bullet scars on his chest," Kevin challenged.

"Hey I'm walking upright, aren't I?" Ronan snatched another brownie and popped it into his mouth whole.

"Today." Fitzgibbon silently made the sign of the cross.

"Did either of you get shifter vibes from him? I want to know if he's a panther or a flamingo or something cool." Greeley grinned.

Carson and Cole exchanged a silent look with each other. "To be honest, I wouldn't know what to look for."

Cole nodded his agreement. "It's possible we've run across hundreds of bears or wolves, but if we don't know the psychic clues that identify them, we're kind of dead in the water. I mean I got nothing overt that identified him as something other than human. Keep in mind there are non-human entities other than shifters."

Ronan's eyes widened. "What do you mean? Like aliens?"

Cole shrugged. "I don't know about that. I was thinking more along the lines of things like gargoyles or griffins. Things more mythological than animal."

"Because all myth is rooted in truth somewhere," Ronan concluded.

"You're all skipping over the most obvious answer. I didn't want to say anything because we hadn't talked about it before." Greeley looked around the table.

"What's that, Boy Wonder?" Ronan snorted.

"Just ask him! Hey, man, are you a shark? Or an eagle? A lion? A tiger? A bear?"

"Oh my!" The table chorused.

"That sounds good in theory." Carson smiled at the teenager, "but what if he doesn't know any of this about himself? He had three psychics poking and prodding him psychically and no one could get through his barrier. He might not know that's an unusual thing. He might not know this is a gift."

"That would be something, huh? To have a gift like that inside of you and not even know it." Greeley looked up at his father.

"This world is full of a lot of unexplainable things, kiddo."

"Don't I know it. You won't believe what book Kaye and I settled on next for our book club!"

"Don't tell me you talked her into reading *Harry Potter*? I can't imagine Kaye reading about the boy wizard." Ronan laughed.

"It's *Fifty Shades*. Isn't it?" Carson howled, slapping Truman's shoulder.

"Oh God," Tennyson moaned. "I'll never be able to get *that* visual out of my head."

"That goes double for me." Fitzgibbon shuddered visibly. "What book? Quick before they can suggest something worse."

"*Twilight*!" Greeley crowed.

"Seriously?" Ronan asked. "The one about the vampires?" He'd never read the books.

Greeley nodded. "The books are YA, so there's no sex. I figured that would work for Kaye."

"Does she know there's vampires and werewolves and stuff like that?"

"That's the best part! She thought it sounded *whimsical*. Her word, not mine."

"I can't believe it." Ten sounded dumbstruck.

"Count me in. I want to join the book club." Ronan raised his hand.

"Me too," Truman said. "Now that the babies are sleeping through the night, I have a bit more time on my hands."

"I know what you should be doing with those hands, *husband*." Carson shot his husband the hairy eyeball. "But count me in too."

"I'm a man of *many* talents, *wife*." Truman nibbled at Carson's neck.

"What the hell. I'll read it too." Fitzgibbon smiled at his son. "How bad can it be?"

"That just leaves Uncle Cole and Uncle Tennyson." Greeley looked back and forth between them.

"I'm out, kid. Sorry. Cassie and I are working on a new project."

"What kind of project? Ohhh..." Greeley's mouth hung open like a fish out of water.

Carson shot a silent look at Tennyson who nodded. "Do you know or are you guessing?" Carson asked.

"I heard the word in my head." Greeley said. His eyes were glued to Cole.

"What word did you hear?" Curiosity tinged Cole's smile.

"Brady." Greeley looked up at Tennyson.

"Jesus Christ, kid." Carson laughed. "Spoiler alert!"

"Nice job, Greeley!" Cole patted the teenager's shoulder. "I thought you were going to say baby or something like that, but you nailed it."

"Is Cassie expecting?" Ronan asked.

Cole shook his head. "Not yet, but your future daughter isn't the only little soul Bertha has been visiting."

"Christ, there must be a whole wing of the heaven nursery dedicated to our family." Ten laughed.

"Good! That might help with Project Gobble." Greeley rubbed his hands together as if he had a diabolical plan he was about to lay out for everyone.

"What the hell is Project Gobble." Ronan had a feeling he knew *what* it was or rather *who* it involved.

"Well, I've been trying to butter Kaye up for the big ask." Greeley held his breath as he met Ten's eyes.

Ten sighed. "You want her to come out here for Thanksgiving." It wasn't a question.

"Don't you, Uncle Ten?"

Ten mumbled something under his breath.

Ronan thought he heard something about "a vat of spiders," but he wasn't going to repeat that out loud.

"Sure," Ten agreed. "If she can behave herself and not hand down a list of rules."

Carson started laughing. "I second that motion. Do you have any idea how hard it was *not* to fornicate with my own husband in my own house? For the love of God."

Truman started to giggle. "What the hell are you talking about? We fornicated plenty! We just had to do it with you gagged."

"Hey!" Fitzgibbon whacked Truman. "My seventeen-year-old son is sitting right here, dumbass!"

"Uh, officer?" Truman turned to Ronan. "This man just assaulted me."

"Snitches get stitches, Tru..." Ronan flashed a wicked grin.

"So, getting back to the point here," Greeley said. "Is Project Gobble a go or no go?"

"It's absolutely a go!" Ten announced. "If my mother stays at your house!"

"I second that motion," Ronan agreed.

"All in favor?" Truman said.

"Aye!" The table chorused.

28

Tennyson

Tennyson hadn't slept well. He'd kept playing the conversation to come with Lorraine McAlpin's mother over and over in his head. By the time it was late enough in the morning to make the call, Ten had no idea what to say to the woman.

In the end, he'd gone with the words Jude Byrne had suggested. Technically, they were the truth. He had been contacted by Tank Hutchins' defense team who was mounting a strong appeal. He and Ronan were not working for Tank. No money or goods had changed hands in exchange for Tennyson's reading of Tank that day at Walpole. If Bradford Hicks insisted on paying for the reading at a later date, Ten would insist he make a donation to the Salem chapter of *Toys for Tots* since Christmas was just around the corner. He'd make sure to tell Hicks that the donation needed to be a sizable one.

It has surprised him when Ellen McAlpin had known who he was when he'd introduced himself. It turned out she was a South Boston girl and had followed the Michael Frye case with special interest, having grown up in a house only two blocks away from the Frye home.

Ellen had cried when Tennyson told her about the Hutchins appeal. She cried harder when he'd asked if he could read Lorraine.

Now, he and Ronan were in the Mustang cruising down I-93 South toward Marina Bay in Quincy to conduct that reading.

"You okay?" Ronan asked.

"I think so." Ten rested his head on Ronan's shoulder. "This still feels so backward to me."

"Every case is different, but yeah, I know what you mean. Are you going to tell Ellen that Tank is innocent?"

Ten picked his head up. He studied his husband's profile for a few seconds, stalling for time. "I don't know. Part of me thinks she has a right to know."

"What is the other part saying?"

"The other part is the coward in me who doesn't want to hurt this woman or get into some kind of shouting match with a grieving family member who's already been through enough."

"I don't think that's cowardly," Ronan said. "There's parts of criminal investigations we keep from family members all the time."

"Yeah, but isn't that because you're investigating them as suspects?"

"Not always. If I was murdered, shot in the head by a killer. Would you want to know the gory details of it? What the killer did with my body afterward? Or that the bullet went through my right eyeball?" Ronan shuddered.

Ten was silent for a minute. "I would, Ronan, because I would find out eventually, right? I mean I'd get those details from your autopsy or from a D.A. Or during the trial when the pictures were shown to the jury. I'd rather know the facts before, so there are no surprises. I get what you're saying though. You hold back some details to save the family grief."

"In this day and age, it's all about transparency, right? I'm not necessarily a fan of that. There's just some information that people don't need to know."

"We'll see how it goes."

"I promise I won't share your secret." Ronan set a hand on Ten's thigh.

Ten nodded and went back to staring out the window.

***

Fifteen minutes later, Ronan was flashing his badge to the security guard at the gate to the condo complex. After they were waved through, Ten got a good look at the buildings overlooking Boston Harbor.

"Wow, this is quite a place." Ronan whistled.

"I like our sleepy little suburb." Ronan had a point though. This complex was off the hook. It had its own marina where pleasure craft and houseboats were moored. It even featured off-season boat storage for residents. Local celebrities called this place home. TV weathermen and sportscasters lived here, along with well-known radio personalities. The location was close to Boston and made for an easy commute.

"This is it here." Ten pointed to the left. There was a large arboretum heralding the main lobby of building number two.

Parking the car, Ronan turned to look at his husband. "You've got this."

Ten nodded. "I'm a little nervous about meeting Ellen. I'll be okay."

"I love you, Ten. I'll be right by your side every step of the way."

Ten nodded and brushed a kiss across Ronan's lips. "Let's do it."

"Here? In the car?" Ronan laughed.

Ten laughed along with him. "Ask me that question again when the weather gets warmer."

"You underestimate my abilities to keep you warm, Nostradamus." Ronan kissed him hard and moved to get out of the car.

Ten knew Ronan could keep him plenty warm. He was just worried about getting stuck in a snowdrift overnight. He followed Ronan out of the car and toward the building.

Ronan announced them at the front desk and shortly after, they were allowed to proceed to the elevator bank. "This is the life, huh?"

Ten shook his head. "I love our townhouse out in the country."

"Me too. I'm becoming quite the country mouse."

Ten laughed as the elevator doors opened on the eleventh floor. He schooled his features and got himself ready to meet Ellen McAlpin.

When they got to unit 1126, Ronan knocked on the door.

Tennyson was about to thank him for being here when the door was opened by Ellen McAlpin. She was a tiny woman with pure white hair. She didn't look much older than fifty, but Ten knew losing a child could have awful effects on a person.

"Tennyson!" Ellen greeted warmly, pulling him in for a hug. "And you must be Ronan! Come in. Please, both of you, come in."

Tennyson entered the well-lit condo and wasn't surprised to see a shrine set up to Lorraine in the living room. There were framed pictures of the young woman taken too soon, along with memorabilia from her life. Her red high school graduation tassel was framed along with her purple college tassel. There was a glass jar filled with movie tickets and another filled with seashells. "This is amazing," Ten said when he heard Ellen approach from behind him.

"It's not much, but these were the things that meant the most to my baby girl." There were tears in Ellen's voice.

"What happened to all of the things in her Charlestown house?" Ronan asked.

"It's all in storage in case those damn vultures need to paw through it again."

"By vultures, do you mean Thomas Hutchins' defense team?" Ten asked gently.

Ellen nodded. "I knew they wouldn't need personal things like this, but they insisted that everything be boxed up and kept for future appeals. Have you ever heard of anything so ludicrous in your entire life?"

"Actually, I have." Ronan offered her a tender smile. "Usually though, the police or crime scene unit will box up what they think they'll need. I haven't heard of an entire apartment being kept on reserve."

"I was about to pack all of Lorraine's things and take them home with me," Ellen sniffled. "I didn't want to disturb her home, but I couldn't keep paying her rent, you know? The day I was going to finally do it, a lawyer showed up with an injunction and would only let me take a few personal possessions, like the movie tickets and Lorraine's diplomas and tassels."

"I'm so sorry, Ellen." Tennyson meant it. He understood the driving force behind what Bradford Hicks had done in his trying to secure Tank Hutchins' freedom at all costs, but on the other hand, Ellen McAlpin had lost her daughter.

"Can I get either of you some coffee or tea?"

Ronan shook his head no.

"I'd love some tea, Ellen. Thank you," Tennyson replied with an easy smile.

Ronan narrowed his eyes at his husband. "What's up with that? You never take tea from strangers."

"I don't see Lorraine here." Ten had been trying to reach out to her since he'd walked through the door but hadn't gotten any response.

"Shouldn't she just be here?" Ronan looked worried.

Ten nodded. He wasn't used to this happening. Usually he showed up for a reading and the spirit in question was ready to go. He got up from the couch and wandered over to the large sliding glass doors that overlooked Boston Harbor. Ten could see the John F. Kennedy Library. It reminded him of the time he'd spent in South Boston with Ronan when he lived there. Ronan loved going for runs out by Columbia Point.

"Lorraine, my name is Tennyson. It would mean so much to your mother if we could speak this morning."

"You don't fool me! You're working for *him*!" a voice hissed back.

Oh, so that was the reason Lorraine wasn't ready to reconnect with her mother. "I can explain that and frankly, you're not going to believe what I'm about to tell you."

"Let me guess, twins?" a sassy voice shot back. "The only thing more cliché than that is the idea of a good twin and an evil twin."

Ten pulled out his phone and pulled up a picture of Tim and Tom Hutchins. "I don't know if you can see this, but, yes. These are the Hutchins twins."

"Son of a bitch!" Lorraine McAlpin appeared in front of Tennyson.

"Hi, Lorraine. It's nice to finally meet you," Tennyson said. "We have a lot to talk about. The main reason I'm here is to reunite you with your mother. I know there are other things you'd like to discuss though."

"You're damn right there are." The harsh look on her face softened. "I do want to speak with my mother. Three years is way too long to go without hearing her voice."

"Here's the tea. I made a cup for Ronan too, just in case," Ellen was carrying a tray with steaming mugs of hot water.

"Let me help with that, Ellen." Ronan rushed to her side and grabbed the tray.

Tennyson turned back to Lorraine. "I promise I can explain all of this to you. Let's give your mother the healing messages she needs first and then I'll give you the answers you deserve."

Lorraine nodded and looked up at her mother. "I can't believe how much she's aged. Did I do that to her?" The heartbreak in her voice was gutting.

"Why don't we find out." Ten said gently. He walked over to the sofa where Ronan was setting out the mugs of steaming water. He'd placed a green tea bag next to Tennyson's cup. "Lorraine is here with us, Ellen."

"I knew it! I could hear you whispering. Can she hear me?" Ellen sat in the chair opposite the sofa.

"She can." Ten turned to Lorraine who was kneeling next to her mother's chair.

"Hi, Mom. I've missed you so much. I stayed away because I didn't want to see how badly my death was upsetting you."

"Lorraine says she hasn't been around because she knew how hard her death would be on you." It was a hard message for Tennyson to deliver. He could see for himself how hard Ellen had taken her daughter's untimely passing. It wasn't just the color of her hair. There was no spark in her eyes either. Ellen seemed to be an empty shell of her former self.

"It hasn't been easy, that was for sure. It got better when that man was convicted, but I knew seeing him in prison orange wouldn't bring my girl back. I'm still alone here." Ellen swiped at her misty eyes.

"Ask my mother if she's still singing." Lorraine didn't take her eyes off Ellen.

"She wants to know if you're still singing."

"Heavens, no." Ellen shook her head. "I learned how to play guitar when I was a little girl and I taught Lorraine when she was about five. We used to duet all the time. Her father hated it. I think it was half the reason he walked out on us when she was ten years old. He was sick of hearing us sing Backstreet Boys songs." Ellen laughed. "There was no way I could ever pick my guitar up again after..." Ellen sunk her head into her hands.

Lorraine reached up to stroke her mother's snow-white hair. "You have to sing again, Mom. To remember me. To celebrate our life together."

Ten felt tears sting his eyes. "She says she wants you to sing again so that you can remember your time together and celebrate your daughter. Don't let that gift you shared die, Ellen," Ten added.

"Is she okay, Tennyson. Does she look okay?" The worry was etched all over Ellen's face. "I saw my baby after what that monster did to her. The medical examiner said that I should just remember her the way she was, but I had to see..." Ellen shook her head as if to clear the memory from her mind's eye. "Does she look like that now?"

Ten shook his head no. "Your daughter is beautiful with her flowing brunette hair. Her smile is lighting up this entire room. When we pass, all of the pain and ills of the physical world stay here, they don't follow us into the spirit world. Lorraine is perfect."

"Thank you, Tennyson," Mother and daughter said together.

"You're welcome." Ten looked at Ronan who gave him a sharp nod. "There's something I need to share with you, Ellen, before we move on to the second part of this reading."

Ronan reached out to take Ten's hand. "A few weeks ago, I got a letter from Tank Hutchins."

Ellen's posture stiffened at the mention of her daughter's killer.

"I know his name is the last thing you want to hear," Ronan said, "but I hope you'll listen to what we have to say."

Lorraine's mother nodded.

"In his letter, Tank said that he was innocent and that he thought Tennyson and I could prove it." Ronan shut his mouth. He looked up at Tennyson who squeezed his hand.

Ellen looked back and forth between Tennyson and Ronan. "How could the two of you prove it? There was DNA evidence. I'm no scientist, but the experts at the trial said the DNA matched Mr. Hutchins."

"That's part of the problem, Ellen. It matched both of them, Tim and Tom," Ronan said. "In the letter, Tom thought that if Tennyson read him, Ten would see that he was innocent of the crime."

"Oh, dear." Ellen's eyes widened. "So, you went to see him. You both went to see my daughter's killer?" Her voice was neutral, betraying no hint of emotion.

"Only I went at first," Ronan said. "All convicted killers claim to be innocent. I figured if he was just another bullshit artist then I didn't want Tennyson wasting his time going down there to meet him. I found his story to be credible."

Ellen clenched her teeth in response to Ronan.

Tennyson could see the visceral response the grieving mother had to Ronan's words. He knew this wasn't going to get any easier. "I was very reluctant to go down to Walpole and meet him. Usually, I'm on the other side of these cases, helping the victim's families. I love my husband, Ellen, and I went to the prison as a favor to him. When I read Tank Hutchins, I found that he was telling the truth. He didn't kill Lorraine."

"And you're never wrong?" Ellen half-shouted.

Ten held out both hands in supplication. "This is the part of Lorraine's story you have to hear. When Ronan and I got here, your daughter wouldn't speak to me because she was angry that I had spoken to her killer."

Ellen shook her head. Her confused eyes darted back and forth between the psychic and the detective. "You just said that Thomas Hutchins *didn't* kill my daughter."

"Tim and Tom are identical twins, Ellen. They look alike and share the same DNA," Ronan said simply. "If Tom wasn't the killer, it must have been..."

"Tim," Ellen said breathlessly.

Ronan nodded. "We need to ask Lorraine what happened the night she was killed."

"Why?" Tears slid down Ellen's cheeks. "Why does my baby need to relive those awful, terrifying last moments of her life?"

"If we have the details of the crime, it will help us get a confession out of the real killer. Like if Lorraine can say he wore a red shirt, we can look for it in Tim's house," Ronan said.

"It's been three years, Ronan. How will that help now?" Ellen sighed, sounding defeated.

Ronan reached a hand out to Ellen. "You'd be surprised what kinds of evidence killers keep as trophies or how resilient DNA is under all kinds of conditions. Not to mention that if we can give the killer details about the crime, it will make him more apt to blurt out something since he thinks we already know what happened."

"You're stronger than you think, Ellen," Ten chimed in.

"I'm ready to tell my story," Lorraine said. She stood up from beside her mother's chair.

"Lorraine is ready to talk. Are you ready to listen?" Ten asked. "I know how hard this is going to be."

Ellen nodded. She reached for a tissue from the box on the table beside her and dabbed at her eyes. She straightened her shoulders, looking Tennyson in the eyes. "I'm ready."

Lorraine paced behind her mother's chair. "I'd been seeing this man named Jack for a few weeks. He was handsome. Kind. He paid for things when we went out. I hadn't told my mother about him because I wasn't ready to introduce them yet. I'd dated a lot of frogs and I wanted to wait until I was sure he was my prince."

Ten turned to Ronan. This was a development he wasn't expecting. "Lorraine says she was dating a man named Jack. She hadn't told you about him, Ellen, because she wasn't sure if he was a keeper yet."

Ronan narrowed his eyes, scanning the notes he'd taken. "Lorraine, we found no phone or electronic records of any communications between you and a man named Jack. Actually, we found no outside communications at all except for well-established people in your circle; your mother, friends, and coworkers."

Lorraine nodded. She gave a rough laugh. "Jack worked for the FBI. He gave me a special phone for us to communicate through that couldn't be traced or hacked. Or, so he said. I realize now that was just a line of bullshit."

Ten's mouth hung open. "She says he gave her phone to use to contact him with. Says he worked for the FBI..."

"What was his last name?" Ronan asked gently.

"Black," Lorraine laughed. "I can't believe I fell for that. Just like the actor. Or like *Men in Black*... God, what an easy mark I was." Tears slipped down her face.

"What's she saying, Tennyson?" Lorraine asked, sounded panicked.

"She realizes that the man played her. That the name he gave her, Jack Black, was fake, and so was their relationship."

Ellen's sharp blue eyes narrowed on Tennyson. "She thinks she was targeted by this man on purpose?"

Lorraine nodded. "He groomed me. Made me fall for him. I have no doubt of that now. What I don't understand is why?"

"She thinks this man preyed on her but doesn't know why." Ten turned to Ronan. "Why would a man do this?"

"He could be a thrill killer," Ronan said thoughtfully. "He could have been a budding serial killer and counted on the fact that twin DNA would save him in the end."

"What do you mean?" Ellen asked.

"Most juries rely solely on DNA evidence to convict, but when you tell them that two people have the same DNA profile, that makes them balk. Most of those cases end in acquittal." Ronan unlocked his phone and flipped through his pictures. "Lorraine, is this Jack?" He held up a picture of Tank and Tim Hutchins."

Ten watched as Lorraine's spirit approached Ronan and got a closer look at the image on the phone. "Oh, Jesus. That's him. The problem is, I don't know which one of them is Jack."

"She says that's the face, but she doesn't know which one of them is the man she dated," Ten relayed.

"What happened *that* night, Lorraine?" Ronan asked.

"Jack called to ask if he could come over and go for a walk. I agreed since it was such a nice night. He texted me on the private phone when he was outside. We walked across the footbridge and into the park. He was telling me that he was ready to take our relationship to the next level. I was so excited that I wasn't really paying attention to anything but the full moon above us. He attacked me from behind, driving me into the ground so hard that it knocked the breath out of me. I had no chance to scream. Before I knew what was happening, I was standing next to my own body watching him stab me."

Ten shut his eyes and said a silent prayer for Lorraine. "It was just like Jude thought. He ambushed her from behind, knocking the wind out of her. She couldn't cry out for help."

"Did she suffer, Tennyson?" Ellen's voice was barely above a whisper.

"No, Ellen." Ten shook his head and reached out to the bereaved mother.

"Will that help you catch him?" Lorraine asked.

"Did you see what he did after...?" Ten asked gently.

Lorraine's brow knit together as she thought about Tennyson's question. "Oh! I saw what he did with the knife and the secret phone."

"You did?" Ten turned to Ronan. "Lorraine saw what the man did with the murder weapon and her phone."

"He dropped them into the storm drain in the park." Lorraine's voice was filled with pride.

"If I show you a picture of the park, do you think you can point out which drain it was?" Ten asked, tapping the screen of his phone.

"There's no need for that, I remember it perfectly. It's right near the parking lot. There's a pink dogwood tree beside it." Lorraine smiled at the psychic.

"Lorraine said he dropped them both into a storm drain near the parking lot with a pink dogwood tree next to it."

"Last question, Lorraine, what was he wearing that night?" Ronan asked, picking up his notebook and pen.

"Black. He was dressed in black jeans and a black tee-shirt. I remembered thinking, how fitting since his last name was Black." She crossed her arms over her chest.

"What are you going to do now that you have additional information about the crime?" Ellen asked.

Tennyson looked to Ronan. He wasn't sure what the answer was to that question.

"I'm going to have to speak to my supervisor about this," Ronan answered. "Knowing the details about the crime from the murder victim is one thing. Knowing where the murder weapon was dropped is another matter entirely. I'm not certain what our next step is, but I know I need to speak to Captain Fitzgibbon first."

Ellen nodded. Understanding filled her eyes. "I know I was angry at you earlier for having spoken with Tom Hutchins. I just wanted someone to pay for killing my daughter. Thinking about it now, I want to make sure that the right person is being punished, not just any person."

Tennyson thought that was a pretty open-minded thing for Ellen to be saying so soon after hearing all of this new information.

Dabbing at her eyes with a fresh tissue, Ellen cleared her throat. "Tennyson, why is my girl still here? Why hasn't she crossed over yet? I want her soul to be at peace."

"I want the same thing for you, Mom. Put away the shrine. Pick up your guitar. Color your hair. Go pink or aqua or pink *and* aqua! *Then* I'll be at peace." Lorraine laughed for the first time.

Ten swiped at his own tears. "She wants you to play the guitar and sing again. Color your hair and put away the shrine. Live your life, Ellen, then Lorraine will be at peace."

Ellen laughed. "I was always partial to pink, like Cyndi Lauper in those new commercials she's doing."

"I say go for it!" Ronan laughed. "I'll be in touch when we learn anything new." He stood up and offered his hand to Ellen.

"Thank you both for coming out here today and letting me talk to my daughter one last time." Ellen hugged Tennyson.

"We'll see each other again, Mom. I promise. Tennyson, tell her to look for pennies. Now that I know she's going to be okay, I'll start leaving them for her. Ones with 1987 on them."

"Start looking for pennies from heaven, Ellen. I have a feeling you'll start finding ones with a very special year on them."

29

Ronan

Ronan dialed Fitzgibbon as soon as he and Tennyson were back in the parking lot of the condo complex. He didn't want to give too much detail over the phone, but he let his boss know there was an important development in the McAlpin case that involved the murder weapon and a possible cell phone. Fitzgibbon wanted Ronan and Ten to meet him in his office as soon as they could get from Quincy to South Boston.

Ronan had been so wrapped up in the idea of finding the murder weapon after three years, that he'd failed to notice that Tennyson hadn't said a word since they'd left Ellen's house. "Hey, you okay?"

Ten turned from the window to look at his husband. "I got a lot of easy forgiveness today. I'm not sure I deserve it."

Ronan reached a hand out to his distraught husband. "You mean from Lorraine and Ellen?"

Ten nodded. "Lorraine knew I'd met with Tank. She was still certain he was her killer at the time, but the look on her face..." Ten sighed. "If looks could kill, I'd be dead twice over. I still don't think Lorraine believed me about Tank's reading."

"I don't blame her."

"What!?" Ten screeched.

"Calm down, sweetheart," Ronan said in his softest tone.

"Calm down? You just said you don't blame a murder victim for not believing one of my readings!" Ten's tinny voice echoed in the small confines of Ronan's Mustang.

"Let me finish what I was going to say." Ronan paused to let Ten catch his breath. "I don't blame Lorraine for believing her own eyes. She knows the man she knew as Jack killed her. She saw us meeting with that man. She had no possible way of knowing Tank had a twin. All she knows is that it's the same face; same man. I'm not doubting you in the slightest."

Tennyson huffed, but remained silent.

"When you showed her the picture of the twins together, do you think that changed her attitude?" Ronan tried again. He hoped taking a different tact with his emotional husband would get him to calm down.

"She was shocked, that was for sure. It was a blow to find out he'd given her a fake name. Then to find out there were two of them..."

"Why didn't she know?" Ronan asked carefully.

"Know what? That Jack had lied to her or that the Hutchins brothers are twins?"

"Either. Both." Ronan would take anything he could get at this moment in time.

Ten sighed as if he were dealing with an exasperating toddler. "I've told you before that dying doesn't answer all of the unanswered questions of the universe. You don't suddenly know what happened to Jimmy Hoffa or who assassinated President Kennedy."

Ronan was trying hard to hold on to his temper. "Yes, I know that, but why wouldn't Lorraine have attended the trial?"

Ten shifted in his seat and looked at Ronan. "In all the years I've been speaking to dead people, I've never once spoken to a soul who has attended their own murder trial. Would you?"

"Hell, yes!" Ronan said without hesitation. "I have so much to live for, Ten. I'm a newlywed with an entire lifetime to spend with my new and sometimes totally annoying husband. I have kids to raise and vacations to take and grandkids to spoil rotten. If someone murdered me, I would be so fucking pissed off that you had damn well better believe I would be at my trial. Front row, center every day until the bastard who killed me was convicted and given the fucking death penalty." Ronan slammed the heel of his hand against the steering wheel.

Ten's lips twitched. "What if it was justifiable homicide?"

Ronan snorted. "Then I'll haunt you to the end of your days, Nostradamus." He flipped on his blinker and pulled into the Boston Police Department parking garage. Nerves prickled up his spine. He had no idea what was in store for him with Fitzgibbon.

***

The office was strangely quiet when Ronan and Tennyson got off the elevator. Everyone was hard at work. No one was shooting the shit or hanging out at anyone else's desk. Something was definitely up.

Walking past O'Dwyer's desk, his fellow detective and friend shot him a sympathetic look that seemed to say "It was nice knowing you."

"Oh, shit," Ronan whispered to Ten.

"Yeah, everyone's on edge. Are we about to get canned and they all know it?" There was a nervous edge to Ten's voice.

"I don't think so. If I were a betting man, I'd guess there's a special guest waiting for us in the Cap's office." Ronan ran a hand through his hair and straightened his tie.

Ten shut his eyes and took a deep breath. "Oh, man!" Ten started to laugh. "You have no idea just how *special*!"

Ronan pulled Tennyson aside. "Why are you laughing?"

"Let's just say that when the captain made the call that he made to inquire what to do about our little fact-finding mission, he had no idea that his special guest would also bring a special guest." Ten bounced his eyebrows at his husband.

"Is he wearing one of his blizzard sweaters?" Ronan snickered.

Ten shook his head no.

"Thank Christ for small favors." Ronan straightened his spine. "Get it together and remember to act surprised when we see them."

"Have you ever met either of them before?" Ten asked.

"I met the police commissioner after Manuel Garcia shot me and then again after Mark Abruzzi shot me. Christ, I really do need to stop getting my ass shot." Ronan shook his head. "Truman was in the room with me when he stopped by that time, which is why you didn't meet him. I've never met the big guy before. You ready?"

Ten nodded and followed Ronan to Fitzgibbon's office door.

Ronan knocked and took another deep breath.

"Come!" Fitzgibbon barked.

Ronan opened the door and saw the Boston Police Commissioner and the governor of Massachusetts sitting in the seats he and Tennyson usually occupied.

"Ronan, Tennyson, I assume you both know who my guests are." Fitzgibbon pointed as if neither man had no idea who the men sitting in his office were.

Ronan shook hands with each man. "It's good to see you again, sir," he said to the Boston Police Commissioner. "Governor." Ronan nodded as they shook hands. He took a moment to glance over at Kevin who looked like he was at the end of his patience.

Tennyson was shaking hands with both men when Ronan turned his attention back to him. "I didn't realize my earlier call would warrant such a response," Ronan said carefully.

"Neither did I," Fitzgibbon muttered.

"Fitzgibbon explained about the letter and your two trips to Walpole, O'Mara. Tell us what happened today," the commissioner said.

"Tennyson read the spirit of Lorraine McAlpin. She told us what happened to her on the night she was murdered. To make a long story short, she was groomed by a man calling himself Jack Black, who claimed to work for the FBI. We were not aware of this man because he was only communicating with her using a burner cell phone. He lured her from her apartment on the night of the murder, attacking her from behind once they were in the park. Once Lorraine was dead, he dropped the murder weapon and her destroyed cell phone into a storm drain near a pink dogwood tree in the park. She indicated it was the only tree of its kind next to a storm drain in the parking lot."

"Did you try to recover the phone?" Fitzgibbon asked.

"No, captain. Once Tennyson and I were in possession of this information, we called you and drove straight here." Ronan knew what Fitzgibbon was doing. Kevin was making sure his boss knew they'd followed procedure.

"We're in a bit of a bind here. Thomas Hutchins has been tried and convicted of this murder," the commissioner said.

"What is the state of his latest appeal?" the governor asked.

"I'm not sure, sir." Ronan shook his head. "So far as I know, they are trying to find evidence that will allow them to petition to have his earlier conviction overturned."

"You conducted a psychic reading for Thomas Hutchins, Mr. Grimm?" the governor asked Tennyson.

"Yes, sir," Tennyson answered. "I was not paid for my time nor was I compensated in any way."

"What's your usual rate for that sort of thing?" His blue eyes danced in the afternoon light coming through the office windows.

"Two hundred an hour, sir, but for you, it's on the house." Ten's smile was bright as the sun. "Your mother is quite a character."

The governor's eyes widened before he schooled his features again. He quickly turned back to Fitzgibbon.

"Out!" Kevin pointed to the door.

Ronan grabbed Tennyson and practically dragged him to the door, shutting it quietly behind him. "Have you lost your damn mind! That's the Governor of Massachusetts!" Ronan felt like he was going to have a heart attack and a stroke at the same time.

"He's going to call me," Ten said simply.

"That's not fair using your mind powers."

"I wasn't using my mind powers. Ronan. Prince, pauper, or governor, he's going to want one last chance to talk to his mother."

"Jesus Christ." Ronan bit his lip to keep from laughing. "You're going to be the death of me, Nostradamus."

"Oh, and by the way, Kevin was totally sporting wood behind his desk."

If he lived to be one hundred, Ronan would never be able to unsee *that* visual.

30

Tennyson couldn't decide if Kaye coming out for Thanksgiving was a blessing or a curse. He, Ronan, Greeley, and Fitzgibbon were all standing at the JetBlue gate waiting for the queen herself to deplane.

"You look like you're about to have kittens," Kevin said from beside him.

"That obvious, huh?" Ten asked. He felt like he was going to toss his cookies.

"Only to people who love you." Kevin elbowed his side.

"Oh good, so my mother won't notice a thing is wrong then." Tennyson started to laugh. He'd spent the last two days since he and Ronan had visited Ellen McAlpin cleaning his house like a maniac.

"Come on, Ten. She agreed to fly out here again only three weeks after the last time. She must miss you."

"No!" Ten turned an angry look at Kevin. "She misses your son!" Ten looked at Greeley who was standing a few feet away, holding a sign he'd made for Kaye. It read, "Welcome, Grandma Kaye!" The sign looked like an entire AC Moore store threw up on it. It was rainbow colored and full of so much glitter that Fitzgibbon's SUV was going to sparkle for years to come.

"Okay, you're probably right. What's important is that she's here through Christmas." Kevin's smile was so bright, it nearly split his face in half.

"What?" Ten felt all of the blood drain out of his face. "That's not funny, Cap. I know we've given you endless shit over you popping wood over the governor, but that's no way to get me back."

Kevin burst out laughing. "When I get you back for outing my man crush, you'll know it. What makes this little bit of news so damn delicious is that it's true!" He slapped Ten hard on the back and pointed to the runway tunnel. "Hark, there's your mother now!" He laughed harder and headed toward Greeley who was calling Kaye's name and waving frantically, as if she were a member of One Direction.

Son of a motherfucking bitch... Why was he always the last one to know everything?

"Greeley!" Kaye Grimm shouted, running toward the equally exuberant teenager. "I missed you so much."

Tennyson felt his lunch rise up in his throat. "Please pinch me to make sure I'm awake," he mumbled to a stunned-looking Ronan.

"Only if you pinch me back. I don't have words for that." Ronan pointed to where Baptist dragon queen and gay teen were hugging the life out of each other. "It's like those videos on the internet where mother tigers are cuddling with baby pigs. The tiger should be eating the pigs."

Ten nodded in agreement. He shut his mouth, so his shock wouldn't be so apparent. "It's against nature, but there it is. Live and in living color."

Fitzgibbon was snapping pictures of the happy reunion on his iPhone. "Isn't this great?"

"Awesome," Ronan deadpanned.

"Fantastic," Ten echoed.

"Party poopers!" Kevin turned back to the huggers. "Hello, Kaye."

"Hello, Kevin. It's good to see you." Kaye was beaming from ear to ear.

"Hello, Mother Grimm." Ronan waved.

"Mother Grimm? Sounds like something out of a twisted fairy tale." Tennyson snickered.

"Ronan," Kaye said coolly. "Hello, Tennyson."

"Hi, Mom. Why don't we go get your luggage?"

"Sure, that will give me time to catch up with my boy." Kaye wrapped her arm around Greeley. "I have something for you in my bag."

"Your boy?" Ten was dumbfounded. He turned and headed for the baggage claim area before he said something he'd regret.

"Where do we stand on the murder weapon and cell phone?" Ronan asked Kevin. "Have we gotten a ruling from your secret lover yet?"

Kevin stopped dead in the middle of the terminal. He shoved a meaty finger into the center of Ronan's chest.

"Play nice, boys!" Kaye said as shc and Greeley walked past them arm in arm.

The fight passed out of Fitzgibbon. "I'm waiting to hear back from the commissioner. Tomorrow is Thanksgiving. I can't imagine we'll hear back on this until Monday. That evidence has been sitting in this storm drain now for three years, another few days isn't going to make any difference. Hell, it might not even be there anymore and if it is, the chance that there's any viable evidence left is one in a million."

Tennyson had considered the same thing. Massachusetts had had its share of blizzards and thunderstorms over the last three years. Just one of those storms alone could have been enough to wash the pieces of the phone away, especially the tiny SIM card. The first rain would have washed any prints or DNA off the knife, but Tennyson knew there was more to the murder weapon than biological evidence. If it was part of a set it could be matched back to the killer.

"Is this something that we need to tell Bradford Hicks and Jude Byrne about?" Ronan asked.

"Not yet." Fitzgibbon shot Ronan a fiery look. "You know better than this, Ronan. We're in a tough spot here."

"We're gonna be in a tougher spot if this goes haywire somehow." Ten shook his head.

Kevin stopped dead again. "What are you talking about?" His green eyes burned. "What do you know?"

"Calm down, Kevin. I don't know anything. Secrets have a way of coming out. You know that. We all know that. If it somehow comes to light that the BPD knew about possible exonerating evidence and didn't do anything about it for days on end, that could look bad for you and the department. People love to shit on my gift until it helps them out of a jam and then you know they'll shit on you for keeping a lid on it." Ten shook his head. This day was getting worse by the minute.

Kevin nodded. "I know that, Tennyson. I have to wait until I get word from my superiors. Isn't there anything you can do with your gift? From a distance?"

Ten thought about that for a minute. He'd heard of remote viewing but had never tried it before. The only person he knew of who had that gift for certain was Madam Aurora. Under any other circumstance he wouldn't mind asking for her help, but in this situation, the fewer people who knew about this potential evidence the better. "There might be a way I can look into things without leaving the house. I'll check into it."

Ronan picked up his hand and pressed a kiss to the back of it.

"Tennyson!" Kaye angry whispered.

Greeley leaned over and said something to her.

"Yes, Mother," Ten said, feeling very weary. He knew what was coming. Kaye was going to dress him down about holding his husband's hand in public.

"You look very nice today." Kaye managed a small smile before she turned back to Greeley and stepped onto the escalator leading down to the baggage claim area.

"We're stuck in *The Twilight Zone*," Ten muttered.

"She's *your* mother," Ronan mumbled back. "I just came along for the ride because we're going out to dinner."

"Shit like that's gonna get you kicked out of your house if you're not careful," Kevin pointed out. "And you know who's sleeping in our spare bedroom, right?"

Ronan turned to Ten. "Have I told you lately how much I love you?"

"Nice save, Columbo."

***

"Greeley, tell me more about this grinch-popping you're doing with the turkey tomorrow," Kaye asked when they were finally settled into Kevin's SUV and were heading north toward Salem.

"It's spatchcocking, Grandma Kaye," he laughed. "It's this thing the big-name chefs on The Food Network do where they cut out the backbone of the turkey and flatten it out."

Kaye frowned. "Young man, I have no idea what you're talking about."

"Think about a book that you open in the middle and lay flat. After I cut out the backbone and flatten it a bit, I'll put a super-secret, fresh herb mixture under its skin and it will cook on the grill for a few hours."

"What's my role in the Thanksgiving festivities?" Kaye sounded excited to participate.

"Chief dragon in charge?" Ten volunteered.

"I heard that," Kaye said from the backseat. "I don't know why you think I'm the enemy here."

"Neither do I, Mom. I must have imagined the last thirteen years." Ten went back to staring out the window and watching the scenery roll by.

"Has everyone picked up or downloaded their copy of *Twilight*?" Greeley jumped in. "It would be awesome if we could start reading together tomorrow night after dinner. Maybe we could take turns reading the first chapter out loud?"

"I downloaded it, but are you sure this book isn't going to scare the pants off me?" Kaye reached over for Greeley's hand.

"You know how to download books, Kaye?" Ronan turned around from the front seat to look at his mother-in-law.

"Yes, Ronan. You all told me that if you bought me the technology that I had to learn how to use it. Greeley and I have read a few books together since you all left Kansas."

"I think that's wonderful, Kaye. What have you read?" Fitzgibbon looked up at her in the rearview mirror.

"We read *Jurassic Park* and *Pride and Prejudice*. The dinosaurs scared me, however, Mr. Darcy was delightful."

"I also enjoyed the witty banter in *P&P*," Greeley agreed. "It's a shame that letter writing is a dying art."

"You write beautifully, Greeley." Kaye patted his hand.

"*Twilight Zone*," Ten whispered.

"What was that, Tennyson?" Kaye asked sharply.

"I said *Twilight*, Mom. Ronan and I need to download our copies. We're joining in the book club too."

"Me too," Fitzgibbon chimed in.

"It will be fun discussing the book with everyone, right, Kaye?" Greeley elbowed her.

"Yes, Greeley."

"Wasn't there news you had to share about Union Chapel?" the teenager prodded.

"You're a very tiring young man to spend time with." Kaye sighed. She patted the left side of her hairdo.

"Uncle Tennyson is going to want to hear this news." Greeley reached up to squeeze Ten's shoulder.

"You mean you didn't tell him?" Kaye sounded shocked.

"It's not my news to tell."

"Hmm." Kaye crossed her arms.

Tennyson prayed for patience. His mother could give stubborn lessons to a pack of mules. Of course, he already knew what the news was. Kaye and Greeley were both broadcasting it like a fifty-thousand-watt radio station, but he'd keep his mouth shut until one of them said it out loud.

"I had a chat with Shelly Brinkman." Kaye shot Greeley a dirty look that asked if he was satisfied now.

"That's great, Kaye!" Ronan said.

"Yeah, well *someone* had to water my tree," she grumped. "According to the book I downloaded, it wasn't going to survive without me for a month."

"You mean the bonsai tree we gave you?" Ten asked. Shelly Brinkman had been Kaye's best friend back in Union Chapel, but they'd had a falling out over Kaye's feelings about Tennyson being gay. Kaye reaching out to Shelly was a step in the right direction. A step Ten hoped his mother would be extending in his and Ronan's direction.

"The bonsai tree my *grandson* gave me," Kaye insisted, sounding more stubborn than ever.

Ten set his head on Ronan's shoulder and prayed Kevin would drive faster.

"Tennyson!" Kaye half-yelled from the backseat.

Ten didn't have the energy to move. "Yes, mother."

"I thought you said you and Ronan were working on making me a grandmother too."

Ten pulled his head off Ronan's shoulder. They both turned around to look at Kaye. "Are you serious?"

"Well, I'm not getting any younger. I like babies."

For lunch? Ten couldn't help but wonder. "We have an appointment at the clinic on December 4th."

"Good, I'll come with you," Kaye announced as if her word decided the matter.

Ronan turned to look at his husband. "*Twilight Zone!*" they said in unison.

31

Ronan

Ronan and Tennyson were still sleeping when their doorbell rang early Thanksgiving morning. Groaning, Ronan rolled over and cracked an eyeball open to read the alarm clock.

"What the hell," Ten muttered.

"It's 6:30am. I've got one guess who's ringing the doorbell and it ain't the Avon Lady."

"It's the dragon lady," Ten giggled, just as the doorbell rang again.

Dixie barked from her dog bed and scampered out of the room.

"Okay, I'm up." Ten stumbled out of bed and grabbed his tee-shirt from off the edge of the bed.

"I'm right behind you." Ronan didn't even bother to comb his fingers through his hair. If his mother-in-law wanted to ring the doorbell at zero-dark-thirty then she deserved to pay the price.

"Mom!" Ten announced when he swung the door wide. Dixie ran between his legs and kept barking at the newcomer. "Dixie, you remember Grandma Kaye. Be nice."

"Awww!" Kaye practically squealed and scooped up the tiny dog. "Hello, love muffin. I missed you. Why do the two of you look like you were still sleeping." Kaye walked past them into the house carrying Dixie.

"We *were* sleeping, Mom." Tennyson raked his fingers through his hair.

"Whatever for? There's work to do!"

"We're only making side dishes, Kaye. Everyone else is making turkeys." Ronan scratched his stomach and headed toward the kitchen. He was going to need coffee, and a lot of it. He'd never seen his mother-in-law first thing in the morning. If she was one of those bright-eyed and bushy-tailed nut-jobs then he was going to need some octane.

"I'll make the coffee, babe." Ten patted Ronan's shoulder. "Mom, if you open the sliding door, Dixie can go out and do her morning duty."

Kaye raised a skeptical eyebrow. "Her morning duty? Are you a soldier, cutie pie?"

Ronan snorted. "Kaye, if you open the sliding door, Dixie can go out and take a piss and a shit. How's that?"

Kaye's nose wrinkled. "Okay, Dixie. Time for your morning duty. I think Grandma will come too so your Daddy can wash his mouth out with soap."

When the glass door slid shut behind Kaye, Ronan burst out laughing.

"You're awful. You know that, right?" Ten giggled.

"Did you see the look on her face when I said shit? It looked like she had a mouthful of it." Ronan slapped a hand on the table, making the salt shaker jump.

"Ronan…" Ten warned.

"I know, babe. She's here. That means she's trying to get along with us. It means we need to try to get along with her." Ronan pulled his husband into his arms. "It's a day for giving thanks. I, for one, am thankful for you and this family we've built from the ground up."

"Me too," Ronan agreed. "I'm still stunned that she wants to come to our baby appointment in two weeks. Greeley must be weaving some kind of magic."

"I certainly hope there is no magic going on in this house!" Kaye said as she led Dixie back into the house.

Tennyson started to laugh. "The only kind of magic going on here, Mom, is the metaphorical kind. Can I make you a cup of coffee?"

"Yes, thank you. Dixie was a good girl out in the yard."

"I'll get her breakfast while Ten gets the coffee started. Kaye, what kind of Thanksgiving meals did you make when Tennyson was little?" Ronan grabbed Dixie's water dish and brought it to the sink to wash out and refill.

"Thanksgiving was always a day of service for us. We'd drive out to one of the larger churches over in Severance that had a food pantry and we'd help prepare the meal. Tennyson was usually on potato peeling duty and then I would cut them up and man the boiling pots of water. David was one of the turkey carvers. We'd both help out in the serving lines too."

"Ten didn't help serve the meals?" Ronan shot his husband a questioning glance.

Ten shook his head. "No, they always kept the kid helpers in the kitchens so that we wouldn't recognize any of our classmates. It was bad enough for the adults to know who among the congregation needed a hand up, but it would have been hell on the kids…" He trailed off.

"Bullies suck!" Ronan set Dixie's food and water dishes in their usual spot. "Breakfast is served, Dixie, my little pixie."

"While I don't agree with your language, I do agree with the sentiment, Ronan," Kaye agreed. "After the meal was over, we'd all pitch in to clean up and our treat was to have Chinese food at the Coral Dragon."

"You didn't eat any of the Thanksgiving fixings at the food pantry?" Ronan asked curiously.

"Oh, heavens no!" Kaye shook her head. "The hardest luck cases knew that if they stuck around or came late, that not only would they get their Thanksgiving meal, but we'd box up the leftovers for them in those Styrofoam take-out containers too. That food was for the needy. We would get a turkey breast and make a Thanksgiving dinner the week after. We'd have mashed potatoes and gravy and cornbread. I think that was Shelly's recipe, Tennyson."

Ten nodded. He set mugs of coffee down in front of his mother and husband before returning to grab the cream and sugar. "I love that recipe. Shelly sent it home with us. Ronan can eat the entire pan by himself. We're making it today."

"Ten says I have to share." Ronan was not happy about that development, but he figured there would be plenty of food to fill up his belly.

"Why are you here with us, Mom. Why aren't you chilling with Greeley?" Ten set a boxed coffee cake on the table and passed out plates.

"Boy wonder is working this morning. Cassie opened her bakery until 10am for last minute Lucy's who need a pie or cupcakes to bring to their gathering. It looks like a nice place from all of the pictures that Greeley's sent me."

Ronan exchanged a silent look with Tennyson who raised an eyebrow in return. "You know, the bakery is only a five-minute ride from here, Kaye."

"Kevin had mentioned that. Why are you telling me this, Ronan?" Kaye gave him a suspicious look.

Ten sighed. "If you give us a minute to change and clean up, we could take you over there so you could surprise Greeley."

"You mean my grandson could wait on me?" Kaye looked enchanted by that idea.

"I think we could arrange that." It struck Ronan in that moment that Kaye kept referring to Greeley as her grandson. He vividly remembered a conversation from a little over a month ago where Kaye pointed out that neither he, Ten, nor Fitzgibbon were related to

Greeley by blood and now here Kaye was considering herself a member of the boy's family. She'd certainly come a long way.

He could almost say the same thing about her relationship with Ten, if there weren't that pesky thirteen-year gap in the middle. He supposed what was important now was that Kaye was here and making an effort. "I'm gonna run upstairs and change. Come with me, Nostradamus. We'll pick out matching shirts."

"Surely the two of you don't need to be *that* cute. Do you?" Kaye called after them.

"What's your game?" Ten asked when they got to their bedroom.

"Just another step in the process." Ronan pulled his tee over his head and shucked out of his sleep pants. He walked to the closet and pulled out a faded pair of Levi's.

"What process is that?" Ten joined him in their walk-in closet and grabbed for pants of his own.

"When Kaye was here for our wedding, she didn't want to see things that were part of our life and that included the bakery and the shop…" Ronan trailed off hoping Ten would see where he was leading.

"You think she might want to see where I work?" Ten sounded dubious.

"I think if Greeley offers to show it to her then anything is possible. Maybe if she sees that the Magick shop isn't filled with ghosts and demons and God knows what else she thinks she's going to find in there, it will be one less thing for her to fear about your life and your gift."

"What do you mean *fear*?" Ten narrowed his eyes before slipping into his shirt.

"It's all about semantics, babe. Think about the word crystal, right. It sounds new age and mystical, but when you see it's just a rock, that takes some of the magic out of it, doesn't it? A dream catcher is just feathers and twine. A tarot is really just a deck of cards with pictures. It's all a matter of perspective and vocabulary."

"And belief," Ten said, as if he'd never looked at it from that point of view before.

"Exactly. Maybe that's all Kaye needs is a different point of view. Greeley has been good at giving her that with other things. Finish changing. I'm gonna call Truman and see if they want us to pick them up coffees or muffins." Ronan smacked a kiss against the side of Ten's head.

"Ronan!" Ten called.

"Yeah, babe?" He turned back to see a happy look on his husband's face.

"If I forget to tell you in the madness of the day, I'm thankful for you."

"That's goes double for me, Ten!" Ronan meant it. No matter what the day had in store for them. It was their first Thanksgiving as a married couple.

32

Tennyson

The line for the bakery was out the door when Ronan drove past it. They ended up having to park around the corner.

"Is the bakery usually this busy?" Kaye asked from the backseat of the Mustang.

"No," Ten said. "Cole mentioned to Cassie that it would be a good idea to open for a few hours this morning for people who needed things at the last minute. It was Bertha's idea, actually."

"Carson and Cole's *dead* mother thought opening the bakery would be a good idea?" Kaye asked, one eyebrow was raised so high, it almost escaped into her hairline.

Instead of answering, Ten hopped out of the Mustang and pulled the seat forward to help his mother out.

"Bertha is a brilliant businesswoman," Ronan said. "She was the one who opened and ran West Side Magick all by herself after she kicked her husband out. She was a single mother raising two small sons and running a fledgling business at the same time." Ronan offered his mother-in-law his arm.

"Don't you mean Bertha *was* a brilliant businesswoman?" Kaye asked.

"No, Mom. Bertha is still very active in everything that goes on in the shop and here at the bakery." Ten held the door open for his mother and husband when it was their turn.

"Oh, wow!" Kaye sounded impressed when she got her first view inside the bakery.

Ten could smell coffee and pumpkin pie. He could go for a slice right now, barring that, he'd love a pumpkin muffin. Cassie made the best muffins in town and they were the size of a softball. Ten's attention was focused on his mother who was trying to catch a glimpse of Greeley over the heads of the other customers in the store.

When they got closer to the counter, Kaye pulled her iPhone out of her purse and tapped on the camera.

"Look at you, Kaye. You're an expert at this." Ronan laughed.

"Greeley was very persistent in teaching me how to take pictures to send to him. Especially selfers. I don't know why he needed to see a picture of me every day, but he insisted."

Ten started to laugh. He knew exactly why Greeley wanted to see a "selfer" of Kaye. It was to make sure she was getting out of bed and taking care of herself after they'd all come back to Massachusetts. He was a clever boy, that was for sure. "It's a selfie, Mom, and I'm sure Greeley was just missing your face."

"Grandma Kaye!" Greeley was all smiles when he saw who his next customer was. "What are you doing here?"

"I wanted to come to see you at work. Ronan was nice enough to drive me. What do you recommend?"

"Everything here is off the hook!" Greeley said loud and proud. "For you though, I'd recommend the carrot cake muffin and a pumpkin spice latte."

Kaye nodded. "You've got yourself a sale, young man." She snapped a couple of pics of Greeley.

"Morning, guys!" Cassie said. She looked like she was wearing half of the dessert case on her apron.

"Hey, Cass! Looks like Bertha was dead on with her idea to open this morning." Ronan grinned.

"She sure was. I know you and Ten are gonna be busy making sides for Thanksgiving dinner, but is there any way you could take Laurel home with you so Cole could come down and help with the rush?"

"Of course! You know how much I love spending time with your mini-me."

"I do. Just don't teach her any more 'Ronan words,' okay?" Cassie grinned. She set two pumpkin lattes and a pastry bag on the counter in front of him.

"What are 'Ronan words?'" Ten asked. He grabbed his latte and the bag containing their pumpkin muffins.

"Ones that would get beeped and then get you fined by the FCC if you said them on television."

"Oh, she means George Carlin's famous *Seven Words You Can't Say on Television*!" Ronan broke out into a wide grin. "Let's see, what were they?"

"I swear to God, Ronan, if Laurel comes home with even one of them…" Cassie trailed off as her next customer stepped up to the counter.

"Even one of what, Ronan?" Kaye asked.

"Leftover Halloween candy, Kaye. We've got a ton of it." Ronan turned and rolled his eyes. "Since we're here, why don't we give you a quick tour around the shop?" Ronan grabbed his latte and waved to Cassie.

"I'll have Cole bring Laurel to you when he comes downstairs," Cassie called over the din of the crowd.

"She looks happier than a duck with a June bug," Kaye lifted a hand to wave back.

"You know the story of how she and Truman used to work together in human resources, right?" Ronan asked.

"What story? Kaye asked.

Tennyson knew what Ronan was trying to do. He was trying to engage Kaye in a story so she wouldn't notice he was leading her right into the store. The overhead lights turned on automatically when they crossed the threshold into the section that housed the books. Oddly enough, this was the part of the store where Tennyson and Ronan met each other back in January.

"They had worked together for years and were best friends," Ronan started as they passed by the crystals. Ronan absently passed his right hand over the bin of fluorite crystals. "Their company needed to fire one of its employees at the beginning of December two years ago and it was up to Truman and Cassie to carry out that process."

"In December? That doesn't sound very charitable." Kaye shook her head.

"It wasn't," Ronan agreed as they passed the candles and dreamcatchers. "The man fired wasn't even offered his Christmas bonus or a severance package. This is where the story gets interesting." Ronan stopped in front of the reading room door. He flipped on the light and motioned for Kaye to go inside.

"I remember this room from the television show." Kaye set Bertha's Tibetan chimes jingling.

"This was the room where Bertha Craig conducted readings with her clients." Ronan set a hand on her chair. "She'd sit here and her clients would sit across from her. The crystal ball in the center of the table was just there for show."

"Ronan, is this where you get me to try to believe in the occult?" Kaye wore a sour look on her face.

"No, Kaye." I'm just telling you a story. Listen, okay?"

Kaye frowned, but kept her mouth closed.

"A few years ago, Bertha got breast cancer. When she was nearing the end of her fight, she begged Carson and Cole to keep the store open even though neither of them had one drop of her talents."

Kaye's brow knit together. "Wait! Both of them have the same powers as Tennyson. How could that be?"

Ten tried to hide his smile, but it just wasn't possible. His mother just admitted, out loud, that he had psychic abilities. He didn't know whether to laugh or cry.

"Back then, neither one of them could have picked the winning horse in a two-horse race." Ronan snorted. "Anyway, after Bertha passed, Carson became a con-man, of sorts, he'd give psychic readings by using the information his clients would voluntarily give him and their own body language."

Kaye looked stunned but didn't say a word.

"On the night that Truman and Cassie fired the worker, Carson was closing up the shop after one of those readings. He was in this room talking to Bertha and he touched the crystal ball when the strangest thing happened. He had a vision. A real vision."

"You expect me to believe that load of malarkey? You just said Carson was a con-artist."

"He was, until that moment." Ronan grinned. "Ask me what the vision was about, Kaye." Ronan nudged her gently.

"What was the vision about, Ronan?" Fake enthusiasm dripped from her voice.

Tennyson couldn't help laughing.

"Carson saw a Christmas party."

"A Christmas party?" Kaye sounded dubious.

"Yes, Kaye, a Christmas party. At this party was the handsomest man he'd ever seen in his life with these glittering green eyes."

"Wait a second. Truman has green eyes."

"Does he?" Ronan turned to Ten. "I'd never noticed that before. Anyway, the handsome, green-eyed man in the vision was holding his arms up like he was being held at gunpoint." Ronan demonstrated.

Kaye gasped. "What happened next?"

The man's body jolted and a ruby-red stain appeared through his white dress shirt before the man crumpled to the floor. A woman appeared over the man and started performing CPR before the vision faded to black."

Kaye stood there stunned for a moment. "I don't know what to say, Ronan."

"Neither did Carson. It was Cole who told him it must have been their mother who sent him the vision and that it was his duty to find and save the green-eyed man."

"A vision brought Truman and Carson together?" Kaye sounded like she didn't quite believe the words that were coming out of her mouth.

Ronan laughed. "There were a few bumps along the way, but yes."

"You call Carson getting shot a *bump* along the way?" Ten asked.

"When you've been shot four times, I guess one puny bullet could be considered a bump in the road," Cole said from behind them.

"Ro!" Laurel screeched, toddling toward him.

"Well, hey there, Petunia!" Ronan scooped the two-year-old up and peppered her face with kisses.

"Thanks for taking her home with you, guys. Mom said opening the bakery this morning would be successful, but she failed to mention there would be a line around the block."

"We'll have a great time cooking together, won't we? You can cut up the potatoes!" Ronan winked at Cole.

"Doggie?" Laurel asked excitedly.

"Oh, you want to see Dixie?"

Laurel nodded her head so hard, she whacked Ronan in the forehead. "Owwie!"

"Do not break my child. Do not teach her any new words. No sugar," Cole cautioned.

"No problem. I was just going to let her play in traffic and talk to strangers." Ronan rolled his eyes.

"Bye, cutie!" Cole smacked a loud kiss to Laurel's head.

"Bye, Daddy!" She held her tiny hand up to wave. "Candy, Ro?" Laurel turned her sweetest smile on Ronan.

"Let's talk about that in the car, okay? You're gonna sit with Grandma Kaye."

"Kaye!" Laurel clapped her hands.

"Hello, sugar plum." Kaye ran her hand through Laurel's blond hair.

"We'll meet you outside. I have to strap her seat in." Ronan whinnied like a horse and galloped out of the room.

Tennyson nodded and waved to Laurel as they left. He was a little nervous to ask Kaye what she thought of the store. It would have been easy enough to just read her, but that was the coward's way out. He led her back into the main store. "Well, what do you think?"

Kaye walked back out into the main part of the store. "It's not really what I expected."

Ten's eyes narrowed. He was expecting the worst to come out of her mouth any second now. "In a good way or a bad way?"

Kaye shook her head and walked over to the main display case where the cash register stood. Inside the glass were several different crystal balls. "These are just polished rocks."

"You're absolutely right. Some people see highly polished, round rocks. Other people see decorations. Other people see tools."

"Tools?" Kaye's brows knit together.

"There are psychics who use crystal balls to channel. It's a tool for them like a hammer is for a carpenter."

"Jesus was a carpenter," Kaye said.

It was like Kaye read his mind. "I was just thinking the same thing, Mom. To some, he was just a man, others think he was a prophet, others think he is the son of God."

"I'm struggling with believing in both." She didn't meet her son's eyes. Instead, she kept staring at the crystal balls in the display case. Some were clear quartz, others rose quartz, there was even one made of amethyst. The most stunning crystal in the case was made of obsidian.

Ten knew Kaye was talking about believing in both Jesus and his own gifts. "Jesus believed in psychics too, Mom. If you think about it, a psychic *is* a prophet. They tell the future. The Bible was against false prophets which over time morphed into including psychics, mystics, and occult practitioners. Anyone or anything that kept people from church or from *donating* to the church."

"That's awfully skeptical." Kaye finally looked up from the display case to meet Tennyson's eyes.

"Don't be naive," Ten cautioned. "Churches run on money."

Kaye nodded. "You've given me a lot to think about."

"It means the world to me that you're thinking about things, Mom."

"Do you think Laurel will let me play with her and Dixie?" Kaye asked.

Ten laughed. "I'll give you a hint. If you put *Frozen* on, she'll love you forever. Why do you think she's nuts for Ronan? He sings with her."

"Ronan sings?" Kaye laughed.

"Badly, Mom. Very badly." Ten shivered. Ronan was the *worst* Elsa ever.

"Hmm, I think this might be a good time to try out the video feature on my phone."

Ten burst out laughing. Kaye was going to give him blackmail fodder over his husband for decades to come.

33

Ronan

Ronan didn't realize how much work it was to peel root vegetables. He had a dozen potatoes, half a dozen yams, carrots, parsnips and turnips, all freshly washed and sitting in front of him.

"How's it going, detective?" Jude Byrne asked from behind him.

"Jesus Christ!" Ronan jumped a mile. "Warn a guy, would you, Byrne. You crept up on me like a cat. What are you, a panther or something?" Ronan was interested to see if the P.I. would rise to the bait.

Jude's golden eyes glowed. "My grandfather always said I had cat-like reflexes. You probably didn't hear me come up from behind you because you were too busy cussing out the vegetables. What the hell did they ever do to you?"

Ronan sneered at the annoying man. Not only did he *not* answer the question about being a panther, he'd overheard his ongoing diatribe against peeling the potatoes. "Who the hell invited you anyway?"

Jude laughed. "Your well-mannered husband. Where is he? I didn't see him or Dixie on my trip through the house."

It was strange too that Ronan hadn't heard their guest knocking on the door. He sure as hell hadn't rung the bell. "Carson was having some kind of turkey emergency, so he went over there to help. Dixie and Laurel went with him. Kaye too, I think."

"Turkey emergency? What the hell is that?"

"Knowing my husband, its code for getting him the hell out of here. I might have been a bit grumpy over my assigned role."

"A *bit* grumpy? You were telling the spuds to bite you!" Jude snorted. "What role did you want, but didn't get? Hamilton? The Phantom? Elphaba from *Wicked*?"

"Funny." Ronan deadpanned. "I wanted to make the gravy which would have required me to go around and get the turkey drippings from Carson, who's making his bird the old-fashioned way and from Greeley, who's spatchcocking his. I could give two fucks about the gravy. I just wanted an excuse to go see how this cutting the turkey in half and unrolling it like the Declaration of Independence works."

Jude stared at Ronan like he'd lost his mind. "Am I having a stroke? What the fuck are the words 'Declaration of Independence' and 'turkey' doing in the same sentence?"

Ronan sighed. How did a man like Jude Byrne get this far in life and not know what the hell he was talking about? "Bobby Flay," Ronan stopped and shot Jude the side eye. "You know who he is, right?"

"Yes, asshole! I'm from the southwest. He's the king of southwestern cuisine. Plus, that ass in a pair of Wranglers? A-fucking-men!" Jude held his right hand to God.

Finally, something they had in common. Ronan was also nuts for Wrangler butts. "Bobby Flay did something on his show called spatchcocking where you cut a turkey's backbone out."

"Ouch!" Jude shivered.

"You do that *after* the bird is already dead." Ronan held his hands out and looked up to the ceiling as if he were looking for a little divine intervention. He didn't get any. This was probably Karma getting him back for all of the times he was a dick to Tennyson. "Anyway, once the backbone is gone, you flatten the turkey out, season it, and throw it on the grill. Greeley thought it looked good, so he's trying it."

"Okay, so why don't I help you with your role and when we're done you can go see Greeley?"

Jude made it sound so simple. Ronan nodded.

"Oh, and by the way, I brought drinks. Eggnog for the sweet tooth's in the crowd, soda, water, and some of those bottled coffee drinks. I left the cooler in the living room."

Ronan turned from the sink to study the man. It was curious that he hadn't brought any booze to Thanksgiving. "No alcohol?"

Jude raised a silent eyebrow as if he were choosing his next words carefully. "With you and Greeley in recovery, I didn't think that was the wisest move. Plus, fire water isn't exactly a friend of mine."

Fire water... Interesting choice of words and the first real clue about Jude Byrne. Ronan would file that tidbit away for later. "Whose idea was it to write to me? Hicks', Tank's or yours?"

Jude grinned at Ronan. "You got another peeler? I'll lend you a hand."

Ronan shook his head. "We've only got the one, but if you grab a knife out of the block, you can start cutting up the potatoes into cubes."

"I wondered how long it would take you to ask *that* question." Jude grabbed a chef's knife and walked around to the opposite side of the island, giving both himself and Ronan plenty of room to work. "I've only been here in Massachusetts for about three years now. The first thing I did, after I found a cheap place to rent, was marathon read the last year of *The Boston Globe* and then *The Herald*. I made a list of all the major crimes, trials, appeals, and fraud cases. You name it, I tracked it. I didn't think your incident with Manuel Garcia and your subsequent trip to rehab was a big deal until the Michael Frye case."

Ronan felt his lower jaw tighten. His stomach tossed at the thought of how Jackie and Ross Frye were spending *another* holiday without their son.

"I don't know if you realize it, Ronan, but you teaming up with Tennyson is a game-changer."

"What do you mean, a game-changer?" Ronan looked up from his spud to lock eyes with the P.I.

"Tennyson is an instant lie detector."

Ronan shook his head. "Not necessarily. There are certain people, yourself included, who can elude his gift. There is one killer in particular who was able to mask the evil inside of him. That little trick almost got me and Ten killed.

"But you knew who *hadn't* killed the little boy, right? Sometimes knowing who isn't guilty is just as important as knowing who is."

Ronan knew the latter part of Jude's question was talking about Tank Hutchins, who, at this moment, was sitting in his 6x8 foot cell at MCI-Cedar Junction about to enjoy a meal of turkey loaf and instant mashed potatoes. "I get what you're saying, but Ten isn't just a robot who can go down a conga line of cons saying 'guilty,' or 'not guilty.' This shit takes a lot out of him. He's a human being with real feelings and emotions. Talking to the dead and their grieving families is gutting."

Jude was silent. He didn't respond to Ronan.

Ronan was beginning to wonder if Jude was just going to ignore that last remark all together.

"It's not always easy dealing with live bodies who find out a loved one's been unfaithful. It can be soul-sucking."

"Why do it then?" Ronan challenged. He had to admit Jude looked almost human in this moment.

"Probably for the same reason Tennyson does. To help people. As hurt as my clients are to find out they're being cheated on today, they all agree it's better than finding out tomorrow."

Ronan understood where Jude was coming from. "How many of your clients actually leave the cheater?"

Jude's smiled. His amber eyes grew warm. "About 70%. When you're serious enough to hire a P.I., you're serious enough to leave 'em high and dry."

Ronan burst out laughing. "Don't tell me *that's* your tag line?"

"Well, this looks like trouble!" Ten walked into the kitchen alone.

"Hey, babe. Where's Laurel and Kaye?"

"They're watching *Frozen* with Uncle Tru. Rumor has it he's a better singer."

Ronan was about to argue with the rumor, but then he remembered he sounded like a dying albatross when he tried to sing *Let It Go*. He let the fight pass out of him. It was better *not* to scar Laurel for life.

"Have you thought about a change in careers?" Ronan asked Jude.

"What like to become a fireman or an astronaut? I think that ship has sailed." The P.I. laughed.

"You never know when an opportunity is just around the corner." Ronan shot Tennyson a silent look.

Ten frowned. He shook his head as if he had no clue what kind of possible message Ronan could be trying to convey.

"There are all kinds of things to investigate that won't suck your soul out of your body. Paranormal things. Ghost hunting kinds of things." Ronan couldn't believe how thick Tennyson was being. His husband wasn't usually *this* dense.

"Ohhh," Tennyson said, seeming to finally be picking up what Ronan was laying down. "Oh?"

"Is he missing a dose of medication?" Jude finished cutting the potatoes and set his knife down. "I'm gonna hit the head while the two of you sort out whatever message *this* was supposed to be."

"Seriously, babe?" Ronan raised an eyebrow at Tennyson.

"What the hell were you trying to tell me?"

"Weren't you the one who told me you and Carson were talking about hiring house cleaners when you expand the business? Jude might not have any psychic gifts, but aren't you going to need someone to do the leg work and investigate the properties to see if there were crimes committed or if someone was murdered in the house or do background checks on the property owners or whatever?"

"You hate that dick, remember?" Ten looked confused.

"Weren't you the one who said it takes one to know one?" Ronan couldn't help grinning.

"Ronan, if we hired this guy, we'd be stuck with him forever. He'd be a part of our family. I mean, he'd be the next..." Words seemed to fail Tennyson.

"Me." Ronan laughed. "I think you're trying to say Jude would be the next me."

Ten sighed. His mouth hung open before he shut it with a click of his teeth. "Yeah. Since the role of loudmouthed dick is already taken, we'd have to find a different one for him to fill."

"For now, just pencil him in as fiery dick. We'll figure it out from there."

"How many times do I have to tell you both that I prefer *genius* dick?" Jude shouted from the bathroom.

34

Tennyson

As unbelievable as Tennyson thought it sounded when they'd discussed it a few weeks back, Thanksgiving dinner prepared at four different houses was on the table, on time, and looking delicious.

They'd all decided Carson and Truman would host the meal this year since all of the gear the babies would need was at their house. Laurel would be fine in a booster seat that Cole and Cassie would bring along with them. They didn't have a table big enough to seat all ten of them, but Fitzgibbon supplied a folding table and chairs that he'd "borrowed" from the office.

All of the food was laid out around the table family style. All that was missing was Tennyson, who was pouring the molten-hot gravy into the gravy boat. "Here we go. Thanksgiving can officially begin now!" He set the gravy in front of Greeley who was practically drooling.

"Okay, everyone, dig in!" Truman surveyed the table, finally grabbing the serving fork and taking a big slice of turkey which, he started cutting up on his plate. "Turkey for my little gobblers!" he announced, setting a pile on each of the babies' high chair trays. Carson was at the ready with his phone to film the moment.

"I still can't believe we made four different turkeys for fourteen people, four of whom are two years old and under," Cole laughed.

"I love it!" Greeley's green eyes glowed. "This is my first real Thanksgiving ever…" Emotion crept into the teenager's voice. He bowed his head.

"It's our first Thanksgiving as a whole family," Tennyson said, wanting to get the attention off Greeley so he could get himself back under control. "I want to try Truman's deep-fried bird. Can you pass it over, Jude?"

"Not until I grab the drumstick." He forked it onto his plate and passed the platter Tennyson's way.

"I want to try Greeley's grinch-popped bird," Kaye said. "Who's got that one?"

"I've got it," Kevin laughed.

"It's spatchcocked, Grandma Kaye."

"I refuse to say that obscene word at the dinner table." She took the tray from Fitzgibbon and served herself.

Ronan bit his tongue. "I think we need to have a contest to determine who's got the best turkey."

"That's not a contest at all, Ronan. I've already won." Ten held his arms up and shook his fists like a prize-fighter.

"How could you have won? You didn't even make a turkey."

"Ohhh, you didn't say we were going to determine who *made* the best turkey. You said we were going to determine who *had* the best turkey. I win hands down!"

"And twice on Sundays." Carson laughed. "He grabbed the mashed potatoes and dumped dollops on each of the babies' trays for them to try.

"What are you doing, *wife*?" Truman asked. "None of them know how to use spoons."

"That's the fun of it!" Carson scooped up some potato on his finger and offered it to Bertha. "Mmm, try this."

Bertha shot her father a quizzical look but did what he asked. She squealed after tasting the buttery spuds and dug into her potatoes with both hands.

"Told you!" Carson stuck his tongue out at his husband.

Seeing that their sister was enjoying the white blob on her tray, Brian and Stephanie joined in. Both babies babbled with apparent joy and started shoveling the potatoes into their mouths with both hands.

"Looks like we might need more potatoes." Ronan laughed. He pulled his phone out to take pictures of the babies. "Don't any of you forget who the potato master was."

"Go, Ronan." Jude golf clapped.

"Okay!" Ten said quickly. "Back to the idea of a turkey contest. "I think I have an idea for first prize."

"You do?" Ronan asked.

Ten nodded. They'd talked about this a few weeks ago, but he wasn't sure if Ronan would remember. "Remember the plan about the boat?"

Ronan tilted his head. "Oh! You want to tell everyone about our idea now?"

"We're all here and the kids are happy, why not?"

"What plan? What boat?" Greeley asked. He was spooning a huge pile of candied yams onto his plate.

"Ronan and I didn't really take an actual honeymoon. We just stayed home and helped Fitzgibbon and Greeley move into their new house, so we thought we would take a cruise after Christmas." Ten turned to Ronan to continue the story.

"There's been so much going on with me and Kevin getting our stupid asses shot and then with Kevin adopting Greeley and Carson and Tru having the babies and everything going on at the shop and the bakery and Kaye losing David, that we though all of you might want to come along with us."

"On a cruise?" Truman's green eyes looked like they were going to bug out of his head. "With three babies who'll be eleven months old and probably walking by then?"

"We thought about that. We would have to be extra careful with them when we're on deck, but with all of the adults around, that shouldn't be a problem." Ronan grinned. "There's a cruise to Bermuda that sails out of Boston, so we wouldn't have to fly. We'd just need to book a car service to drive us to the cruise terminal. After a day and a half at sea, we dock in Hamilton and the ship stays there until we sail back to Boston on Thursday of that week. Ten and I thought that would be better than island hopping. Greeley and Kevin knew about this idea already, but what does everyone else think?" Ronan looked around the table.

"We're in!" Fitzgibbon said without even consulting Greeley.

Cole started to laugh. "Cass was just saying the other night that she wanted to go on vacation. Ask and you shall receive."

"Carson, Truman, what about you guys?" Tennyson turned to look at the babies whose faces were covered in mashed potatoes. They seemed to all get a look at each other at the same time and started giggling.

Truman picked up his phone and started filming the babies laughing at each other. "We're in! The last time my chest saw the sun was when Bertha threw up on me at our Fourth of July barbeque and it was easier to just take my shirt off than to wear baby puke."

"What about you, Jude?"

"I'm invited?" Jude sounded stunned.

"So long as you don't act like a di-"

"Ronan!" Kaye yelled sharply.

"What?" Ronan sounded offended. "I was going to say so long as he doesn't act like a ditz." He smiled angelically at his mother-in-law. "What did you think I was going to say, Kaye?"

"I, well…" Kaye trailed off. She focused on folding the napkin in her lap.

"You're invited too, Mom. Same rule as Jude though. You can't act like a ditz either." Ten winked at his husband.

"Really, Tennyson. I never act like a ditz."

"Good, so you're in too!" Ronan laughed. "So, back to the turkey contest. The chef of the winning bird goes on the trip for free. Our treat!" Ronan pointed back and forth between himself and Tennyson. "The loser does the dishes! We'll vote after dessert."

35

Ronan

Ronan was so stuffed that he would swear he wouldn't be able to eat again until Monday at the very least. He was sitting, half-awake, on Truman's sofa, with the dogs all piled around him. He was fat, happy, and warm. Add to that, the Cowboy's game was on television. Life was good.

"Well, Jesus Christ! Aren't you King Mutton!" a sarcastic voice crowed.

"Fuck off, Jude. You're just jealous." Ronan didn't bother to open his eyes.

"Oh good, I'm glad I caught you both getting along." Fitzgibbon swept past Jude into the living room. "Are you some kind of tiny dog whisperer, Ronan? Christ, they flock to you like you have treats in your pocket."

"More like he soaked his underoos in Kibbles and Bits." Jude drawled, sounding bitter.

"Can both of you go screw and leave me to enjoy my food coma in the company of these three lovely ladies. Can't you see we're trying to watch the football game?"

"How can you watch the game with your eyes shut, ditz?" Jude chuckled. "Nice save by the way."

Ronan laughed. His blue eyes popped open. "I need to be fast on my feet when my mother-in-law is in town."

"They're starting to wrap up the leftovers in there, so I thought now would be a good time to talk about the case."

"On Thanksgiving?" Jude sounded like he thought Fitzgibbon had lost his mind.

"Crime doesn't take a holiday, son!" Ronan drawled in his best impersonation of Fitzgibbon.

"No," Jude shook his head. "I could give a fuck what day it is. I just meant with all of these other people here." He pointed toward the kitchen.

Ronan could hear laughter coming from the kitchen. The babies were banging on their high chair trays and babbling up a storm and Laurel could come running in here at any second. Even though he'd said it in a dickish way, Ronan knew where Jude was coming from. "Cap will make it quick."

"I'm just waiting on Ten. He said he'd be right in. He and Carson were in the middle of a conversation about rocks and Aquarius. That's when I tuned out." Fitzgibbon shook his head.

"In this crowd it might take a few minutes to get himself out of the nine conversations he's got himself in the middle of." Thanksgiving dinner had been a crazy train. Once talk of the trip to Bermuda simmered down, everyone broke off into different factions. Ronan heard Greeley and Kaye talking about going to IKEA for Black Friday. Truman had wondered if he still had a bathing suit that fit him. Fitzgibbon and Jude were talking about the Patriots' shit offensive line. Carson babbled with the babies as he'd heaped yams on their tray, while Cassie and Cole whispered about something amongst themselves. At one time or another Ten had a hand in all of those conversations and started a few of his own.

Ronan, for his part, had sat back and listened to the madness around him. He passed dishes around the table and ate his share of the meal. For him though, having his family surrounding him was the best part of this day. For the last few years, he'd spent Thanksgiving with his old partner from Homicide, Tony Abruzzi and his wife, Carlie.

After the outcome of the Max Harmon case and the fallout that came after, he and Tennyson hadn't seen Tony or Carlie in months. They hadn't come to the wedding or even sent a card. It had been upsetting to Ronan, but he'd understood. He'd never shut the door on the friendship he'd shared with Tony, but if his friend was looking to rekindle it, the ball was in his court. Still, Ronan couldn't help but think of him today.

Ronan had lost his mother, Erin, a few weeks after he'd graduated from the police academy. This was the first time since then that he'd felt like he'd spent Thanksgiving with a family of his own.

"Here I am." Tennyson announced as he walked into the living room. "Carson was showing me pictures of pink sand beaches. He's so excited, I think he wants to leave today." Ten took a seat next to Fitzgibbon. "Reporting for duty, Cap."

"Where are we with this case?" Fitzgibbon was obviously wasting no time with small talk.

"Isn't that what we should be asking you? Aren't we still dead in the water with being able to retrieve the murder weapon and the cell phone?" Ronan asked.

Fitzgibbon nodded. "Yes, Ronan, but when do we ever stop investigating and sit with our thumbs up our asses? That's right, never!" Fitzgibbon answered his own question. "If I were handling this investigation, I would get my ass back to Charlestown and talk to Tim Hutchins. You might also want to talk to his mother and see where the hell things went so wrong with her sons."

Jude narrowed his eyes. "What do you mean, Fitzgibbon? I've met Jennifer Hutchins and she's a good mother."

Kevin narrowed his eyes right back. "Oh really, genius dick? If she's such a good mother then why did one twin let the other twin go to prison for the murder he committed?" He stood up. "Oh yeah, mother of the fucking year! Give the woman a trophy!" He stalked back toward the kitchen. "I'm gonna need some pie soon!" He practically thundered.

Ronan looked over at Tennyson who he could see was trying not to laugh. "He's really part of the family now, Ten."

"What the hell are you talking about, Ronan?" Jude didn't sound like he was in the mood for riddles.

"Fitzgibbon named you. We have no choice, we've got to keep you now." Ronan was not pleased with that development. Fitzgibbon only got *that* pissed off at you if he really liked you.

Jude looked perplexed. "What the hell did Fitzgibbon name me?"

"Genius dick!" Ten and Ronan crowed together.

"What's that old saying?" Ten tapped a finger against the side of his head. "Oh, yeah. Be careful what you wish for. You just might get it."

Jude shot him a dirty look and crossed his arms over his chest.

"You said you wanted to be called genius dick and your wish came true! Bet you're thinking now you should have wished for a million bucks and a ticket out of Boston, huh?" Ronan moved off the couch. "Now that all of you assholes have ruined my food coma, let's go eat some pie!"

The table was set for dessert when Ronan walked into the kitchen. At each spot was a square of paper and something to write with. Ronan assumed this was to tally the votes for the turkey contest.

"Oh good. So nice of the *newlyweds* to join us."

"Jeez, Carson, it's not like we were doing it on your couch. Not with Sadie watching us. She has such penetrating eyes." Ronan shuddered.

"Have a seat. I'm dying to try a piece of Cassie's pumpkin pie." Carson sounded grumpier than usual.

Ronan tipped Carson a mock salute but took his seat.

"Write down the type of bird that was your favorite to avoid confusion. Just to recap, we had a traditional turkey, a brined bird, the deep-fried turkey and the spatchcocked creation. Ready? Set. Vote!" Carson shouted.

It wasn't even close for Ronan. He scribbled his answer down on the paper, folded it and stuck it in the bowl. He looked over at Tennyson's paper and saw that his husband had written down the same thing. He had a feeling the vote was going to go to Team Spatchcock, that was if people could spell it. If not, there were going to be some pretty hilarious attempts.

When all of the responses were in the bowl, Carson pushed it over to Tennyson and Ronan. "Since you're giving away the prize, you should be the ones to tally the votes."

"I'll read them out and you keep count?" Ronan asked Ten.

Ten nodded, grabbing a napkin and a pen. "This is so exciting. It makes me feel like Vanna White!"

The absolute last person Ronan wanted to be was Pat Sajak. He had a whiney voice and was way too short. "I'll play Bob Barker then!" Ronan pulled out the first ballot. "One vote for grinch-popping. Hmm, I wonder who wrote that, Kaye?"

"Ballots are supposed to be secret." Kaye frowned at Ronan before grinning at Greeley and patting his hand.

"Spat-flopping." Ronan recognized the writing as Carson's. Interesting that he'd vote against his own traditional turkey.

"Trench-dropping." Truman's block printing. Ronan noticed a trend developing.

"Spatchcocking. Atta boy, Greeley! Not only did you vote for yourself, you spelled it right!"

"If you don't vote for yourself, no one else will." The teenager beamed with pride.

"Cut out my backbone and flatten me out, accompanied by an illustration of a turkey holding its wings over its eyes." Ronan held the ballot up for everyone to see. He wondered who the artist was, since he didn't recognize the handwriting.

"Flat-bopping." Ronan laughed. This was getting ridiculous. The writing looked like Cole's.

"Fart-stopping." That was Fitzgibbon's messy scrawl.

"Art-whopping!" In Cassie's elegant hand.

"Splash-shopping." Tennyson's vote

"And lastly, the Bobby Flay way, because one of us can't spell worth a damn. It's unanimous, Greeley wins."

Greeley's mouth hung open. He took a deep breath, looking like he was about to make a speech and promptly burst into tears.

Ronan felt himself getting a little emotional too. If anyone deserved to sail away from Boston for a little fun in the sun after all he'd been through, it was Greeley Fitzgibbon.

36

Tennyson

Since the contest had really been more of a massacre, everyone chipped in to help with the dishes. Laurel had reached the end of her endurance after her turkey cupcake, so Cole had packed her and his leftovers up and they'd headed home. Greeley was so excited to start researching Bermuda with Kaye, that they'd headed out shortly after that, with Fitzgibbon promising to make gobbler sandwiches later on. Jude had said his goodbyes minutes later when all three babies exploded in their pants and started laughing hysterically at each other.

"That's our cue to leave too!" Tennyson started looking around in the fridge for the bag of leftovers with their name on it.

"Oh no, Mr. Moms. Hold it right there." Truman stood in the kitchen door holding a laughing Bertha out in front of him. "The two of you have your appointment with the surrogacy service in twelve days. Carson and I have been looking for an opportunity to speak with you about that and I think this is the perfect moment."

"Ah, Truman, I don't know how to say this in a way that won't hurt your feelings, but your daughter smells like something crawled up her butt and died."

Truman raised an eyebrow. "Oh, and I suppose your sainted daughter is going to shit vanilla?"

Tennyson let a strangled giggle escape his lips. "I was thinking raspberry or maybe even lavender."

"Someone take the baby before I start cracking skulls!" Truman's voice brooked no argument.

Ronan swallowed so hard his throat clicked, but he stepped forward. With his arms stretched out as far as they would reach, he took the baby from a suddenly militant Truman.

"Looks like we got here just in time, Erin!" Bertha Craig cackled.

"Front row seats!" Erin O'Mara agreed.

"Sweet, merciful Christ, baby Bertha, what did you eat?" Ronan gagged.

"The same thing you ate, Ronan. People food." Truman laughed. "Lesson number one, baby shit changes dramatically when they switch from formula and baby food to real human food."

"I brought pajamas for all three of them and..." Carson stopped short when he caught sight of Ronan holding Bertha and gagging. "Hi, Mom. Hi, Erin."

Both women were laughing too hard to speak. They waved instead.

"Are you gonna stand there and watch, Nostradamus, or are you going to help me?" Ronan dry heaved again.

"I'm not sure I know what to do. Carson, can we use a lifeline here?" Baby Bertha was still laughing like she'd heard the funniest joke ever. Tennyson had no idea where to start with the baby.

"You're going to give Bertha a bath in the sink. What do you think the first thing the person *not* holding the baby should do?" Carson was biting his bottom lip.

Tennyson had no clue. They were going to bathe the baby. Baths required water. Aha! That was it. "Turn on the water and find a temperature that's safe for her skin." That seemed like a safe bet.

"Perfect. Now Ronan, since you're holding the baby, what do you think you should do?" Carson had taken on a school teacher tone.

"Keep breathing through my mouth so I don't barf on your baby." Ronan deadpanned.

"Breathing is good, since you're holding my child." Carson rolled his eyes. "Since Bertha's still dressed why don't you try taking off her dress and tights."

"What I would give to have Handsome take off my dress and tights," Bertha Craig sighed.

Erin laughed. "You realize that's my son your sighing over."

"Hell, yeah!" Bertha laughed.

Ronan sat the baby on the counter and undid the snaps on the back of her dress. He started to work the white and red material up toward her head when he gagged again.

"Jesus, Ronan, what now?" Tennyson had his left elbow under the faucet testing the water temperature. It was warm on his arm, but not hot.

"It's all up her back." Ronan's voice was weak. "The shit is all over my hand and it's still warm." He held up his hand to show Tennyson. He gagged again.

Ten gagged too.

"Shit! I wish we had popcorn!" Bertha cackled. "This is priceless!"

"You just said shit!" Erin was laughing so hard she was gasping for breath.

Ronan finally got the little dress over baby Bertha's head. "Ten, I'm gonna hold her up. You peel down the tights."

"Uh, Ronan. It's *in* her tights. What if it leaks out onto the counter?"

"Maybe you should hold her over the sink, Tenny?" Bertha suggested between fits of the giggles.

"Hey! No fair helping, Mom!" Carson called out.

"Carson, you have to give them some help! I've got two other grandbabies in the other room rolling around in their own shit. If Tweedle-Dee and Tweedle-Dumber keep up at this pace, it's gonna fossilize. Do you want that?"

"I guess not," Carson grumped.

"Hold her over the sink and I'll try to get her tights off," Ten suggested. He was going to have a long talk with Carson later about friends letting friends twist in the wind.

Ronan held the baby over the sink and Tennyson managed to pull her tights off. He held them up. "What do I do with them?"

"I think we should burn them in the backyard," Ten suggested.

"Here." Truman held open a plastic grocery bag. "We'll put all of the soiled clothes in here and I'll take care of them when everyone is clean. Next is her diaper. Keep her over the sink for that too. Take a breath over your shoulder before you open it." Truman patted Ronan's shoulder and backed away.

"Okay, Ten. Do it," Ronan urged.

Ten peeled back the tabs and caught the diaper as it came off. He'd swear it weighed five pounds. "Holy shit, honey! No wonder this thing overflowed!" Ten gagged again. He rolled the diaper up the way he'd seen Carson do a million times in the last few months and used the fastenings to secure it shut.

"Now you can hose off her little bum and wash her off. See the purple bottle? That's her soap. Here's a washcloth." Carson set a pink cloth next to Ronan. He also set pink footie pajamas and a fresh diaper nearby along with a fuzzy octopus towel.

"Oh, man. I didn't realize babies needed so much stuff." Ronan held the wet baby while Ten reached for the soap and cloth.

"That's why we wanted to have this talk with you. It's so exciting to talk about picking out a redheaded surrogate and getting pregnant, but there's so much more that comes after that we weren't prepared for."

"I'm guessing you're not talking about baby showers and midnight feedings either." Ronan asked.

Tennyson saw that the baby was clean and soap-free. He grabbed the octopus towel and held it out for the wet baby. "We're ready for number two."

Ronan gagged again. "Can we can it with the baby shit jokes?"

"I meant baby number two. I had no idea a human being could turn that shade of green, babe." Ronan was going to need some TLC later, once they escaped this fresh hell.

"What's Handsome gonna do when his little miss shits her britches like this?" Bertha asked.

"Jesus, Bertha." Ten shook his head and rubbed the towel over the baby's downy head to dry her hair.

"What's she saying?" Ronan asked curiously.

Ten snorted. "She wants to know what you're going to do when our baby shits her britches like this?"

Ronan laughed. "I imagine I'll think it's the cutest shit ever. I'll take pictures of it. Call up Fitzgibbon so he can come over and see it. Then, I'll get you to change her." He batted his eyes at Tennyson.

"Is it too late for an annulment?" Ten rolled his eyes.

"Okay, Ten, you're up!" Truman held Brian out to him, while Carson scooped Bertha out of his arms.

"You remember the night when they all got the puking bug?" Truman asked.

Carson nodded. He sat down at the bar with Bertha and got her ready for her diaper. "It was like 7pm on a Friday night. One minute they were all fine, playing on the floor with each other and us. The next minute, they were all erupting like Vesuvius and screeching." Carson shook his head as if he was trying to shake free of the memory. "I remember freezing. I had no idea what to do in that moment. My babies were all sick and I couldn't move."

"What was worse was I remember being pissed at Carson. The kids were all sick and screaming their heads off and he was frozen like a deer in the headlights. I screamed at him. Something awful like, 'Are you gonna do something or stand there and watch our kids die, asshole?' I'll regret saying that for the rest of my life."

Carson zipped up Bertha's footie pajamas and cuddled her against his chest. "Yeah, that was pretty bad, but it snapped me out of my trance. I grabbed Bertha and Stephanie and raced upstairs with them. I figured if they were throwing up, they'd be doing this soon too." He pointed in the direction of the loaded diaper Ten was peeling off of Brian. "The best place for them was our giant bathtub."

"They ended up spiking fevers and we couldn't get a hold of our pediatrician. It was the worst night of our lives," Truman chimed in. "I called you the next morning to see if you could stop by at lunchtime."

"I remember that," Ronan said, taking a wet and now clean Brian from Tennyson. "That started our baby lunch dates, where I'd bring you lunch and play with the babies and you'd take a nap."

"That's another thing I wanted to warn you about, Ten," Carson said. "Our gifts dull down the more tired we are. There are days when I'm dragging so bad that Mom has to wake my ass up when I doze off in the reading room. This parenthood thing is truly exhausting." His bloodshot eyes told the tale.

"Being a parent is never easy, Carson, but at least you have Truman. He's a true partner." Bertha smiled at her son.

"That's really sweet, Mom." Carson turned to his husband. "Mom called you a true partner."

"Thanks, Bertha. I have a true partner too; thanks to the way you raised your son. I can never thank you enough for that." Truman's eyes started getting misty.

"Okay, enough of this *Days of our Lives* bullshit. Let's get back to the juicy stuff. When's Ronan gonna donate his spunk? I want to be there for that!"

"MOM!" Carson's face turned beet-red.

Tennyson burst out laughing.

"What? What did Bertha say? She wants to be the one to give *me* a bath, right? She wants to wash my tushy and rinse me off, right?" Ronan was all smiles.

Tennyson was torn. Did he tell his husband the truth or did he lie straight to his face? "Yup, you got it exactly, Ronan! There was also mentioning of powdering dat ass."

"I knew it. Bertha, you dirty girl." Ronan winked in her general direction.

"I'll get you for this, Tennyson." Bertha crossed her arms over her chest and frowned at him.

"Go kiss our daughter goodnight, would you? Don't you have better things to do than flirt with my husband?" Ten blew a wet kiss in her direction. "Erin, try to keep her on the straight and narrow, would you?" Ten pleaded.

"Try and stop Hurricane Bertha? Not on your life. Tell my boy I love him. I'll see you both tomorrow." Erin waved.

"Toodles, boys!" Bertha was gone.

"Okay, I need a minute before we tackle Stephanie." Ronan fanned his face and ran toward the bathroom.

"Okay, liar, liar, pants on fire," Truman laughed. "What did my mother-in-law *really* say? The two of you turned redder than a Fourth of July lobster."

Carson leaned over and whispered in his ear.

"You're shitting me?" Truman burst out laughing.

Carson shook his head. "Not shitting you."

Truman turned to Tennyson.

"I shit you not!" Ten agreed. He'd take that secret to his grave.

37

Ronan

The next day found Ronan driving back down I-93 South toward Cambridge. He didn't know how he'd gotten talked into doing this little favor. It must have been the product of his sex addled brain.

"I hate Cambridge. Fucking yuppies. Fucking earth-crunchy college students thinking they can change the world," Ronan grumbled.

"Who the hell pissed in your Cheerios?" Ten asked from the passenger seat of the Mustang.

"You!" Ronan growled.

"Me?" Ten half-screeched. "I was the one sucking your dick in the shower! Jesus, I've still got the tile imprints in my knees for God's sake."

Ronan smashed the heel of his hand against the steering wheel. "You did that to trick me into driving to Cambridge to pick up Jude Fucking Law!"

Tennyson started to laugh. "Ah, don't you mean Jude fucking *Byrne*?"

"No! The only way I can get through this is to imagine it's Jude Law we're picking up." There was a faint smile in Ronan's tone.

"I have no words for that." Ten shook his head. "*The Talented Mr. Ripley,* Jude Law or *Sherlock Holmes,* Jude Law? Because that *Holmes* toupee sucked..." Ten trailed off.

"You're *not* helping." Ronan felt his lips curl into a snarl.

"Why are you so pissy? We're going to Cambridge, *not* Cedar Junction. You make it sound like we've got to drive an hour out of our way or something."

"You know Jude rubs me wrong." Rubs him wrong was an understatement. He'd been okay to hang out with yesterday, until his comment about Jennifer Hutchins being a good mother. That wiped out any good will helping to prepare the Thanksgiving meal had earned the *genius* dick.

"I thought the two of you were besties now after you peeled and chopped root vegetables together. Hell, I thought the next step for the two of you would be making friendship bracelets and braiding each other's hair at a sleepover."

"Ten, he thinks Jennifer Hutchins is mother of the year. I just can't wrap my head around that." He couldn't get his gut to stop churning over the mere thought of that notion.

"Explain to me why that offends you so much. Calmly, though. I can see that vein starting to pop in your forehead. I'm not in the mood for a side trip to Mass General to get you treated for an aneurism."

Ronan took a deep breath. "One son brutally killed a woman and let his brother take the rap for it. Where was Mother of the Year in all of this?"

"Stuck in the middle, I'd say. Probably a common spot for her."

"What do you mean?" Ronan challenged.

"One son brutally killed a woman, but which one? What if she doesn't know either? It would be one thing if she was covering for the *real* killer, but what a helpless feeling it must be if she doesn't know who killed Lorraine McAlpin either." Ten set a hand on Ronan's knee.

Ronan was silent, chewing on Tennyson's words. He couldn't help thinking about Carson and Truman's kids. He knew they loved those babies equally. What would they do if one of them was accused of committing a crime? How would they side with one child over another? "Yeah," Ronan muttered.

It wasn't that he didn't see where Tennyson was coming from, it was that they were pulling down Jude's street. He didn't want to have this conversation with Jude in the car.

"There he is." Ten pointed to Papi's, a Dominican Restaurant. Jude was standing on the sidewalk in front of the entrance. He was dressed in a leather bomber jacket and was rocking worn jeans and Ray-Bans. "Of course, he looks like something out of fucking *Top Gun*."

"You're just pissed because he makes a better Maverick than you." Ten rolled his eyes and unbuckled his seatbelt. He hopped out of the car when Ronan put it in park.

"Are you sure you don't want to take my Thunderbird? It has four doors." Jude pointed down the street to where the car was parked.

Ronan had half a mind to drive off and leave the annoying man standing on the sidewalk with his dick in his hand, but that would also mean leaving Tennyson. He knew damn well if he did that, there would be no repeat of this morning's bitchin' shower scene for long time to come, leaving him with *his* dick in his hand. "Shut up and get in, Cinderella. If you don't like the ride, you can take your own pumpkin coach."

"Christ O'Mara, did the bluebird of *unhappiness* shit in your eye this morning?" Jude climbed into the backseat.

"We're going to ruin this family, Byrne," Ronan muttered. "Pardon the fuck out of me if I'm not giddy about it."

"What do you mean we're going to *ruin* this family? I don't know what kind of fairy tale world *you* live in, Ronan, but the family is in shreds." Jude met Ronan's angry eyes in the rearview mirror.

"What do *you* mean?" Ten turned around so he could see Jude.

"I know how much you love your husband, Tennyson. Only God knows why, but you do. If you were in the Hutchins' situation with your husband and Ronan's twin brother's DNA was found at a murder scene, how could your relationship with him ever be the same again?"

"I thought Michelle Hutchins said Tim was home with her the night of the murder?" Ronan sounded confused.

"She did," Jude agreed. "One of the first things Hicks had me do when I took this job was to sit on the Hutchins' home. I shadowed the house and the family for weeks. They don't share the same bed. They fight all the time and they don't do anything together. If the kids have an event, like a ball game, only one parent goes. They're holding on by a thread. According to my sources, their marriage wasn't like this before Lorraine McAlpin was murdered."

"Fine then, when Tennyson reads Tim Hutchins and we find out that he's Lorraine's killer then that thread is going to snap. Not only is that revelation going to send his marriage crashing to the ground but it's going to devastate Jennifer Hutchins. Unless she already knows the truth, Byrne. Tell me she doesn't already know Tim is the real killer."

"Without Tennyson's gift, I have no way of knowing what she knows. What I do know is that she did the best she could as a single mother with twin sons and only a high school education. She worked two, sometimes three jobs to keep food on the table and the lights turned on to cook it. Most of the time it was store-brand macaroni and cheese and hot dogs. I guess what I'm saying is that there are some people who will do anything to keep their family together.

Ronan was no stranger to the struggles of a single mother. His own father had skipped out on him and Erin before he could walk. He knew without a shadow of a doubt that if he'd committed a crime, Erin would have hauled his ass into the police station herself to turn him in herself. "I get that."

"But as a cop, you can't condone it," Jude jumped in.

"What do you want me to say, Jude?" Ronan shot him an angry look in the rearview mirror. "That it's fine to harbor a fugitive? That you should cover for your son who's a family man and send the divorcee to prison for possibly the rest of his life?"

"Uh, Ronan? This is the street." Ten pointed to the next right.

Taking the turn, Ronan looked for the row house marked 243. Spotting it, he parked the car and turned around to look at Jude, who he realized was essentially trapped in the backseat of the car. "Look, I get that this is a no-win situation for a lot of reasons. Tank Hutchins asked for our help and he's getting it. It's not my job to judge what kind of mother Jennifer Hutchins was to her twin sons. It's also not my job to judge what kind of brother Tim is to Tank. I just want the truth to come out today. It might not even make a difference." Yanking the keys out of the ignition, Ronan climbed out of the car, pulling the seat forward so Jude could get out too.

"What the hell do you mean it might not even make a difference?" Jude grabbed Ronan's arm and spun the detective around.

"Take your hand off me, Byrne. I'm not in the fucking mood."

Jude didn't take his hand of Ronan. He grabbed him with the other hand too, standing toe to toe with him. He was a few inches taller than the cop.

It wasn't very often someone towered over Ronan, but Jude Byrne did by a couple of inches. He could feel the other man's fingers digging into both arms.

"What do you mean it might not make a difference," Jude repeated, this time hissing his question.

"The murder weapon and the destroyed cell phone are still sitting at the bottom of a fucking drain pipe or have possibly been flushed into the Boston sewer system where there are rats the size of VWs. We may never get permission to go in and try to discover that evidence because your client has already been convicted of this crime. Massachusetts Appeals Court judges don't overturn solid convictions based on psychic readings. Now, take your fucking hands off me!" Ronan shoved hard against Jude's broad chest, sending the P.I. stumbling back a few steps before he was able to stop his backward momentum.

"Jesus Christ you two, we're on a public street. Stop the fight club bullshit. If you need to have a dick measuring contest, do it in private. The last thing either of you needs is to end up in the gossip column of *The Herald*." Tennyson headed for the steps leading up to the Hutchins' front door.

"I'd win," Jude proclaimed.

"The fuck you would." Ronan gave the private dick another shove for good measure and followed behind his husband.

38

Tennyson

Tennyson heard the last exchange between his husband and Jude Byrne. Never one to count Ronan out of anything, he'd grudgingly admit Jude would probably give his husband a run for his money. The man had the biggest hands he'd ever seen, shy of the guys who played in the NBA.

Climbing the stairs to the Hutchins' row house, Ten shook his head. The last thing he needed to be thinking about at a time like this was who would win a hypothetical dick measuring contest. He was about to ring the bell when he heard a commotion going on inside the house.

"When are you ever going to trust me again, Michelle?" a man shouted.

"When you can prove to me you didn't murder that woman, Tim!" Came Michelle's response.

"Is there a problem, Tennyson?" Jude asked from behind him.

Ten held up a hand, hoping Jude would get the message to be quiet. He heard Ronan moving up the stairs quickly from behind.

"I didn't kill her! They convicted Tank! When is that ever going to be enough for you!" Tim screamed.

"I think now's a good time to ring the bell." Ronan moved past Tennyson to do just that.

"Who the hell are you expecting, Tim?" Michelle yelled.

Tim yanked the door open. Frustration was apparent on his face. "What?" He blinked and took in the strangers on his doorsteps. "Hey, I know you." He pointed at Tennyson. "*Why* do I know you?"

Before Tennyson could answer, Michelle was at the door pushing her husband aside. "You're Tennyson Grimm, the psychic, and you're his partner, the cop, Ronan. You, I don't know from Adam."

Ronan flashed Michelle an annoyed look and his badge. "I'm detective Ronan O'Mara from the Boston Police Department. This is Jude Byrne. Do you mind if we come in? This is the kind of conversation that would be better to have inside, rather than out here where your neighbors could overhear us."

Too late for that, Tennyson couldn't help but thinking. There were already several curious people out on their stoops already.

"Come in, please." Michelle held the door wide open for them. "Pardon the look of the house." She didn't bother to explain why it looked like a tornado had blown through their living room. Toys were strewn everywhere in the living room. Dirty dishes were piled up in the sink and on the stove. The trash was overflowing with old pizza boxes and take-out bags.

Tennyson didn't need a reason for the state of the house and it wasn't because he was psychic. When you fought with your spouse 24/7, who the hell had time to cook or clean?

Michelle and Tim both hurried over to the dining room table they grabbed the piles of bills, magazines and newspapers and moved them into the kitchen. "Please sit," Tim directed. "Can we get you coffee, tea, or water?"

"No thanks, we grabbed something from Dunkin Donuts on the way." Tennyson took a seat in the middle of the rectangular table. When he set his hands on the wood, they landed in something sticky. No doubt this was where one of the Hutchins' three kids sat.

"I don't mean to be rude, but who is Jude Byrne and why are the three of you showing up on my doorstep unannounced like this?" Michelle Hutchins sat down heavily in the chair at the head of the table.

Tennyson waited until everyone was seated at the table until he started to speak," Do you want to start us off, Jude?" Ten figured the P.I. should be the one to explain who he was and what brought them all together.

Jude took a deep breath and turned to Tim Hutchins. "I'm a private investigator who was hired by Bradford Hicks on behalf of your brother."

"I knew it. I fucking knew *Tank* had to be in the middle of this shit storm somewhere." Michelle went to get up from the table.

"Why don't we hear them out before we fly off the handle and get all dramatic, Michelle?" Tim turned back to Jude. "Please continue Mr. Byrne."

"Tank has strenuously proclaimed his innocence since the day he was arrested. He wasn't happy with the attorney who represented him in the original trial, which is why he hired Bradford Hicks for the appeal."

"How much is *that* gonna fucking cost us?" Michelle sneered.

"Actually, Mr. Hicks has agreed to take the case on pro bono." Jude smiled at Michelle.

"What does Cher's dead husband gotta do with how much this new lawyer is gonna cost?" Michelle asked, sounding bewildered.

Tennyson bit his lip to keep from laughing. He kept from looking at Ronan because he knew he'd lose it if he saw the look on his husband's face. "Bradford Hicks is taking the case for free."

"Oh, well, why didn't you just say that in the first place?" Annoyance rang through her voice.

"Anyway, Tank had read a lot in the papers about Tennyson and the work he'd done with the Boston Police Department's Cold Case Unit. He figured if a psychic could help solve those kinds of cases, why couldn't a psychic be used to figure out who really killed Lorraine McAlpin?"

"Oh! I see what's going on here! You're here to somehow get my husband tangled up in this mess. The cops said he had nothing to do with it. Trump's right, this is a witch hunt!" Michelle shrieked.

"Mrs. Hutchins, sit down and shut up!" Ronan commanded. "This is going to go a lot smoother and faster if you would listen more and talk less. This isn't a witch hunt. Your brother-in-law wrote me a letter asking for my help. He claimed he'd been wrongly convicted and said that Tennyson's gifts could prove it. We took a trip to Walpole and Ten read him. Tank did not kill Lorraine."

"I fucking knew-"

Ronan held up his hand for silence and flashed the woman his sternest look. Oddly enough, it shut her up. "After we spoke with Tank, we spoke with Lorraine McAlpin's spirit. She claims the man in this picture killed her." Ronan pressed buttons on his phone and flipped it around to show Tim.

"That's a pic of me and Tank from Ryan's Baptism a few years ago," Tim said. "Which one of us did Lorraine's spirit pick out?"

"That's just the thing, Tim. She didn't know which one of you killed her," Tennyson said gently. "What she was able to tell us was that she'd been dating her killer."

Michelle opened her mouth, but Ronan reaching back for his handcuffs and letting them clank onto the surface of the table was enough to get her to swallow her words.

"I swear to you, Tennyson, I didn't know that woman. I'd never seen her a day in my life until the moment her picture flashed across the morning news to announce that she'd been found murdered a few miles from here."

Ten nodded at the obviously upset man. "Tank's people are working on an appeal. Ronan is looking for the truth. All I want to do is read you to see if you killed Lorraine, Tim."

Tim looked down at his folded hands. "You have no idea how hard these last three years have been on me, my wife, and our whole family. I've lost my job, my brother, my marriage is hanging by a thread and my mother has no idea which one of us killed that woman. Do it, Tennyson. I want to prove to everyone," Tim looked his wife in the eye, "that I was not the one who ended this woman's life."

"What if he did it, Tennyson?" Michelle asked, staring daggers at Ronan.

"A psychic reading is not admissible as evidence in a Massachusetts courtroom, but I will tell you this, Michelle. If Tim killed that girl, I will not rest until he and Tank have switched places. Am I understood?" Ronan's blue eyes never left Michelle's.

She gave Ronan a sharp nod and quickly looked away.

Tennyson shut his eyes and tried to center himself. There was so much chaos and bad feeling in this house. He could sense years of mistrust and bitterness coating the walls like an extra-thick layer of paint.

Scanning through Tim, he couldn't find any evidence of the murder or of Lorraine McAlpin. The woman said she'd dated "Jack" for a few months and Ten wasn't picking up any of those memories or of the fake FBI cover story. Knowing so much was riding on this, he read Tim again.

"Well?" Michelle's shrill voice rang through the quiet room.

Ten startled, his dark eyes opened. He turned to his husband. "You're not going to believe this, but Tim didn't kill Lorraine."

Ronan's eyes narrowed. "What do you mean Tim didn't kill Lorraine? Are you sure?"

"I read him twice. That's why it took so long." Ten got up from the table and pulled Ronan aside. "I also didn't get any memories of him dating Lorraine or of him making up the FBI cover story."

"I've gotta call Fitzgibbon. I promised to keep him in the loop every step of the way." Ronan grabbed his phone off the table and headed toward the front door.

"Mom?" Tim Hutchins crowed into his phone. "You know that Salem psychic you love? Yeah, that one! He's standing in my dining room. He did a reading and said I didn't kill that girl. What? Yeah, he said it. I know…"

"You okay?" Jude asked, pulling Tennyson's attention away from a jubilant Tim.

Ten nodded. "Ronan went to call Fitzgibbon. I'm not sure what we do now. I think I need to read Tank again."

Jude's eyes narrowed. "What do you mean you need to read Tank *again*?" The P.I. took a menacing step closer. "You said he didn't kill Lorraine."

Tennyson felt a shiver of fear snake up his spine. "We didn't have the information about Lorraine dating her killer and him posing as an FBI agent. When I interviewed Tank at the prison, there was a lot of background residue there that was interfering with my gift and making me feel sick."

"So, what? This is what you do when things don't go your way? You make excuses, Grimm?" Jude sounded like he was about to go nuclear on the psychic.

"You're going to want to take a step back from my husband, *Byrne*," Ronan snarled. "Move now, or I'll move you and you won't like the way I'll do it."

Jude took a step back. He spun on his heels to face Ronan.

Tennyson sagged backward. He never felt like he was in danger from Jude Byrne, but he sure as hell wouldn't want to be on the wrong side of that man. The way he and Ronan were staring each other down reminded him of Rocky and the Russian right before their big fight at the end of *Rocky IV*. Tennyson's money was on the hometown boy, but if it came to blows, the fight was going to be bloody.

39

Ronan

The incident with Jude Byrne in the Hutchins' dining room was as close as he'd come to swinging on a friend in a long time. How dare that ignorant prick accuse Tennyson of making excuses for the way his reading with Tank had gone a few weeks back.

When Fitzgibbon showed up a short time later, Ronan was able to calm down a bit more. The feeling didn't last long though. Jennifer Hutchins, Tank and Tim's mother, had arrived moments after that.

"Why don't we all have a seat at the table?" Fitzgibbon tried to herd everyone in that direction. "Tennyson, catch Mrs. Hutchins up on everything that's happened so far."

"Tom sent Ronan and I a letter asking us to help prove his innocence. When I went to the prison to read him, my gift told me he was innocent. When I read Tim an hour ago, I got the same result."

Jennifer Hutchins' face morphed from a look of pure joy to one of confusion. "How is that possible Tennyson? The prosecutor said the blood found on that poor girl's body belonged to Tom. He said DNA doesn't lie."

"The trial was rigged, Jennifer, just like President Trump says. It was rigged against my brother-in-law. Those bastards probably planted blood at the crime scene and now they are going to use that evidence to say my husband killed that girl."

Ronan felt his stomach pitch. The words "President" and "Trump" just didn't belong next to each other in a sentence. "To the best of your knowledge, Tim, had either you or your brother gone for blood work in the days leading up to the crime?"

Tim cocked his head to the side and seemed to be thinking about the question. "Not that I can remember, but I'm sure a quick check of our medical records would confirm that we hadn't."

"The fly in the ointment, Jennifer," Tennyson said, "is that when I showed Lorraine's spirit a picture of your sons, she said one of them was the man who killed her."

"Tennyson, is it possible your gift is on the blink again?" Fitzgibbon asked.

"What?" Ten's mouth hung open as if he couldn't believe Fitzgibbon's question.

"What did you just say, Cap?" Ronan was halfway out of his seat, his hands clenched into fists, before he realized what he was doing and sat back down.

"You both heard me. When you came back from the prison, Tennyson said there was a lot of background interference from the fifty years' worth of hinky murderer and rapist energy that had built up in that place. Isn't it possible that shit kept you from getting a concise reading?"

"No, captain, that *isn't* possible." Tennyson turned to Ronan.

Ronan could see the bewildered look in his husband's eyes. Anger was churning in his gut. He was angry enough to rip Fitzgibbon's traitorous spine out and beat the man with it. How fucking dare he even suggest something was wrong with Ten's gift.

"I might be able to explain why the *asshole* psychic can't figure out who killed the McAlpin bitch!" a menacing voice said from the front door.

Jennifer gasped, nearly falling out of her chair.

Ronan turned toward the door and couldn't believe his eyes. At first it was the Tim Hutchins' doppelgänger that caught his immediate attention, but what he quickly focused on next was the handgun he had pointed at Jennifer Hutchins. "Who the fuck are *you*?" Ronan slid slowly out of his seat.

The stranger laughed. It was a sound filled with gravel and years of hard living. "You wanna field that question, *Mommy?*" He kicked the front door closed with a slam and managed to lock it without taking the gun off Jennifer.

Ronan used that time to position himself in front of Tennyson. "Triplets?" Ronan gasped in disbelief. He blinked a few times just to be sure his eyes weren't deceiving him.

"Master of the fucking obvious, eh, Detective O'Mara?" The man kept his eyes on his mother. He was dressed in black jeans and a black tee-shirt. He wore a dark Carhartt jacket over it.

"Travis, why don't we talk about this calmly and *without* the gun," Tennyson suggested. He stood up and managed to move out from behind Ronan.

"My name isn't Travis, you psychic freak!" The gun swung at Tennyson, but Travis's hand was steady.

Tennyson's hands came up slowly. "Okay, Shane, then. Why don't you tell me your story?"

He shook the gun at Tennyson. "Don't you know it already? You're the *psychic.*"

Ten shrugged. "Yeah, I know your story, but I don't need to use my gift to see you've been waiting a very long time for this moment, right? To share this story with your *real* mother? So, maybe you'll put down the gun and tell her everything you've had to keep bottled up inside you all these years. Trust me, we're all on the edge of our seat to hear every word."

"The gun stays, asshole! I'm not stupid. There's two cops and a P.I. in this room, plus you with your brain powers. I didn't come this far only to get lit on fire by some damn mind freak." Shane was obviously angry but seemed to be in complete control of his emotions.

"You're thinking of a Stephen King novel, Shane. People can't *really* set things on fire with their minds."

Jude shot Tennyson an are-you-fucking-kidding-me look. Tennyson ignored him.

"Tell the story," Tennyson urged. His voice was gentle and calm, with no hint that a semi-automatic weapon was aimed in his direction.

Ronan's heart was in his chest. He could see a shaft of sunlight shining off the barrel of the gun that was pointed right at Tennyson. If Shane pulled the trigger, there was nothing he could do to save his husband. All he could do now was pray Bertha and Erin were here just in case things went bad.

Shane tilted his neck to the left, the joints cracked grotesquely. "According to the Boston City Hall Department of Public Records, I was born Travis Hutchins on May 1, 1986 to Jennifer Hutchins and Jake Sparks. I was the third of three brothers born that day. Thomas and Timothy Hutchins were born before me. Public records don't say why what happened next happened, but on May 3, 1986, I was adopted by Betsy and Richard McNamara of Rochester, New Hampshire. The birth announcement in *The Boston Globe* said that Thomas and Timothy went home on May 4th. You care to fill in the details, *Mommy*?" Shane sneered.

Jennifer's skin had gone so pale, she was practically transparent. Her mouth opened but no sound came out.

"Speak, woman!" Shane thundered. His arm holding the gun swung from Tennyson back to Jennifer.

Jennifer yelped and lost her balance, nearly falling out of her chair for the second time. Tim reached out a hand to steady his mother.

"Shane, I'm so sorry for what you went through, but it doesn't have to be like this. Just put the gun down and we can talk," Tim pleaded with his triplet.

"Fuck you!" Shane roared, the gun coming to rest on his triplet brother. "Look at you, Mr. All-American! Nice house, pretty wife, three kids. What the hell do you know about suffering? Huh?"

Tim's mouth shut with an audible clack of his teeth.

"Jennifer," Tennyson said gently. "Why don't you fill in the blanks for Shane?"

Ronan couldn't help thinking this would be the voice Tennyson would use with their little miss when she was refusing to eat her broccoli or go to sleep. He whispered a silent prayer that he would get to hear Tennyson negotiate terms with their daughter-to-be.

Clearing her throat, Jennifer sat up a bit straighter in her seat. "I was nineteen years old when Jake knocked me up."

"Oh, cry me a friggen river!" Shane rolled his eyes toward the ceiling.

"Shane, you wanted answers and she's giving them to you. Let's hear her out, hmm?" Ten's voice was soothing and suggestive, as if he were interested in hearing the story too.

Shane huffed a rough breath but didn't contradict Tennyson.

"I was working as a cashier at Star Market and Jake was a mechanic. We didn't have a lot of money and no health insurance. I had one ultrasound and the doctor told me it was twins." Tears were shining in Jennifer's eyes. "Jake was pissed. He didn't want one baby, forget two. He was on the verge of walking out then, but we got an apartment in Roslindale near his job and we made it work."

"The perfect picture of domestic bliss." Shane's lips curled into a cruel snarl.

"No." Jennifer shook her head. "Jake was a drunk. He knocked me around when he'd had a few. That was what sent me into labor. They wouldn't allow him into the delivery room because he was so wasted. I ended up having to deliver you boys alone. Worst pain of my life." She shrugged. "I thought I was done after Tim was born, but then the doctor said there was a third baby. I thought he was joking, but a few minutes later…" Jennifer trailed off.

"A few minutes later what?" Shane thundered. He stalked to the table, yanking Jennifer out of her seat by her arm. "What?"

She shrieked. "Don't hurt me! Please don't hurt me." Jennifer was trying to pull away from her enraged son, but Shane kept yanking her back against him.

"Tell me what happened, *Mom*!" Spittle flew from his lips to land on her face.

"He was little. The third baby was so little. It was like the other two ganged up on him and all he got were the scraps."

"He? Don't you mean *me*?" Shane screamed in her face.

Jennifer nodded.

"Why did you give me up?" Shane gave her arm a shake.

"When Jake sobered up, he was allowed in the room to see me. He was pissed that there were three babies. Told me I had a decision to make. That I could have him and two babies, because that was the original deal, or I could have three babies without him." Tears spilled down Jennifer's face.

Ronan felt rooted to the floor. What a terrible position to have been put in. He would never have chosen another man over his own flesh and blood, not even Tennyson. He slid his eyes over to Fitzgibbon who was staring at him. The look in his eyes was asking what in hell took so long for Ronan to glance his way.

Fitzgibbon threw his eyes toward Shane, indicating that he planned to inch toward the crazed man.

Ronan knew it was a bad idea. They were both armed, but neither had body armor, nor did the five other adults in the house with them. He took a slow, sliding step forward, managing to get in front of Tennyson again. He shot his husband a look telling him to stay there. Not that Tennyson was going to pay attention to that. Ronan knew he would do anything, including throwing himself in the line of fire, to keep Jennifer safe.

"Gee, let me guess which option you picked! You selfish bitch!" He shoved Jennifer hard, sending her sailing across the kitchen. She crashed into the refrigerator with thump and a rattle of glass bottles.

"I should have kept you!" Jennifer wailed, holding her grossly twisted left wrist close to her chest. "He left after two weeks anyway. I thought we'd have a better shot to make it as a family with two paychecks, but he couldn't stand all the crying."

"How did you decide, *Mom*? Was it eenie meenie miney mo? Did you pick the baby who came out last? The one with the least amount of hair? How did you choose who to keep and who to throw away? Why was it me?" Shane raged. The gun was pointed at Jennifer's head.

"Y-You were the smallest. The runt of the litter, Jake said. He didn't want such a scrawny baby." Jennifer gasped, seeming to realize her mistake instantly. "Sh-Shane, I-I didn't feel that way. Jake did."

Shane roared. It sounded primal, like he was letting all of the hurt inside of him escape. He took a step toward his mother when Tennyson spoke.

"Shane, what about your adoptive family?" Ten had taken another step forward and was now in front of Ronan again. The crazed man stopped dead in his tracks. "My adoptive family?" Shane blinked a few times as if he realized he needed to get himself back under control. "My mother was a saint. An angel on earth. All she ever wanted was a child. I was her dream come true." Shane's gruff voice sounded almost tender.

"What happened to her?" Ten asked gently.

"You fucking know what happened, asshole! Say it! Say what happened!" Shane's voice broke with the emotion.

Ten sighed. It was filled with profound sadness. "Ovarian cancer when you were seven. The diagnosis came too late. She died holding you in her arms."

"What about your adoptive father?" Ronan asked, needing to get the attention off Tennyson. He knew Shane could snap at any second and just start firing.

"Dick McNamara lived up to his name. My mother was all he had. Once the dirt was shoveled over her grave, he took his grief out on me. Started beating me. Starving me. Used to punish me by making me kneel on rice. I'm scarred for life."

Tennyson shivered. "You killed him…"

"God damned fucking right I did! Fucker had a bad heart. I sped things along with rat poison in his food. I stood over him while he died calling him every name in the book and telling him how I was the one responsible for that moment. The last words he heard were how much I fucking hated him." Shane McNamara smiled. It was full of sharp teeth and venom. "While I was doing CPR on his corpse and waiting for the EMTs to come save my dearly departed *Daddy*, I decided my next move would be to find you next, Mom."

Ten gasped so hard he nearly doubled over.

Shane laughed. He swung the gun toward Tennyson. "Finally figured it out, *psychic*?"

Ten nodded. He struggled to take a deep breath. "Revenge," he wheezed.

"God damned right. At long fucking last. Say goodbye, bitch!"

Shane turned toward Jennifer, raised the gun, and fired.

40

Tennyson

Tennyson's ears were ringing. Ronan was shouting something at him but he couldn't hear the words. Whatever it was Ronan was saying must have been pretty important because he kept repeating them over and over. The next thing he knew, Ronan was pulling his hands away from his ears.

"Get down!" Jude shouted. He was running toward where Shane was standing over Jennifer's prone body.

Tennyson could see what was going to happen next in his mind. He tried to shout a warning but it was too late. There was nothing he could do to stop what was coming.

Shane spun around at the sound of Jude's voice. He raised the gun and fired again, hitting Jude in the shoulder. The slug didn't slow Jude down. On the contrary, it only enraged him further. Letting out a feral yell, the P.I. hurled himself at Shane, knocking them both into the kitchen counter near the sink.

Jude had grabbed for Shane's gun and now the two men were battling over it.

Grabbing Ronan's arm, Tennyson tried to yank his husband to the floor, but Ronan wasn't budging. Out of the corner of his eye, Ten caught the movement of Tim grabbing Michelle's hand and pulling her toward the back door. He could only hope they would call 911 once they got to safety.

"Jude get down!" Fitzgibbon ordered, sounding every bit the police captain he was. Kevin had his weapon drawn and had it pointed at Shane. His finger was on the trigger.

Jude kicked out at Shane's left knee and that sent them both sprawling to the kitchen floor. Both men were scrabbling, trying to get the upper hand, when the gun fired again.

"Jude!" Ten shouted, pulling away from Ronan and running to his friend's side. "Kevin, call 911, now!" Ten fell to the floor and managed to roll Jude over. His left thigh was covered in blood. Shane was struggling to get up. "That's two of you. You're next, psychic." He tried to pull his arm out from under Jude's body.

"Fuck you, asshole!" Ten punched Shane in face, knocking the man unconscious. He got up on his knees to pull his belt off.

"Jesus Christ, Ten." Ronan slid onto the floor next to him. "Where the hell'd you learn to do that?"

"From you, Rambo! You want to help me with this tourniquet, so Jude doesn't bleed to death in this hellhole?"

"Uh, can you save me first and fight later?" Jude's voice was weak.

Wrapping the belt under Jude's leg, Ten secured it above the bullet wound and threaded it through the buckle.

"Pull harder, babe," Ronan advised.

"Do you mind not flirting. Christ, I'm fucking bleeding to death here!" Jude moaned.

"Harder, Ten. Let's not make genius dick's prophecy reality, huh?"

"He'd be the one haunting *me*, not you." Ten pulled the end of the belt with all his strength.

"Jesus! Fuck! Ouch!"

"Here, let me lock it in." Ronan slid the prong into belt hole.

"Let's move Jude so I can cuff Shane. The last thing we need is this fucker waking up free," Fitzgibbon said.

"I'll grab his good leg. You take his shoulder," Ronan directed.

"There's a bullet in that shoulder, asshole," Jude hissed.

"At least I didn't drop you." Fitzgibbon grinned. He reached over Tennyson and Ronan for a paper towel, which he used to grab Shane's gun. He moved it to the dining room table before cuffing the still unconscious man. Sirens wailed in the distance.

Ronan went to check on Jennifer, while Fitzgibbon stayed with Shane. "She's still breathing," Ronan announced.

"She'll be fine," Tennyson said. "Long road to recovery with a lot of therapy, but she'll be okay."

"You fucking knew I was gonna get shot, didn't you?" Jude half-growled.

Ten shrugged.

"You've got two bullets in you and you're bleeding all over the place. How is it possible you sound stronger now than you did ten minutes ago?" Ronan looked shocked.

"I've always been a quick healer." Jude managed to smile.

"Quick healer? We're talking about hunks of lead penetrating your body, not scabbed knees from falling off your bike."

Jude ignored Ronan. "Why didn't you tell me, you son-of-a-bitch?" he demanded.

"Watch your tone unless you want a third bullet to join the other two." Ronan growled good-naturedly.

Ten set a hand on Jude's good shoulder. "You changed history when you made your move, Jude. I saw it play out after you shouted for us to get down. There was no time to warn you. History changed like this." He snapped his fingers.

"I changed history? What was supposed to happen?" Jude's eyes narrowed. "Was I going to get shot anyway? Did I die?"

Ten was about to tell him Ronan was going to get shot again when the BPD burst through the door. "Later." Ten patted Jude's good shoulder.

The EMTs charged in after the police cleared the scene. They started tending to Jude and Jennifer.

"Come with me, Nostradamus." Ronan pulled Tennyson toward the front door and then outside.

The cold November wind bit into his skin. The chill was soon gone when Ronan wrapped him in his arms. "You okay?"

Ten nodded against his shoulder. "I am now."

"I was gonna get shot again, wasn't I? That's why you kept edging in front of me." Ronan's voice was tight with emotion.

Ten whimpered against Ronan's neck and held on to his husband tighter.

Ronan pulled back and looked into Tennyson's misty dark eyes. "Are you kidding me? Byrne save me? I *hate* that asshole!"

"No, you don't, Ronan. It's a funny schtick, but you don't hate him. How could you? You're the same person."

Ronan's upper lip curled into a snarl. "Now that's just plain mean."

"It's true. Carson said you're destined to be besties." Ten kissed him hard.

"Don't count on it. I have plenty of besties. I don't need any more. Especially not rude, heroic, bastards who heal like Deadpool."

"That's the grumpy cat I know and love." Ten patted his cheek.

"How did I know you'd be involved in this somewhere O'Mara?" a handsome patrolman asked.

"You must be psychic, Owens." Ronan rolled his eyes.

"Fitz is in there giving his statement to my captain. He's so detailed that we'll be here for an hour."

"Add an 's' to that, man. Grab coffee and a sandwich. It's gonna be a long ass day for you."

"Ronan." Ten gave his husband's arm a tug as the EMTs carried a stretcher out of the Hutchins' house. It was shrouded in a sheet. They set it down on the sidewalk.

"We're sorry, Ronan," the ginger medic said. "We did everything we could. There was just too much blood loss."

Ronan's face was a mask of shock as he pulled back the sheet. The body on the stretcher was Jude Byrne. "Oh, Jesus Christ," he whispered. "I never got to tell him he really wasn't a dick, that he was a good man. My friend."

"Gotcha, asshole!" Jude's golden eyes popped open.

The EMTs burst out laughing.

"You dirty bastard!" Ronan threw the sheet back down over Jude's face. "Did you know about this?" He asked Tennyson.

Of course, Tennyson knew about this. He was psychic and he'd seen the rise and fall of the sheet as Jude breathed. "No, Ronan," he lied through his teeth. "I was just as surprised as you were!" He crossed his fingers behind his back. The lie didn't count if you crossed your fingers. At least that was the rule on the playground back in Kansas.

"Okay, we've got to get him to the hospital. Beth Israel, Tennyson. You coming with us, detective?"

An evil grin spread across Ronan's face. "Yeah, you can revive him *after* I kill him." Ronan dug into his back pocket and pulled out the keys to the Mustang. He tossed them to Tennyson, who in his shock, nearly dropped them on the ground. "Don't crash her, babe. I'll see you later." He smacked a kiss to Ten's cheek and hopped into the back of the ambulance.

Tennyson watched as the ambulance pulled out into the street with the lights flashing and sirens wailing. He shut his eyes, saying a silent prayer thanking God for not taking his husband from him today.

41

Ronan

The ride to the hospital was surprisingly quiet. The paramedic monitored Jude's vitals and Ronan monitored Jude. The P.I. laid calmly with his eyes shut.

"Stop staring at my chest. I'm still breathing, asshole." Jude cracked open a golden eye.

"Why did you do that?" Ronan asked, still in shock himself.

"What?" Jude opened his eyes fully, before narrowing them to study Ronan. "Save your ass?"

Ronan nodded. "Play the hero. You didn't have a gun."

"Didn't need one. I was going for Shane's."

"I think we can all see how spectacularly well that worked out for you; bullet in the shoulder and another one in the thigh. McNamara, meanwhile, walked away without a scratch."

"Not true, he got one hell of a right hook from Tennyson. That boy's gonna need an x-ray. I bet he broke his hand."

Ronan shook his head. "I had no idea he could do that. He watches a lot of *Law and Order*. I guess he was doing more than just staring at Stabler's ass."

"Stabler has a mighty fine ass. I'd tap it." Jude giggled. "Why doesn't my leg hurt anymore? Am I all better? Ro, let's go for ice cream. Tell me a story. Unicorns rock!" Jude's eyes slid shut.

"The drugs just kick in?" Ronan laughed.

"Yup, kind of like an elephant when it gets darted out on the plains of the Serengeti. It takes a while for it to go down, but when it does, it goes down *hard*." The EMT grinned.

Ronan laughed. "You just made my day. It will be my pleasure to tell him that story later. Is he going to remember any of this when he wakes up?"

The EMT shook his head no.

Trying to hide his smile, Ronan picked up Jude's hand. "Thanks for saving my life today."

Jude's fiery eyes popped open. "Tenny isn't the only one with a present." Jude winked and passed out.

Ronan set Jude's hand back on the gurney and leaned back against the side wall of the ambulance. How the hell did Jude know that Bertha Craig sometimes called his husband Tenny? More importantly, what did he mean when he said Ten isn't the only one with a present? Present as in right now? Or a present as in a gift, like being able to see into the future and stop his stupid ass from getting shot. Again.

There wasn't too much time for Ronan to think about Jude's cryptic words. They were pulling in to the ER at Beth Israel Medical Center. He hopped out of the way when the emergency room staff opened the ambulance doors.

As they rolled Jude past, Ronan started to compile a list of all the people he needed to call, starting with Bradford Hicks. What upset him the most was that in all the time they'd known each other, Ronan had never once asked about Jude's family, nor had his mysterious friend volunteered the information.

"Detective O'Mara?" a nurse in blue scrubs asked.

"Yes?"

"Will you come with me, please? I'll take you to the family waiting room."

Ronan nodded and followed along. It struck him that this is what Ten went through when he had been shot back in August.

"Does Mr. Byrne have any family we can contact?"

"I'm not sure. We haven't known him that long. He's been consulting on a case with the BPD." Ronan was sure he'd be forgiven for the little white lie he'd just told. "My husband and I are the only friends he has in Boston."

The nurse nodded. "I'll keep you updated on his surgery."

"Take care of him. He's one of us." Ronan touched the BPD badge attached to his hip.

The nurse, whose nametag read, "Angel," nodded and left the room.

Ronan took a seat in one of the cushioned chairs. There were a lot of phone calls that needed to be made but they'd hold for a few minutes. His hands were shaking and he was starting to feel like he was going to throw up. He knew it was the adrenaline rush starting to wear off. He'd never been overly kind to Jude Byrne, but thanks to him, Ronan was going to get to go home with Tennyson tonight instead of being the one getting prepped for surgery.

"Ronan!" Ten called as he rushed into the waiting room.

"What's wrong? Did you crash my car?" He caught his husband as Ten flew into his arms.

"No! But I wouldn't mind one of those babies for Christmas!" Ten laughed as he held his husband tight. "Are *you* okay? I could feel something was wrong with you the second I walked into this hospital."

"He saved me and I've been a dick to him all along."

"To be fair, he's been a dick to you too." Ten pulled back to look into his husband's eyes. "There will be plenty of time to make it up to each other when he's home recuperating with us."

"With us?" Ronan half-roared.

"What, we're supposed to leave him in that tiny Cambridge walk-up apartment all alone with two useless limbs?" Ten pulled away from Ronan. "Jude's right. You are an asshole!"

Ronan's mouth fell open, but no sound came out. He was about to plead his case with Ten when his husband let out a strangled laugh. Jude Byrne wasn't the only asshole in his life, not that Ronan was going to say that out loud. He was a lot of things, but stupid wasn't one of them. He knew damn well that oh-fuck-you-almost-died sex was the hottest kind there was. "We've got stairs too, you know. What am I supposed to? Carry him around like a bride over the threshold? He looks like he's a heavy bastard."

"We'll cross that bridge when we get to it. Just so you know, I called Bradford Hicks after the ambulance left. I also called Carson, who's going to let everyone else know what's up. Truman's gonna grab Dixie for us. Fitzgibbon will be along as soon as he's done at the scene."

"Listen, there's something I need to talk to you about before everyone else gets here." Ronan took Ten's hand and guided him to a nearby couch.

"What is it?" Ten seemed to be studying him.

"In the ambulance, when Jude started to get loopy from the pain meds they were giving him, I figured it was a good time to thank him for saving my life. The EMT said he wouldn't remember any of this conversation anyway, so, you know..."

Ten rolled his eyes but didn't interrupt.

"He looked like he was out cold, which is why I spoke to him, but I guess he wasn't. His eyes popped open and he said to me, 'Tenny isn't the only one with a present,' and then he passed out. What do you think it means?"

"It's a real head scratcher, isn't it?" Ten tried to get up from his seat, but Ronan reached out to stop him.

"Oh, no you don't. You stay right here and explain this me."

"Fine," Ten sighed. "He could mean one of two things. Present as in past, *present*, future. Or, what I think is more likely is that he meant present as in *gift*. It's not a huge jump to think Tenny is a nickname for Tennyson. I mean, shit, it's the first five letters of my name, but when you couple it with the fact that Bertha calls me that when I'm upset, then I think it's more than coincidence."

"You don't believe in coincidence."

Ten nodded. "That's reason number two I think he's got some kind of a gift. Keep in mind that I can't read him at all. He might not be psychic per se, but maybe have a highly developed sense of intuition. In his job, he would need that to keep himself safe from enraged spouses or equally enraged people who've had their medical disability fraud uncovered."

"So, explain how he heard Bertha call you Tenny."

"There are a couple of reasons for that. Bertha could have appeared to him in a dream. Jude could have heard some of a conversation when she was present, or he could have used his intuition to reason it out. Plus, you said he was under the influence of the pain meds and sometimes that loosens us up to gifts we didn't know we had, making us more receptive."

"What, you mean like when your car radio starts picking up a far-off station and the signal is staticky?"

"Right, I think it would be more accurate to say when the signal comes in and out as if you were turning the volume dial up and down, but yeah, same kind of thing. Without being able to read him, we might never know what happened in the ambulance, since he isn't the most open of men."

"I was thinking about that when they were unloading him from the ambulance. He's never said a word about his family or where he's from."

"We'll be his family for now." Ten nodded. "On to the other news of the day, I'm sure Fitzgibbon will fill you in later, but Shane McNamara engineered Lorraine McAlpin's murder to destroy the family that gave him up. He said he left his DNA at the crime scene on purpose, knowing it would lead back to Tim or Tank Hutchins. Shane didn't much care which, figuring each brother would know they didn't kill the girl and would blame the other. Whichever one ended up in jail would know his brother sent him there and their mother would be caught in the middle."

"Jesus Christ. Do you think Jude is running from something like that?"

"For his sake, I sure hope not. People leave home for a lot of reasons, Ronan. I'm proof of that."

"Thank God, Nostradamus. I hate to think how dull and boring my life would be without you in it."

Ten rested his head on Ronan's shoulder. "Eleven days to our appointment with the surrogacy clinic."

Ronan started to laugh. "This is going to work our first time out."

"What makes you say that?"

"A little bird told me."

Ten laughed along with him. "A little miss you mean?"

"Maybe."

"On our wedding day, she whispered something to me."

"I remember. She said 'I love you to Dublin and back,' just like my mom used to say to me."

Ten nodded. He pressed a kiss against Ronan's neck. "She whispered something else. Something I kept to myself. I know so much with my gift and you're lucky enough to still have the gift of surprise in your life."

"What else did our little miss tell you? Winning lottery numbers? The name of our first female president?"

Ten chuckled. "Her birthday."

Ronan took a sharp breath. "Ten, I'm blown away. That she's real. That's she's ours. That I'm worthy of this gift."

"You're stalling. Do you want to know?"

On a day where he likely could have died, there was nothing he wanted to know more than the day when his daughter would take her first breath in this world. "Yeah. Tell me."

Ten leaned over and whispered the date in Ronan's ear.

"Valentine's Day?" Ronan burst out laughing. "She's not even here yet and already she's got a flair for the dramatic."

"There's no doubt she's your daughter."

There was no doubt Ronan O'Mara was the luckiest man alive.

Thanks to Jude Byrne.

EPILOGUE

Tennyson

Christmas morning...

The wait was killing Tennyson. He was sitting on the floor in front of the Christmas tree. Dixie was sitting in his lap looking dazzled by the white lights on the tree. Everyone was gathered in their living room waiting for Christmas to start, with the exception of Cole, Cassie, and Laurel.

"I hope everything's okay." Ronan joined Ten on the floor.

"I'm sure everything's fine. Laurel probably didn't want to leave her toys," Kaye said.

"Or they're getting a little last-minute Santa nookie," Jude said from the couch, his injured leg propped up on the coffee table.

"Last-minute nookie isn't possible with a two-year-old in the house." Carson laughed. "At least with the babies, we can pen them up and go at it like-"

"Hey, asshole! My son is in the room!" Fitzgibbon barked.

"Hey asshole, our babies are in the room!" Truman barked right back. "Swear jar!"

"Guys, it's Christmas! Can we please not say asshole!" Tennyson pinched the bridge of his nose. He felt a headache coming on.

"You just said asshole!" Ronan pointed out.

"You're in the thick of it now, Tenny! Asshole soup!" Bertha Craig cackled.

"Eeeeee!" all three babies screeched.

"I think that's their way of saying 'swear jar,' Mom. Merry Christmas."

"Merry Christmas to you too, Carson. You know they're saying Mimi!" She hugged her oldest son. "Where's Cole?" She winked.

"You know where he is," Carson whispered.

"Hey, no whispering about me behind my back on Christmas, Bertha. If you're gonna talk about my fine ass, say it loud, say it proud." Ronan laughed.

"Tell handsome that those damn flannel pants do nothing for him. He gets a two for originality. He needs some of those form-fitting pants. What do you call them, spankings?"

Carson and Tennyson burst out laughing. "You mean spanks?" Carson asked.

"No, I think she actually meant spankings." Ten shook his head. He hoped Santa brought him a big-ass bottle of Advil. "Bertha gave you a two, babe. Apparently, your pants aren't tight enough for her exacting standards."

"Now, as for this red-hot babe." Bertha sat next to Jude on the sofa. "He's a perfect ten."

"Are you sure you want to say that, Bertha? It's gonna start World War III." Oh, yeah. Ten had a headache.

"I'm Bertha's new love muffin, huh?" Jude grinned. "Suck it, O'Mara!"

"No one is sucking anything! What the hell is this, kindergarten?" Fitzgibbon shook his head. "Maybe we should start opening presents?"

"Cole and Cassie are here now." Carson got up from his seat. "I'll go help them wrangle Laurel. She's super-excited about seeing us all." He winked at Tennyson.

"What's going on with all the winking? If I didn't know better, I'd think you all were coming down with a raging case of pink eye." Ronan looked confused.

"Patience, young Jedi. All will be explained." Ten kissed his husband.

"Sissy, Ro!" Laurel announced when she came into the house a few minutes later. She ran to him holding a new doll.

Ronan laughed. "It's not the first time I've been called that before, but it is the first time by a toddler. "Merry Christmas, cutie pie. What have you got there?"

"Sissy, Ro!" She said louder this time.

"Okay! I heard you the first time!" He went for the zipper of her heavy winter jacket.

"We *all* heard her!" Jude snorted. "Twice."

Ronan took off the little girl's coat and got a look at her shirt.

"Oh! I get it. 'I'm the big sister!' he read from her tee-shirt.

"Sissy!" Laurel tapped her chest.

"Congratulations, honey! You're gonna be the best big sister ever!" Ronan pulled the little girl into his arms. "Is that what you and Carson have been winking about all morning?"

"Yup!" Ten leaned over to hug Laurel too.

"I guess the word is out?" Cole asked.

Fitzgibbon clapped the man on the back. "Laurel raced into the living room calling Ronan a sissy."

Cole barked out a quick laugh before covering it with a cough. "Sorry I missed that."

"No worries, man! I recorded it!" Jude held up his iPhone.

"Of course, you did, asshole!" Ronan muttered.

"Asshole!" Laurel parroted faster than Tennyson could slap a hand over her mouth.

"That's my girl!" Bertha cackled.

"Am I late for the grand unveiling?" Erin O'Mara asked, making a sudden appearance of her own.

"What is this, a game show?" Bertha asked. "Did I win a candy-apple red heaven-mobile?"

"Erin's here," Tennyson announced. "She wants to know if she's late for the grand unveiling." This was what Tennyson was equal measures nervous and excited about. He had two giant surprises this morning, but this was only the first one.

"No." Ronan laughed. "You're not late for the grand unveiling, Mom. Merry Christmas by the way. Ten, while we're waiting, why don't we start with our present to everyone first, okay?"

"Sure, babe." He dropped a kiss on Ronan's head and got up from the floor. A lot had changed in the five weeks since the Hutchins case had wrapped up, both professionally, and for him and Ronan personally.

Once Shane McNamara aka Travis Hutchins, the missing triplet, had been taken to police headquarters he'd started singing like Lin-Manuel Miranda on opening night. Not only had he recapped his life with his adoptive father, Dick, he'd also given more details on how he'd poisoned the man with arsenic. That had all been confirmed after the man's body had been exhumed for an autopsy.

The story only got more diabolical from there. Shane went on to detail how he'd found his birth family through public records and how he'd spent an entire year stalking Jennifer, Tank and Tim's entire family, including his three small nephews. Once he had the lay of the land, as it were, he'd started planning how he was going to exact his revenge.

Lorraine McAlpin, as it turned out, was a nice woman who'd helped Shane pick out a tasty frozen dinner at a local grocery store one night. She was in the wrong place at the wrong time and had, unfortunately, made a perfect victim for Shane to use against his birth family.

Ronan and Fitzgibbon had been the ones to take Shane's confession. He refused to speak with anyone else. Tennyson had seen the way the daily sessions with Shane had worn both his husband and Kevin down. It had been his job, when all was said and done, to go in and see if Shane had been telling the truth. He had been. Every disgusting, vile word of it.

The confession had been enough to get Tank's conviction overturned. He was released from MCI-Cedar Junction on December 23, just in time to reunite with his fractured family for the holidays. Tennyson didn't even want to think about what Christmas morning looked like in the Hutchins' house. Tank was a free man and that's all that mattered.

Once all of the identical bright red boxes were handed out to everyone, Ten took his seat back on the floor with Ronan. "Okay everyone, go for it!"

"This is so exciting! I wish I had a box too!" Bertha grumped.

Ten reached under the tree and pulled out two more identical boxes. "Here you go, ladies!" He couldn't help wrapping two extra boxes for Bertha and Erin.

"Tenny!" Bertha crowed. "I didn't get you anything!"

"Oh, no? You've only given me everything. You've kept watch over me, Ronan, and our daughter. You've kept our entire family safe. You're my mentor. My best friend. You saved my life in August. Do you really need me to go on?" Tennyson knew he could. If he did, they'd be here for hours.

"These are cruise ship tickets to Bermuda!" Truman shouted.

"That's what we got too!" Cassie gasped.

"Me too!" Kaye sounded stunned.

"What the hell?" Jude shot Ronan an angry look. "You asshole! I knew there was something up when you kept pushing me off booking my own cabin."

Tennyson burst out laughing. "I can explain, but only if Jude promises to stop using *that* word."

"I make no guarantees. Especially if you people keep being so damn nice to me when I've been nothing but an asshole."

"Damn right," Ronan muttered.

Life had certainly been interesting with Jude Byrne under their roof for the last month. After spending nearly a week in the hospital, Ronan and Tennyson had been able to take Jude home with them. His shoulder wound had been the easier of the two to deal with, but the leg wound required crutches. Getting a two hundred-fifty-pound man up the stairs had been no easy feat. Jude's surly disposition hadn't made things any easier.

Jude had been as ornery as a lion with four sore paws in the process. Ronan was damn lucky he was still a free man. Ten could count at least five separate occasions where it almost came to blows.

"When I called the cruise line to ask about getting so many cabins in a row together, the rep I talked to asked for my name and when I told him, he lost his fool mind." Ten laughed. Losing his fool mind was a gross understatement of what had happened. It actually reminded Ten of footage of Beatles concerts when women would faint on the spot after seeing the Fab Four. "Anyway, once he calmed back down, he put me on hold."

"That sounds like pretty crappy customer service to me! I hope you reported his butt!" Jude looked proud of himself for controlling his language.

Ten rolled his eyes. "His supervisor came back on the phone and started talking about their celebrity cruises and would I like to book one." He set his hand on Ronan's shoulder. "I started thinking well, if Luke Bryan is in the next cabin, then sure thing, chicken wing! But that wasn't what he was talking about."

"Shit! Jude sighed. "We're not cruising with Oprah, are we? Seven days at sea listening to stories about her and Gayle and hearing lectures on the benefits of Kale."

Fitzgibbon whacked Jude's shoulder. "Shut up and listen. Don't make me gag you. On second thought, you'd probably like that."

"Oh, he would!" Betha cackled.

"Anyway, the supervisor asked if I wanted to *be* the celebrity. Cruise with Tennyson Grimm! I'd do group readings and private readings and I'd even be a show headliner one night."

"Are you serious?" Carson laughed. "Ten, that's awesome!"

"He said if I agreed to do it, I could bring some friends along for free! So, Merry Christmas everyone!"

"You're kidding, Ten, right?" Kevin asked. He hauled Ten into his arms, nearly hugging the life out of him.

"Nope!" Ten said when he could breathe again. "We also get some free shore excursions too. There's a brochure in the box that lists them. We can learn to SCUBA dive or go on a glass bottom boat or snorkel with turtles. There's a neat zoo/aquarium with free-range lemurs too."

"Let's do that, Grandma Kaye! I want to meet lemurs!" Greeley's green eyes glittered with excitement.

"Tennyson, I still can't believe that…" Kaye trailed off.

"Maybe you'll come to one of my group readings, Mom and see how my work changes lives." It was a long shot, but an offer worth making.

Kaye looked like she was thinking it over and about to say something when the doorbell rang.

"Who could that be? We're all here. Aren't we?" Fitzgibbon asked. His hand went to his hip where his gun usually sat.

"Showtime!" Bertha and Erin shouted at once.

"I'll get it!" Ronan bounced up from the floor and practically ran for the door. Dixie was strangely silent. Usually, she barked her head off when the doorbell rang.

Tennyson stood up as well. He was fighting back tears. This was going to be a huge moment.

"Everyone, I'd like you all to meet Emilyn Cassidy." Ronan led a redheaded young woman who looked to be about twenty-five years old into the living room. Strawberry blonde was probably a better way to describe her, with eyes almost the exact shade of blue as Ronan's. He helped her out of her coat and moved to hang it up in the hall.

Tennyson walked over to them and gave the young woman a hug. "You're all going to get the chance to get to know Emilyn very well over the next little while. She's going to be..." Ten paused. The tears he was trying so hard to battle back slipped free.

"She's going to be our daughter's mother." The emotion was thick in Ronan's voice.

"Hi, everyone! Ten and Ronan have told me so much about you. Hi Bertha and Erin."

"You can see us, sugar?" Bertha asked.

Emilyn nodded. "I sure can!"

Carson's mouth hung open. He looked like he was in a daze. He raised his hand like he was back in the third grade and had a question.

"Yes, Carson." Emilyn grinned like she knew what he was about to ask.

"We've been looking to hire an astrologer and crystal healer at West Side Magick. When can you start?" His blue eyes were as big as saucers.

"Hold on one second, Carson!" Erin laughed. "I need a minute with the mother of my granddaughter if you don't mind."

"A moment, Tennyson?" Ronan grabbed his husband's arm without waiting for an answer.

Ten laughed and let Ronan drag him into the kitchen. "Surprise!"

"She's a psychic too?" Ronan's mouth hung open.

Ten hadn't told Ronan this little tidbit. He just nodded.

"Is little miss going to get Emilyn's gifts?" Ronan sounded dazed.

"In spades, Ronan. Are you mad?" Ten crossed his fingers. Some things were just meant to be. Ronan had fallen in love with the young woman's profile. Emilyn was bright and curious with a knack for LGBTQ charity work. Tennyson had known the moment he'd met her how psychically gifted she was. He'd known instantly this was the right woman to help them create their family.

"Will she grow up being able to see Erin?" Ronan sounded hopeful.

Ten nodded, holding his breath.

"I could never be mad. I'm thrilled!"

"Our daughter's going to be an Aquarius. She'll be charming, impulsive, independent, and stubborn. We're going to have our hands full, Ronan."

"Already studying up on Astrology, huh?"

"Spoiler alert, you will be too. There's something under the tree with your name on it to get you started."

"Aquarius for Dummies?" Ronan asked.

"Let's go find out. Merry Christmas, my handsome husband."

"Right back at you, Nostradamus!"

Beyond the Grave, a Cold Case Psychic spinoff novella, featuring Tennyson Grimm and Ronan O'Mara is now available!

Museum curator, Harrison Kirkpatrick, has been fascinated by the American Revolution since childhood, but never in his wildest dreams did he ever imagine falling in love from afar with a soldier who fought for America's freedom. Through a series of events too wild to be believed, Harrison is thrown back in time to 1775 mere days before the Battle of Bunker Hill and finds himself at the business end of a musket held by the very man he has been pining for.

Massachusetts Militiaman, Gannon Chalmers, does not know what to make of the strange man he finds wandering around Bunker Hill days before his unit is to engage the British Redcoats. Is this man friend or foe? What he does know is that there is an undeniable attraction growing between them that he must resist at all costs.

As the battle draws closer, so do Gannon and Harrison. Can they deny the passion threatening to explode between them like a powder keg? Or will Gannon's abundance of caution keep him from giving in to the one man who could lay claim to his heart? On the brink of a war that will change the history of the world, the pair must decide what price they are willing to pay for freedom, and how much they are willing to sacrifice for love.

Dead in the Water, Cold Case Psychic Book 7 is now available!

Cold Case Detective, Ronan O'Mara, has set sail on the honeymoon of his dreams to sunny Bermuda. He's looking forward to a week of fun in the sun with his husband, Tennyson, but nothing is going as planned. From a fight between Truman and Carson that's threatening to break up their marriage, to Captain Fitzgibbon's on-again, off-again lover not showing up to meet the ship, to dealing with his always challenging mother-in-law, to frenemy, Jude Byrne, showing up with a suitcase loaded with sex toys and lube, Ronan has all he can do to stay sane. Psychic, Tennyson Grimm, is on the ship to work as well as honeymoon. The cruise ship line has hired him to be the "celebrity" on their celebrity cruise. In between private and group readings reuniting family members with those who have crossed over, Ten is running himself ragged trying to put the pieces of Truman and Carson's marriage back together and trying to keep Jude from horn dogging after the ship's captain, all while trying to squeeze in a few stolen, passionate moments with his husband. He isn't having much luck.

During the return trip to Boston, Ronan and Tennyson are enjoying a performance of Murder Mystery Night staged by the ship's crew. When the crewmember playing the murder victim turns up dead for real, Ronan and Tennyson must set "fun in the sun" aside when the ship's captain turns out to be their number one suspect.

Putting the clues together, the Boston detectives corner the cagey killer who takes someone close to them hostage. Can Tennyson and Ronan save the day before they end up dead in the water?

Made in the USA
Middletown, DE
19 May 2020